# FRACTURED
# BREATHS

COVER:

Model: Rachael Baltese

Photographer: Christopher John of CJC Photography

Designer: Parajunkee Design

FORMATTING

Parajunkee Design

EDITING:

Mandy Smith - Raw Books Editing - RawBooksBabe@gmail.com

:: created in the USA :::

# FRACTURED
# BREATHS

## ZOEY DERRICK

*For all those who are surviving*
*life and all its challenges.*

# OTHER BOOKS
# BY ZOEY DERRICK

*Contemporary Romance:*
*Finding Love's Wings*
*Chasing Love's Wings*
*Irresitibly Undeniable*

*Contemporary Erotic Romance:*
*One Week - Standalone*

*Erotic Romance:*
*Claiming Addison*
*Craving Talon*
*Redeeming Kyle*
*Taming Dex*
*Devouring Raine*
*Defining Us*

*Contemporary Erotic, M/M Romance:*
*Aryn's Desire*

*Paranormal Romance:*
*Give Me Reason*
*Give Me Hope*
*Give Me Desire*
*Give Me Love*

"Some people *live* life. Others survive it. *I am surviving* life, but *surviving* is no longer enough."

ONE.

Two.

Three...

Four...five, six, seven, eight...months.

That only accounts for the time I've been here. I put the makeshift mattress back in its place, covering the tick marks etched into the rotting floorboards. The marks don't count the previous four months at another place or the seven months at another. One year and seven months. It took me more than nine months to figure out I was actually two weeks off. Those two weeks were spent in a daze as I healed in the darkness, unable to track the time. Meals weren't delivered with any sense of regularity so keeping time was nearly impossible.

I remember it like it was yesterday, though. It was winter break, just after New Year's in New York City, the place I called home my entire life. My father was once a respected New York City Police Detective. I snort. Some respected detective he was when he went and got himself killed. It was later on that I learned my kidnapping was retaliation toward my father. It only worked as long as those who had taken me believed my father gave a rat's ass about me. As the months progressed, his loyalty to the force proved to be nothing but a bunch of lies and misplaced trust. I've since been arrested three times, and not one person in my father's old squad seemed to look at me twice. All those supposed 'cop' friends haven't even bothered looking for me. It's been over a year since I was ripped from the streets that were my peaceful

life. I was barely sixteen.

I flip open the cheap burner phone, checking the date.

"Happy eighteenth birthday, Livia," I whisper to myself. I can't even smile because who the fuck cares. My 'driver's license' says I'm twenty-two and my birthday was three months ago.

"Sorcha." Shit. I close the phone and tuck it back into my tiny purse, but not before powering it off. If they find out my phone was on inside the house, they'll lock me away in the basement. But not before making sure I'm punished for my actions.

"What?" I snap back, hoping my delayed response doesn't catch unwanted attention. Sorcha is my street name, though it's one of several I've had over the last almost two years. It is one of my favorites.

The door that separates my area from the rest of the house flies open and beyond it is the one they call Fat Tony. He's more of a Slob Tony with his greasy hair, a dirty white t-shirt underneath some fucked up tropical looking piece of shit that hangs open. The evidence of too many beers pushes his slacks to capacity. I don't look at him too long before turning my eyes toward the floor. It doesn't matter that I have a photographic memory and I already know what they look like. They won't care and won't appreciate me staring for too long. "You're up," the slob declares.

I sigh before plastering on a fake smile and looking up at him, pretending to be uninterested isn't an option. Appearing overly interested raises too many suspicions about my motive for being on duty tonight. If I argue with him, or show him how I feel, I'll get my head pistol-whipped and my ass handed over to one of Fat 'Slob' Tony's goons. "Where'm I goin'?" My Brooklyn accent is strong, my New York attitude

even stronger.

"Deets will take you."

I get off the makeshift mattress of folded blankets and straighten my blue sequined halter top mini dress. I slide my feet into the matching pumps before giving myself one last look in the mirror. I got ready over an hour ago, nothing else to do. How anyone finds any of us attractive is beyond me. We're nothing but skin stretched tight over bones, with hollow cheeks and eyes too big for our faces because food is a luxury that the slob refuses to indulge in. What food we eat is the food we buy with what little money we're given. I notice the bruise under my eye is fading, but even covered by makeup it's still visible. Nothing more I can do about it. My dark hair looks strung out and stringy, giving the perfect illusion of a drug addicted prostitute. Just the way they like me. The bruise around my eye was from my big mouth getting the better of me.

I've never touched a drug in my life. Partaking in all things drug related means I lose what little grip I have left on who I am, where I'm going and how I'm going to get there. Though I still haven't figured that all out.

Each night I walk out of this shithole with the confidence that tonight is the night. Tonight is the night I'm going to get away, but each night I come crawling back here like an idiot.

I rub the back of my neck as a gentle reminder to myself that I'm tagged, like a dog. If I run, they'll hunt me down, beat me, rape me and maybe, if I'm lucky, they'll kill me.

It's pretty pathetic that I've welcomed the inevitable prostitution or solicitation arrest. It's a nice little reprieve from coming back to this shithole. At least there I get hot food and an actual mattress to sleep on, even if it's just for a night. I've nailed drunken and drugged up, which usually

means they're forced to keep me overnight until I sober up.

The slob tosses me out the door and right into Deets's waiting paws. "Let's go, sweetheart." The pet name sends a chill up my spine as he grabs my arm and forcibly drags me toward the waiting black Escalade.

A long time ago they quit hooding me when they took me places because I keep coming back. I've somehow managed to gain their trust. Unlike the other girls who were dumb enough to run away the moment they got the chance, I've always returned. I learned long ago I needed to mind my p's and q's so they'd loosen the reins on me, if only for a little while. And my persistence has paid off. I'm usually taken to the location, told what room I'm supposed to go into and then left there until I call for my pick-up. Usually an hour or two later.

Deets roughly shoves me into the backseat of the Escalade and someone else, Vinnie, or some shit like that, is waiting in the driver's seat. See, no one in the organization wants to handle the trafficked girls voluntarily. But when they piss off the big boss, they get sent here for pussy control.

I'm one of nine girls in the house currently. It's a lot for this bunch of idiots, though not uncommon in the organization. The big guns usually keep this house smaller, around four or five girls, but the slob has gotten careless and maybe even a little reckless. The smaller numbers draw a lot less attention, but nope, they're getting greedy or they're getting desperate. Or, I shiver at the thought, they're getting ready to ship off the girls.

Because I've been around the longest, the girls come running to me. For some reason, once they realize their fate, they lean on me for answers. At first, I hated it. I hated that the girls got attached to me because when I decide running is finally going to happen, I don't need them running to Fat

Tony when I don't show up. That will give me less time to get away. Now, not so much. I never had anyone to cling to when I got here, so I see the value in being that girl for these girls. They're less scared and more cooperative. Then again, I'm the one they all come running to when they got problems.

The problems I can deal with, I do. Usually it's the emotional bullshit that comes from girls, especially ones as young as the lot that's shown up lately. Fourteen, fifteen, maybe even sixteen if I had to wager a guess. When they come here that young, they get moved out of the city and sometimes out of the country pretty quick. The problems I can't handle on my own, I'm stuck running to the slob with. Yeah, telling Fat Tony when one of his girls gets knocked up is never fun. The girls leave and never come back.

The first time it happened, I was naïve enough to believe the slob, to believe he'd taken her to a different house. Until four days later when I caught a glimpse of the morning paper being put out in one of the hotels I was working in. On the cover was a girl, her eyes closed, laid out on a metal table with a headline that read something about Jane Doe's body found...help identify her. A couple days after that, they'd identified the body. Though I never got to read the article, it made my chest hurt. She was a good girl, a friend of mine. Next to me, she'd been with Tony the longest.

The memory sends an icy shiver down my spine.

After that, I knew the drill. So without telling the girls what their fate would be, I stressed the importance of birth control and condoms. Most girls got wise after it happened a couple more times and when they went to the doctor, because the slob made us all go, they got the shot behind Tony's back. Meanwhile, Tony and his goons handed us birth control pills the minute we woke up.

The moron behind the wheel drives off down the road and I slide over to the middle of the bench seat because I like to be a pain in the ass. The only problem with that is Deets and his grabby hands. The goons aren't supposed to touch the girls, well, unless they've come up with a reason to punish them. It doesn't matter how big or small the transgression is or even how non-existent it is, they always find a way.

I smack his hand away when he reaches for my thigh. "You know damn well what Fat Tony will do to that hand if you don't keep it off me," I sneer.

"He don't scare me, sweetheart." I shiver at his tone. I know damn well nobody scares Deets. He's fucking insane. I bite my tongue. The urge to say something back, something smart, is too great and it's better to stay in his good graces. Though smacking away his hand is enough to earn me another black eye, or getting bent over the arm of the sofa while the slob jerks off watching Deets fuck me.

I look into the rearview mirror, redirecting my thoughts from what Deets and his little pecker will do to me later tonight and I catch a glimpse in the rearview mirror as a black sedan with dark tinted windows pulls out behind us. I smile inside.

The cops are coming for Fat Tony and they ain't playin'. These two fuck-knuckles ain't got one damn clue. Ah, the perk of being the captured one – the innocent one. A small sense of satisfaction washes over me. Maybe, just maybe, I'll get picked up tonight. I let the thought vaporize before I let the hope take hold.

I'm tired of Fat Tony's bullshit, and what's even worse is I'm tired of Big Daddy's bullfuck. I'm ready to turn them all in if I'm given the chance again. Of course, my last arrest was before we moved into this house.

I'm over their shit. I should have turned them in a year ago. I've come to the conclusion that a life six feet underground has got to be a million times better than this.

My name is Livia Meadow Fazio, and I'm the daughter of Mercutio Fazio, ex-number one-inside cop for the biggest mobster in New York City.

I am a whore because my father fucked up.

I am part of one of the largest sex trafficking rings in the United States because my father couldn't keep his nose out of places it didn't belong.

My father is dead and I'm paying the price.

# CHAPTER ONE
## WORKING GIRL.

*Bryan*

"DUDE, a strip club? Really?" I glare at Liam, my best friend and bodyguard, as we pull into the parking lot of a Phoenix, Arizona strip club.

"Why the hell not? At least it's dark in there. You can hide in the shadows and I highly doubt anyone will recognize you."

He has a point, but that's not the point. "So, we can deal with the headlines tomorrow too?"

"Look around, no one here cares, all they care about is the piece of ass wiggling in their faces." He ushers me ahead of him and I hand the bouncer my ID, my fake one.

Once we're inside the club, Liam ushers me toward a roped off area in probably the darkest corner of the club. "Besides, it will give the media something new to print," he tacks on when we're out of earshot of most people. The music is loud, but not obnoxious. The patrons of the joint are quite loud. Being inside a crowded club has its advantages as far as staying in the shadows, but the more people present; the more likely it is I'll be recognized.

Realizing Liam is set on being here tonight, I decide to make the best of it. I simply shrug and lead the way to the VIP area.

I need a night of mindless, mind-numbing nothing. A chance to escape the outside world, or maybe even spark new headlines. The media outlets have been filled with nothing but the big bad breakup between me and Heather, an up and coming pop-singer. I won't lie. I was shocked it managed to stay out of the news for more than four months. Then again, our relationship was over three weeks into our little charade.

Sure, Heather was a sweet girl, but it was never going to work between us. I knew three weeks into the relationship; it just took me another month to end it. I guess I put too much faith in the idea that maybe I'd found someone worth keeping around or that I would change my tune about her. It never happened.

I pull myself from the memories of Heather and the bad tabloid headlines as I take in the sight of two rather large men standing on either side of the roped off entry of the obviously improvised VIP area of the club.

Strip clubs used to be a tradition for me and Liam. My concerts always ran late into the night but being amped up on adrenaline from the show made settling down impossible. So, we did the only thing open, we hit the strip clubs. In each new city we'd check out the local flavor. Eventually it grew tiresome and boring. It was a great escape from the crazy that is my life, but eventually it became redundant and boring. I will admit that some places were better than others, but Phoenix has never been one of my favorites. Plastic has always been a popular choice amongst Phoenix strippers and I don't like the plastic ones.

I should have stayed in my hotel room, but after months of being on the road, confined to a bus and a schedule not my own, I'm ready to wrap up this business so that I can take a few months off and get back into the studio. That's why I'm here in Phoenix. We arrived this morning and by the afternoon I was already going stir crazy, but like most things, I should have waited until tomorrow to come into town. My meeting isn't until then and we could have easily flown in right before and right back out after to avoid going stir-crazy in a hotel room.

Liam and I take our seats and he smiles at me. I give him a small smile back. I'm not too sure about tonight, but I give him the best I can manage and remind myself that this is

going to be better than bad hotel TV.

The club is dark, typical for strip clubs, and the décor is mostly black chairs, tables and nearly black carpeting. There are purple accents and the accent lighting is neon pink. Reminds me more of a dance club than a strip club.

Being a 'VIP' has its advantages. It doesn't take more than a minute before the two bouncers let a petite blonde with overdone makeup past the ropes. She's carrying a tray in her hand, wearing pasties over the nipples of her tiny tits and a pair of barely there shorts and fuck me heels. She leans over between me and Liam, showing off her lack of cleavage. "What can I do you for, boys?" she purrs.

"Crown, neat," Liam orders then looks at me.

"The same," I tell her.

"Perfect, I'm Mary and I'll be your server tonight. Can I get you anyone else?" She winks at Liam. I snort softly before taking in his relaxed form. He's attractive as hell, of course. He's Scottish for crying out loud. Most girls usually live for the accent, but the coppery red hair helps accentuate his attractiveness, and that's all before he opens his mouth to talk.

"You'll do," he smirks. His accent is purposefully thicker than normal. He's working himself tonight and I just shake my head. If he wanted to pick up women, we could have done that in a bar. At least there he would have a better chance of picking up something he could take home with him.

Mary giggles with fake enthusiasm and she gives him a little shimmy before sauntering out of the area.

"You know, mate," I say leaning forward and mocking his accent, "You might have better luck getting laid in a bar than a strip club."

He chuckles, "Right, but this way I can flirt with anything and know they're not going to beg to come home with me."

I laugh at his logic. His accent is softer now. I've heard the man talk in a normal American accent on several occasions, well, until he gets enough liquor in him.

Woman are always drawn to him, always have been. I'm pretty sure I owe half the woman I've ever been with to having him around. Sharing women is something we've done frequently, and while I'm not at all into men, he's definitely open about who and what he is.

The music in the club shifts.

I roll my eyes.

"Who the hell dances to this shit?" I snort.

Liam turns his eyes toward the stage. "Apparently she does."

I follow his line of sight to a drop dead gorgeous, leggy blonde wearing a cowboy hat, flannel crop top and shorter than should be legal daisy-duke shorts. My jaw falls slack as a remix of my song 'Somebody's Cowgirl' starts to play. It's been a Top 50 hit for the last fourteen weeks. The longest I've ever had a song on the charts.

*Sorcha*

Hip thrust left...

Hip thrust right...

Leg up, leg down...

Grab the pole and spin around.

Don't forget to smile... you got this...

Yup, they are totally eating this shit up.

Come down off the pole, pull off the hat... shake out the

hair and toss the hat.

It's the same routine, the same mundane everything.

Crawl across the floor.

Dollars everywhere.

Pick them up, dance in their faces, practically rub their faces in your crotch.

Smile and bring them between your tits.

They scream, holler... "Take it off!"

Dirty bastards.

But I do it. Every single night I do it over and over again.

Untie the top. Shimmy a little, slide the top off and give them a little show before moving my hands seductively down my torso to the button on my shorts. I got this, let's work it.

Pants unbuttoned, more dollars come out.

They haven't even seen my tits. Jesus, these men are pigs.

I smile when I see the lone woman sitting next to her husband. She's trying everything she can to prove to him or herself that she's not enjoying this.

I love a challenge.

I take a step back, grab the pole again and swing around it before climbing the pole and flinging myself upside down, right in her direction. I see the smile playing at her lips as I unhook my bra while hanging upside down. I squeeze my tits together before revealing them to her and I get my reward. She blushes bright red. I wink at her.

I slide my bra and shirt off just in time to put my hands down to catch myself. I slowly gain my balance and release the pole from between my legs before bringing my feet down into a straight split.

I grab hold of my tits, bringing one up close to my mouth,

my nipple is hard as hell as I bring it to my mouth and flick my tongue across it. She blushes further and the guys scream a little louder. Egged on and not wanting to get in trouble for focusing too much on one person, I crawl my way around the stage before I stand up and lean against the pole.

I seductively lower my shorts as my eyes scan the room. They land on a pair of too bright eyes watching me from the VIP area of the club. The face, I recognize the face, but I can't place him.

The panic rises from inside me. His eyes are locked on me as I continue to dance my way around the stage, but I can't stop my own eyes from finding his. I do my best to tease him, but unlike the woman, there is something different about him. I blow him a kiss before turning my back on him. I see the twitch of a smile before I return to the woman in the front row.

Deciding to give her a little more than she bargained for, I dance in front of her, leaning off the stage to get closer to her with my arms on either side of her chair.

"Hello gorgeous, come here often?" I tease and she giggles. Her husband or whoever he is, watches with rapt attention as I chair dance for his girl.

I bring my tits to either side of her face and shake them slightly. She takes in a deep breath through her nose and she takes in my vanilla cherry scent.

The song is coming to an end, so I pull myself back. Women are the most fun to tease and of course, to dance for. "I'll be back," I mouth and wink. She smiles a little wider and I collect the rest of the money from the group of men and finish out my song.

I collect my things as Donnie the DJ announces, "Sorcha, ladies and gentlemen, isn't she fucking gorgeous?" The crowd erupts in cheers as I finish collecting money and move

toward the curtain.

As I do, Mister Bright Eyes is standing at the corner of the stage holding out money for me to take. It isn't until I'm a foot or so away from him that I see what he is holding out to me.

I snatch it a little too hard from his hand, give him a wink and disappear backstage just as Scarlet steps between the curtains for her spin onstage.

I hurry to the dressing room. My mind wanders a thousand miles a minute trying to decide where I met that guy before.

Seeing someone I know and not recognizing him immediately has me on edge. I start to pack my shit up, ready to bolt from the club, when my boss Harry comes into the room. "Veeps want you."

My eyes snap to his and I quickly shake my head. "I have to go."

"Like fucking hell you do. They want you, you'll go." He steps in a little too close, grabs my arm tightly, and spins me around. "Listen here, princess, you fucking work for me."

"Yes, sir," I mumble.

"Good, now freshen up and get your ass out there." He releases me and turns to leave but he turns back just steps from the door. "Forty percent," he reminds me.

He says it because he, no doubt, saw the hundred-dollar bill VIP-Man handed me as I left the stage.

"Yeah, yeah." My New York accent comes out without meaning to. Harry leaves the dressing room.

I lean into the mirror, checking my makeup for any flaws. Fidgeting, really. My hands shake and I realize in that moment I am on edge tonight and this is not going to go

well. Anyone willing to offer a stripper a hundred dollar bill at the end of a dance spells trouble. Bringing that much attention to myself is not something I strive for. Yes, I'm a stripper, but that doesn't mean I like the attention.

# CHAPTER TWO
## INNOCENCE LOST.

*Sorcha*

SOMETIMES, shit happens when you least expect it.

Tonight is no exception.

"Thanks, Tiny," I whisper as one of CatTails' bouncers opens the rope for me.

In an instant, I see Mister Bright-Eyes looking me up and down. "Howdy, darlin'." I use my fake Southern accent to entice him a little further, hoping if I hear his voice, I might be able to put two and two together, but he doesn't say a word. He simply pats his lap, an invitation for me to sit with him.

I plaster a fake, interested smile on my lips and skirt the coffee table. He opens his legs for me and I set my little bag down, purposefully putting my ass in his face. I hear him breathe in hard as a lull in the music hits at the same time. My fake smile turns a little more real and I wiggle my ass.

Being a stripper was never my dream job, but it is a job that pays amazingly well. It also beats the alternative. I spent years as a worthless whore. Short of continuing as a prostitute, this is the next best thing. I work at least two nights a week letting creepy old men drool all over me and make good money doing it. Then again, selling my body isn't anything new.

I've somehow managed to keep it from my best friend. She has no clue. I gave her some line about picking up extra shifts at the restaurant where I supposedly work. She also doesn't ask for a lot of details, so I don't have to lie to her beyond telling her I'm going to work. I make enough money to pay my bills, that's all she needs to know.

*Nothing has changed.* The little voice in my head reminds me of this nearly every night since I've walked into this club.

I sit down on his lap. "How we doin', sugar?" I ask him.

"Better," he smirks.

"Got a name?"

"Kyle." Hmm, not what I expected.

"Sorcha."

He cocks an eyebrow at me, reading through me. "Your real name?"

I smirk. "When you give me yours, I'll give you mine," I tell him.

"Fair enough. Can I get you a drink?"

I shake my head. "I think I'm supposed to ask you that."

"No, you're supposed to ask if I want a dance," he smirks. If I don't start dancing soon, Tiny will come in here.

"So what will it be?"

"Whatever you want."

"That's a loaded statement," I tell him before standing up.

The song playing is coming to an end, so let it finish while I set myself up. As much as I enjoy strip-teasing for these guys, he's already seen what I have to offer, so I reach behind my neck and unhook the halter top I threw on before coming out here.

Our eyes meet as I do this and I'm lost in them. Distracted and off my game is not something that goes over well with me and it makes me falter a little. "I know you from somewhere," I share quietly, but I know he heard me when the smile on his lips fades a little.

"No, you don't," he says, his voice a little harsh, but his eyes never leave mine. I do my best to shrug it off when 'Pour It Up' by Rihanna starts to play and I know Darby is on stage behind me.

I start to dance for the mysterious man who calls himself Kyle as the song kicks off. His eyes never leave mine and I can't seem to pull my own away from him. No matter how hard I try, it's like I'm entranced by him.

The song kicks up a notch and I turn around, ceasing our eye contact, giving me a chance to clear my head as I bend over, backing up slightly and bouncing my ass closer to him. He spreads his legs a little wider, granting me access and I take advantage. I back up until I feel his pant legs brush along my skin and then I feel the warmth of his body caress mine. My nipples were hard as pebbles the moment I pulled off my top, but the mix of his body heat and the coolness of the club have them painfully hard.

I dip down until my ass is rubbing on his crotch. His deep intake of breath is matched by my own. Guys having hard-ons is just a part of the job, but never in the time I've been doing this have I felt anything like this. He's definitely packing some heat.

A spark connects between us and this dance suddenly turns into something so much more than just a little lap dance as a desire I haven't felt in more than eight years rocks through me.

My mind races back to that night. The first night I slept with a man, willingly.

*"Where's Deets?" I ask the guy behind the wheel. I used to think his name was Vinnie, but that was just because it's easier if I don't ever learn their real names. Over the last couple of weeks I learned his real name is actually some crazy Italian name, but he's called Leo for short. He has short black hair and a New York accent, typical for these parts*

*"He's off tonight," he says as he opens the back door of the Escalade.*

*"So you got stuck with me?" My voice betrays the relief I*

*feel, but he doesn't seem to notice.*

*He gives me a shy, sly smile and a little nod that only I can see. He's handsome. His dark hair is a contrast to his ice blue eyes.*

*"Good," I give him a small smile as I slide into the back of the SUV. He closes the door and slides behind the wheel. "Where we going?" I ask, hopeful.*

*"You know I can't tell you that." His voice has a softness to it that I'm not used to, it's oddly comforting.*

*"Can't fault a girl for trying." I smile and his eyes meet mine in the rearview mirror. I slide into the center of the backseat and lean forward. "You're not like the other guys, are you?" I ask, but he silences me with a 'Shh' and points to an inconspicuous spot on the dashboard.*

*"I'm just like them all," he tells me, but there is something in his voice that's different. Not just the softer edge, but the demeanor behind it. It makes me a little uneasy so I lean back in my seat and say nothing. Though it doesn't go unnoticed when the black, unmarked vehicle pulls out behind us again.*

*You'd think after two weeks of being followed they'd have noticed by now, but they haven't yet or at least they haven't given us any indication that they have. Regardless, I sit in silence as Leo drives me toward my destination for tonight.*

*After twenty minutes and some obnoxious traffic, Leo pulls in front of a hotel, not one I've been too before and I find it rather odd Fat Tony would allow this to happen, but I let it go as Leo parks the car and turns off the ignition. "What are you-" he cuts me off with a finger to his lips, telling me to shut up.*

*"You're here," he says and climbs out of the car, skirting the front bumper to my door. He opens it and I slide out as best I can in the super tight, charcoal grey shift dress. My heels click against the concrete as I do. Leo, ever the gentle-*

*man, extends his hand to me and I take it as he helps me out of the vehicle. He wraps his hand around my waist, pulling me against him. His erection presses between us along the small of my back. I groan as real desire rushes through my veins.*

"Where'd you go?" A deep voice interrupts my memory and I am suddenly back in the dingy strip club and I'm no longer dancing.

"I'm sorry, I..." What do I tell him?

"Don't worry about it," he says softly as the song ends.

"No, I have to worry about it." Panic rises as I realize I never finished my dance for him. Shit. The next song starts and its Britney Spears's 'I'm a Slave 4 U' and I do my best to make up for the first one. "This one's on me." I give him a reassuring smile but he's not buying it. His eyes are searching mine, hoping to see something in them and it makes me even more uneasy. But I do my best, giving him what he's paying for.

Breaking eye contact with him leaves me feeling cold and alone, but I can't bring myself to turn around and look at him again. There is some part of me that feels like he's going to see right through my façade and read all my secrets. We can't have that.

## Liam

"What do you mean you lost her?"

"Exactly that. Somewhere in Northern California. Her trail went cold. We can only assume she's dead or she took on a whole new identity and this time, she got it right."

"But if we can't find her, how do we know *they* can't?" I ask Declan. He's the last of my ears and eyes inside the Bureau where I used to work.

"You just answered your own question, my friend. If we can't find her, neither can they."

"Well, I've found her," I tell him sternly.

"What do you mean, you've found her?" Declan's shock is evident through the phone. "Where is she?"

"About forty feet away from me."

I end the call as the song ends. The girl I spent two years searching for, the girl I believed to be dead, is very much alive.

## *Bryan*

"Thank you," I tell her as I hand her three hundred dollars.

"I can't take this."

"Sure, you can," She hands me back two of the three bills.

"No, I can't. If I take that, I have to pay *him*."

"It's our secret."

She snorts, "Thanks, but nothing is a secret in this club."

Behind Sorcha, my dancer for the last fifteen minutes, comes Liam. He's carrying three drinks in his hands. "Stay," I insist.

She leans down and whispers in my ear, "If I stay, you'll have to pay for my time."

"Good, then stay."

I can tell she's racking her brain for some excuse to get out of here, but she smiles at me then stands up. "If you want me stay, ask me to dance again."

"Then dance again." I wink at her and she shakes her head.

"I could take you in the back for a little more one on one attention," she offers.

"Drinks are here." Liam's accent rings through as he sets

down what he brought from the bar.

At the same time, Sorcha freezes in place and her eyes narrow on me.

"Help yourself, lass," Liam says.

Sorcha slowly turns around and studies the man standing next to her. Two things happen at once. First Liam smiles sweetly at her in a way I've never seen before. The look is meant to be reassuring, but Sorcha, well, her eyes go wide, her body shakes in a way I can only describe as fear before looking from him, back to me then back to him. "Leo..." she breathes.

"No, sorry, lass, the name's Liam." He extends his hand to her but she refuses to take it. She stares at it intently.

"No, it's not," she snaps before grabbing her clothes and charging through the ropes of the VIP area and disappearing behind the doorway of beaded curtains.

"What the fuck was that all about?" I ask Liam.

"Bureau shit," is all he gives me before slamming back one of the drinks on the table. He surprises me further by slamming back a second one before looking at me. "You ready to go?"

"Me?" I point to my chest. "This was your idea in the first place."

"Right, well, I'm ready to go if you are."

I shrug, slam back the last drink on the table, throw a couple hundreds down on top of it and stand up. "One of these days, Bureau business isn't going to last as an excuse. That girl definitely knows you from somewhere and as far as I'm concerned, you've never worked in Phoenix. So...either you need to start talking, or find another place to work."

I charge past him toward the door, not bothering to care

where I'm going until I'm outside.

"Bryan, wait." Liam calls from behind me. "Listen," he grabs my shoulder and spins me around and continues, "I can't tell you everything, okay, but I know her, from an undercover job in New York about eight years ago. I can't go into details, but I just got off the phone with Declan. He's been looking for her for a few years now."

"Why?" I ask, but before he can answer me someone comes up behind us and I hear the telltale cock of a gun before I see her standing behind Liam.

"Why are you here?" she growls at Liam.

"I just came with my boss," Liam says looking at me but talking to her.

"Is this really necessary?" I ask.

"Shut up," she looks over his shoulder at me.

"Listen, lass, we don't want no trouble."

"Trouble? You think this is trouble? This is nothing compared to what you're going to face unless you start talking. Who sent you?"

Pain flits across Liam's eyes, followed by defeat. "I'm not who you think I am, Livia."

Liam jumps as the woman behind him presses the gun further into his back. "I am not Livia," she growls.

"You're not Sorcha anymore either, Livia."

"Becca, damn it, my name is Becca." Tears form in her eyes. "Why are you here, Leo? Did they send you here to find me?"

"Put the gun down and we can talk," Liam says.

In a flash, she disappears, running around the building before either one of us can go after her. I start running toward her but Liam stops me. "Don't, let her go."

"We need to call the cops," I tell him but he just glares at me. "Are you insane?"

"Listen, she didn't hurt me, or you, just let it go."

I shake my head. "Un-fucking-believable." Just then we are illuminated with headlights as an older model Honda comes around the corner. Liam pushes me out of the way as she drives past us hurriedly. She's looking straight ahead but it's obvious she's crying. "You're a prick." I shove him off me and turn toward the car. "Let's go."

COMING home to an empty apartment is not good. Ireland, my roommate and best friend, well, as good of a friend as she can be given the fact I've lied to her from day one, is gone.

She left me a note on the counter that said she was going away for the weekend. I fold the note up and take a lighter to it, burning it in the sink before running water over it and washing it down the drain. Fuck her.

Becca: where are you going?

Ireland: New York

"Fuck!"

Becca: What the hell is in New York?

Ireland: Dyson. He's flying me out there for the weekend.

Becca: Guess we really do need to talk.

Ireland: When I get home, k?

Becca: K. Don't get dead.

Of all the fucking places in this godforsaken country she could go, why in the hell does it have to be New York?

I go into my room and slam the door, despite no one being here to hear how pissed off I am. I go straight for my bed and reach underneath it. I quickly find my duffle bag and pull it out. Inside the bag is another small bag and I pull it out, sorting through the stack of passports and IDs I've managed to get my hands on over the years and go digging for one I know I haven't used in Phoenix yet. Once I have it out of the bag, I stuff the rest back inside and then pull out the tattered envelope and check its contents.

"Time to start over," I mumble to myself before shoving the envelope full of cash into my purse along with the ID and passport. "A hotel for tonight."

Guilt runs rampant through me as my happy, peaceful world shatters.

* * *

Reese: I guess Ireland isn't coming tonight.

Becca: So, I heard. Want me to pick you up?

Reese: Nah, I'm good. What time will you be there?

Becca: Doors open at seven.

Reese: See you then.

Reese is more Ireland's friend than he is mine. I adore him, of course, but he likes to pry into things he shouldn't mess with, like me. But regardless of that, he's always been there for Ireland, especially when I couldn't be. I've never been able to handle the overly emotional side of people and these last couple of weeks with Ireland have been trying for me.

Her mom died. It's sad, and I'm sorry she's gone, but I don't know how to deal with that. I was little when my mother died and I don't remember her. Couple that with the fact that my father betrayed me in the worst way possible and I don't have much sympathy for missing or lost parents. They're useless as far as I'm concerned.

If Ireland hadn't bailed on Reese and me tonight, I wouldn't be here. I would have bailed myself. Ireland is off in New York with her old new boyfriend – she knew him as a kid. We'd planned to attend this concert months ago. It

was supposed to be a fun night out with the three of us, but after the events of the last couple days, I don't feel like being here. Since we graduated, the three of us haven't hung out as much. With Reese working and Ireland and I moving, we can never seem to coordinate our schedules. I felt guilty about Ireland not coming, so I came. I owe it to Reese. At least with the music pumping and people having a good time, I can work the corners and stay out of sight, right? Right.

## Bryan

"Hey man, I thought you were leaving tonight?" Tristan asks me as I take a seat at the bar. He's back there working his magic and his charm. Though it's not needed.

"I decided to hang around, check out the show. See the bar." I smile at him as he washes some glasses. "Need a hand back there?"

"Nah, man, we're good. Just getting ready for the madness to ensue," he laughs. "What can I get you?"

"Crown, neat."

"You got it." He turns for the bottle behind him and more people filter into the bar.

Tonight, one of my good friends is playing Tristan and Cami's bar in Phoenix and while I originally had no intention of bothering Liam tonight, I realized he needed something to do to keep his mind off that chick from the other night. For the last twenty-four hours, Liam has been on edge and on the phone with one of his buddies. All I could surmise from the conversations is he's been trying to find out more information about her.

I shake my head, shaking off the memory of what happened. He refuses to tell me what the whole ordeal was about. Instead he ignores me or tells me to forget about it. I

have a hard time doing that, and I don't understand why.

*She's a fucking stripper.* I remind myself for the thousandth time since Thursday night.

*Imagine that headline.*

"Did you and Cami get everything straightened out today?" Tristan asks as he slides my drink across the bar. I take him in for a minute. He's gorgeous, of course. Who in Hollywood isn't? He's got shaggy, dirty blonde hair that makes the girls go crazy for him and a body to match. It's hard to believe a man of his stature is tending bar at a club in Phoenix, Arizona, but his happiness is evident.

I know it wasn't always this way, but a couple years ago he met his wife Cami and they have one son, Jaden.

Cami is the owner of Bold International, Inc., a huge Los Angeles based agency that specializes in celebrities, musicians and athlete services. It's how I ended up with my own personal PR Rep, Raine, who is married to 69 Bottles drummer Dex Harris, when I moved companies a few months ago. I wanted Addison, but Cami insisted it was a conflict of interest given Addison's blooming music career.

"We did," I finally answer him. "The tour will start in September and run through early December. We're also going to work on some dates after the New Year, but she wants to wait and see how these dates shake out."

"Damn, that's a long time," he says with a shake of his head. "I have no idea how you do it, Bryan. I really don't."

I smile wide at him. "For the same reasons you get in front of the camera. It's a high that never goes away, my friend."

He holds up a glass, toasting me. "There is that."

"To the high," I smirk and we slam back our drinks.

Tristan puts his glass in the sink beneath him as someone

calls for his attention. He holds up a finger, indicating for me to give him a minute. I nod and he moves to the end of the bar.

"Reese, what's up, brother?" Tristan says to the man he's helping. They smack their hands together before grabbing thumbs. I imagine there'd be a chest bump in there somewhere if the bar wasn't between them.

"Not much, you ready for tonight?"

Tristan snorts, "You know it. What can I get you?"

"Malibu-"

"She's here?" Tristan cuts him off to ask.

"Yeah man, Ireland was supposed to be here too, but someone whisked her away to New York." Reese cocks an eyebrow at Tristan. "So it's me and her."

"Alright, I'll let the other bartenders know."

"Thanks, man." Reese smiles. "I'll have the Pina and an amaretto sour."

"You got it," Tristan says before coming back in front of me.

"I should ask you what that was all about," I jest.

Tristan snorts a laugh and goes about making Reese's drinks. "Nothing really. We have a regular who comes in here and likes to get drunk. She's a friend of a friend, so we keep a close eye on her. The bartenders know to lighten her drinks. Despite that, she manages to get drunk anyway."

"So why not kick her out, permanently?"

"Because, she's not disruptive, just..." He looks up, looks around, then his eyes meet mine before he leans in and whispers, "She usually ends up going home with some random guy. More often than not, when we leave for the night, her car is the last one in the lot."

29

I nod my head in understanding before Tristan slides me another Crown and goes to hand Reese his drinks.

I sit at the bar people watching while Tristan continues filling drink orders until the doors finally open onto the back patio. Reese returned one more time for a refill before then. I never got a glimpse of who he's here with. I was hoping to find out who I should steer clear of before the concert began but I never caught sight of her.

## Becca

"Want to come home with me?" I shudder. The guy I've been dancing with for the last few songs has been putting the moves on me hard. I can't say I blame him, I look hot tonight. Even Reese lost his jaw when he saw me.

"It'll cost ya," I tell the guy.

"You're a hooker."

I roll my eyes. "No, I'm an escort," I retort.

'How much?" Is he serious? This dude doesn't have three nickels to rub together.

"Two-hundred."

"Let's go." He grabs my hand and leads me from the patio and into the bar area where he deposits what's left of his drink on a high-top before leading me out the front door.

"I'm serious," I tell him.

"I have no doubt you are. Still taking you home."

That evil chill of commitment slides up my spine, but I dutifully follow the nicely dressed, hair is too perfect man to his Infinity. Not what I expected from him, but it works. Maybe he does have the money. "I don't take credit cards." For the first time in my life, I find myself trying to work my way out of a transaction and I don't understand why.

"I have cash," he says as he opens the door to his car and I slide in.

*Liam*

"You good here?" I ask Bryan.

"Yeah, where you going?"

"I need to go check on something. Will you be alright to get back to the hotel?"

"Of course, but what the hell is going on with you?" he urges. He's been pestering me since last night at the strip club and I've yet to explain it all to him and it pisses me off. Some stories are better left told when they are resolved or by the person they belong to in the first place.

I saw the look in his eyes when he saw her. It wasn't a look of hunger but one of desire and longing. There is something about that girl that has Bryan entranced and I know that feeling.

"I'll explain, soon, I promise, but right now, I need to handle something."

He grabs my arm. "You do realize I'm the one paying you for protection, right? Not her."

I pull my arm from his grasp. "Understood, sir." He scowls at me. "This is something that goes back to my days in the Bureau and I just need to see that she's alright."

"Then go. But damn it, Liam, you better figure out how to explain this to me or I will have you removed. I can't have you distracted by some old piece of ass you-"

I cut him off with a growl. "She is not some piece of ass, Bryan. She's a protected witness."

His eyes widen slightly but they soften with understanding. "Get out of here," he breathes but his voice is

stern. I don't argue with him as I go chasing after her and the man she left with.

When I make it to the parking lot, they are just climbing into a silver Infinity and I race toward the rented SUV and climb inside, turning the engine over and powering off the headlights. The car pulls out of the lot.

I watch them carefully for direction before I pull out behind them and follow them down the street. They're oblivious to my presence and when we come to the first light, he pulls into the turning lane.

I flip on my headlights, pretending like I forgot them and pull up behind them. The road we are on has several other cars on it so it shouldn't be too suspicious and I hope to fall back.

The light changes and he makes a U-Turn before heading back south. I follow behind him but keep my distance and a slightly slower pace. The cars that had gotten stopped behind me catch up and I'm lost in them, increasing my pace and never losing sight of the car she's in.

After ten minutes we're pulling up to a house and he parks the car in the driveway. I drive past them, down the street and turn. I keep going until I'm out of sight before swinging around, killing the headlights and parking where I can see them getting out of the car. Once they are inside, I pull around the corner and in front of a house a couple houses down, giving me a better view of the house and an easier chance at seeing her leave.

I sit... and I wait.

After about an hour of sitting there, Bryan texted me that he'd returned to the hotel.

Another hour after that a cab showed up in front of the house. I quickly jot down the medallion number before

she comes out and gets into the back of the cab. Her hair is pulled up and her make-up is a little disheveled, confirming my theory. I shake my head.

"Why, Livia?" I ask myself as I watch the cab spin around before leaving the neighborhood and I follow them. This time I don't keep my distance. I stay close. The likelihood she's paying attention is slim. Then again, she knew the cops were tailing her all those years ago.

*"What are we doing here?" Livia asks me. Her eyes scared and confused.*

*"We need to talk," I tell her.*

*"We have nothing to talk about. But you do know that Fat Tony..."*

*"Fuck him," I spat before turning away from her in frustration. "Don't worry, you'll leave here with money."*

*"You? You're my 'date' for tonight?" The disdain I hear in her voice is evident.*

*"More or less, but I have no intention of-"*

*"Why not?" she interrupts before she slides the straps of her dress off her shoulders and it falls to the floor. My cock grows hard in an instant. She's fucking gorgeous, too fucking skinny but gorgeous as fuck.*

*"Put it on."*

*She shakes her head, her brown hair flying around. "If I don't do this, Tony will know."*

*"Fuck him." I reach into my back pocket and pull my wallet out and grab two large ones and set them on the credenza near me. "You'll go back with your money."*

*"So if you don't want to fuck me, what exactly are we doing here, Leo?"*

*"We need to talk, but you need to put your clothes back on first."*

*"No," she refuses and sits on the edge of the bed. My breathing falters and my eyes inadvertently roam over her body. Her nipples are tight pebbles atop her gorgeous C-cups. They're a beautiful brown tone and it makes my mouth water. She's watching me and she tries to seduce me by spreading her legs for me to view her naked pussy. The nub of her clit peaks out between her bare lips.*

*"Jesus, Livia."*

*She panics, her body goes into motion, closing her legs and scooting back onto the bed, curling around herself. "How...?" She doesn't finish and I instantly realize my mistake.*

The memory of that first night, the night I lied through my teeth to help her see and understand that she could trust me, she needed to trust me. My lie wasn't entirely a lie, but I never shared the fact I was an FBI Agent, undercover. Instead, I spun the web of lies I'd found myself in over the course of the three years I'd been inside Vito Ricci's organization.

I told her Vito was not happy with Tony's way of running things so he sent me in to figure shit out and I needed Livia's help. And help me she did. Through her I could gather enough intel to help the Bureau take down the organization, but first, I'd had to help Livia.

We pull up to a hotel, one that's...wait a minute; this is the same hotel where Bryan is staying. Why is she here?

I park my car in front of the Valet and hop out, tossing him the keys and my room number before running inside after her. She heads straight for the elevators and I follow her, keeping my distance as she punches the button.

A million and one questions are going through my mind, the biggest one being whether she's here to see someone, a client.

She steps inside and I wait a moment before darting toward it, catching it before it closes all the way. I slip inside and look over at her. She's not paying attention to me, not in the slightest, but just as the doors are about to close, she bolts for it.

I grab her around her waist and cover her mouth. "Livia, relax."

She does instantly and the doors close. We start upward toward whatever floor she pushed.

I spin her around and press her against the back of the elevator, holding her there while I turn around and stop the elevator. My hand is still over her mouth. Her eyes are wide. "If I release your mouth, are you going to scream?" She nods. "Stubborn as always, I see," I mutter. "I will not hurt you, Livia." Her eyes widen, but the mention of a long lost name forces her to settle a little. "I just want to talk to you. Will you scream?" This time, she shakes her head. "Good, now, are you here to see Kyle?" She stiffens under me again and vehemently shakes her head. I release her mouth, but I don't release my hold on her.

"Why are you here?" she asks, her voice shaky. Her eyes dart over to the elevator panel as it beeps.

"Is there a problem?" A disembodied voice breaks the silence and I have no choice but to put the elevator back in motion.

"No," I answer as the elevator unlocks itself and starts to climb toward the eighth floor, two floors below Bryan. "Are you staying here?" I ask her and she nods. "We need to talk," I tell her. When the elevator doors open, I don't give her much choice as I grab her hand and pull her down the

hallway. "Which one?" I demand.

"Eight-nineteen." Her voice is soft, but I can sense her fear. I need to find a way to ease her a bit.

I turn to her. "Kevin McKinney is looking for you."

She tenses and rips her hand from mine. "How do you know that name?"

"He was my partner."

"You're a cop?"

"Was. Now, can we talk?"

She nods and leads me two more doors down before she digs out her keycard and slides it in. She holds the door open for me. I nod and reach up to cup her cheek, to comfort her, but she pulls away from me. I frown at her and move further into her room.

It's just a standard room, nothing more than any normal hotel room, but it's obvious she's been here for a few days but not much more than that. "What do you want, Leo?"

I frown. "My name is not Leo. Leo was my cover." I let my accent shine through a little more. Once she can hear and understand that I am anything but Italian, I'm hoping she will trust me a little more.

"So what's your real name?" She tosses her key card on the desk near the door and folds her arms over her chest.

"Liam, Liam Callahan."

"You promised to protect me. To keep me safe. But when they came for us..." Her voice cracks with tears, fear and something else, pain.

"I was there, Livia..."

"No, you weren't. They locked me up like some fucking lab rat. Interrogated me for days before they finally released me. I never saw you again."

"I was there the night they raided the house. I was hidden by my tactical gear. If something went wrong, if someone got away, I couldn't risk any one of them running back to Vito and blowing my cover."

"This is all so fucked up, you understand this, right? You promised you'd keep me safe, that you'd get me out of there."

I turn on her, "I did get you out of there, didn't I? You're safe, you're alive and you are still fucking turning tricks." My anger comes through in a way I never intended it to. She fights back with every ounce of the Livia Fazio I know.

"Fuck you, it's not like you or your fucking goons handed me much of an opportunity to get myself right. You forced me out of the city, handed me a new identity, a shitty fucking apartment and no one to keep an eye on me. I've spent the last eight years moving from city to city, state to state, praying like hell Vito and his goons wouldn't find me. I did what I had to do to survive then and I'm doing what I have to do to survive now."

She turns toward the door and opens it. "Get out."

"I'm not done talking."

"I don't give a flying fuck. Get the fuck out of my room before I call the cops."

I approach her. "Yeah, 'cause that will go over real well, sweetheart...with your solicitation record."

The next thing I know, her hand connects with my cheek.

I ignore it and I pull my business card from my pocket, holding it out to her. "If you want more answers, this is how you reach me. We're leaving tomorrow."

"Do they know?"

"Who? The Feds? Or Vito?"

"Both?"

"The Feds? Yes. Vito and his gang of idiots were taken down and off the streets before you were released from custody. They were never coming after you, which is why no one was handling you."

"You can't know that," she breathes but she refuses to meet my eyes.

"Look at me." She doesn't. "Look at me, Livia, so you know that what I tell you is the truth." Finally her eyes meet mine. "You were nothing but a whore in the chains of Vito's gang." Her eyes narrow at me. "No one gives a shit and no one knows who gave them up."

"They always know."

"Well, the information you gave me, I turned over to the Feds. With more than four years of undercover work, trust me, I didn't learn anything from you that I didn't already know." My voice takes on a cold edge, one she recognizes immediately. Her reaction, however, is not what I expected.

She spits in my face.

I grab her chin and push her against the door. "I needed to know whether or not you were the woman I thought you were. I needed to know whether or not you were willing to turn on Tony and Deets for all their bullshit. I did what I had to do to make sure you stayed safe."

"By fucking me over?" Her voice is soft, hurt.

I cock my head at her. "What. I had. To do," I state sternly.

"You used me." I release her chin.

I snort, "That's rich, considering what you do for a living."

She tries to smack me again but this time I stop her, grabbing her by the wrist and holding it tightly. "I had no fucking choice," she pleads.

"Then, but you do now." I push her arm away and walk out

the door. She doesn't argue with me; she slams the door shut behind me.

My heart is hammering in my chest as the pain of seeing the pain in her eyes rips through me.

> Unknown Number: There's a party on Saturday, Blu 8:00 – Ireland would love to see you.
>
> Becca: Who is this?
>
> Unknown Number: Dyson – Ireland's boyfriend.
>
> Becca: Not sure that's a good idea.
>
> Dyson: I don't know what happened between the two of you, but she needs her best friend.

It's been four months since Leo, or Liam, whatever his name is, accosted me in the hotel elevator.

In those four months, everything has changed.

The mention of Ireland brings back the memory of telling her I was moving out. It turned out to be so much harder than I'd expected it to be. Before my encounter with Liam, I was sure Vito and the Ricci crime family were still looking for me.

Now, I'm not so sure. w

I'm pretty sure Liam never knew how I ended up the only Italian-American whore in Ricci's arsenal, which tells me I'm not out of the woods just yet. Despite his belief that I was only a whore, I'm afraid I was much more than that to them.

Sure, Ireland and I had our moments, just like most friends do, but I do love her like a sister and maybe it's time to start treating her like one. This is why it was so hard to ruin a good thing. I need to find it in me to uproot my life and move on.

I distanced myself when she started asking too many questions and I can't even begin to imagine what she's going to say, do, or even think when and if I finally come clean

to her about my past, about who I am. Not to mention that boyfriend of hers. Her association with me and my past can't be good for his business. It's not good for anyone's business.

But before I can do that, I have to find a way to repair my relationship with her first. How? I have no clue, but tomorrow night's party might be the best place to start.

Becca: I'll come.
Dyson: Good, we'll see you then.

Now I'm sitting in the parking lot of Blu Phoenix. My favorite bar. The same bar Reese and I saw the concert without Ireland, the same night Leo became Liam and my whole life changed, again. I've been coming here since the joint opened and even though they try to hide it, the bartenders and owners take care of me. That's probably a good thing.

Even though I've never been busted when I've been here working the room for a little cash on the side it bothers me that I'm working an establishment I enjoy going to. Not to mention the ramifications the bar could face if I were ever busted here.

I watch the entrance for a little while. Not to many people coming and definitely no one is going. I see a couple people I recognize, but they're people I can't put names to. I've seen them somewhere, but they're gone before I can put two and two together.

There are bouncers at the door, though I've never seen them before, at least not in this capacity. They're dressed nice in dress pants and button-up shirts. Most of them are packing, which is either a good thing, or a bad thing, I'm not sure which. Regardless, everyone who has showed up has

been let in. Until now. A man, dressed for a night of drinking and dancing gets turned away from the door. Then shortly after that, another couple of girls get turned away.

It's invitation only.

Shit. How am I going to get in there?

When the crowd is inside I finally decide to get out of the car and head for the door. "What's the worst that can happen? They turn me away?" I mumble as I approach the door.

"Sorry, ma'am, there's a private party tonight."

"I was invited."

"What's your name?"

"Becca, Becca Carpenter?" I say as a question versus a statement and the guy starts talking into his headset.

"We have a Becca Carpenter outside, says she was invited?" There is brief pause, before he says, "Okay, thanks." He turns back to me and says, "Wait here."

"Why do I have to wait...?"

The door behind him opens and out steps a well-dressed man with copper red hair. I slouch. "Sorry guys, I made a mistake." I turn on my heel and start walking quickly toward my car.

"Becca, wait!"

I shake my head and throw my hands up in frustration.

"Don't make me say it."

I turn on my heel again and charge back toward Liam. "Might as well, you've blown up everything else in my life, now you're blocking me from a party I was invited to."

"I assure you, they don't need a..."

I slap him across the face so hard it makes my hand sting before he can get the word out of his mouth. "I am not a

whore."

"Look, I'm sorry, alright. I'm pissed off at you."

"What the fuck did I ever do to you?" I snap.

"Oh, I don't know, Livia, you broke your promise. It makes me feel like everything you ever said to me, every time you were ever scared or unsure, feel like a fucking act. You continue behaving the same way I risked my life, my job and my station within the Ricci family for to get you out of that house and out of that situation. It's a slap in the goddamn face."

"Why did you care so much? Why did you care so much about me?"

He runs his hand over his hair. He's frustrated, but he doesn't say anything, he just stares at me.

"You should have just left me there to die."

"I felt the need to protect you."

"Why me and not them?"

"Because, growing up, your father was my best friend."

I freeze, staring blankly at him. The mention of my father hasn't been brought up in close to ten years.

"It was because of your father that I convinced the FBI to look into the Ricci family. That got them to finally take the accusations your father made toward them more seriously."

"My father was a dirty cop," I sneer at him.

"Yes and no. Look, this isn't something we can talk about in a parking lot of a party you're supposed to be attending, and it's not a conversation that can be held in a matter of minutes. Look," he reaches into his back pocket and pulls out his wallet. He pulls something from a hidden pocket and hands it to me. "He was my friend. I was deep inside the family when your father got killed. I spent the next two

years trying like hell to track you down, to get you to trust me, to get you out of there. Despite what you think, no one ever stopped looking for you. I," he points at himself with his thumb, "never gave up."

I wipe a stray tear from my cheek and stare at the photograph of a much younger version of my father standing next to a redheaded boy in front of an ice cream shop in the Bronx, a place my father took me frequently when I was younger. "That was his favorite place to go," I sniff.

Liam smiles at me. "I met you there, more than a few times, in fact."

I look at him, trying to place him, but like everything else lately, I get the familiarity but can't place him exactly. "I don't remember that, I'm sorry."

He nods and takes the picture from me and carefully returns it to his wallet. "I know. It's okay. You were little then. My job with the Bureau took up the majority of my life, I didn't have the time I wanted to have with your father."

"Why are you here?" I finally find something to change the subject. "Is he here? The guy from the club the other night?" The worry about my 'other job' sneaks into my voice and he catches it.

"He is, though his name isn't Kyle, it's Bryan. I assure you, he won't say anything to anyone."

Bryan...Bryan... the strip club...the song. "Bryan Hayes?" My voice cracks.

Liam cocks a smirk at me before bringing his finger to his lips and shushing me. "He has just as much to lose by outing you as you do. Trust me, the secret is safe."

I nod in understanding and he turns to leave. "You coming?"

"In a minute. I need a minute."

He nods. "They'll let you in this time."

"Thanks."

"Oh, by the way, I love the new hair color."

I grab a strand and look at it. The blonde is now gone, replaced by blue-black, my natural hair color. I look back at him and smile. "Thanks."

## *Bryan*

Liam comes back inside and finds me. "We need to talk a minute."

"Sure, what's up?"

He leads me toward the corner, away from everyone.

"Do you remember the stripper?"

I snort a laugh, "How could I forget her?"

"She's here."

"Fuck, are you kidding..."

"Shh, Jesus, lower your voice and take a deep one. She's a friend of Ireland and Dyson, who are friends with Cami and Tristan." He looks over his shoulder and indicates across the room. "The fiery redhead," he says before turning back to whisper in my ear. My eyes land on the slightly pregnant redhead who's busy talking with Dex, his woman, plus Derek Hunter and his wife as Liam continues talking. "I told her your name. She put two and two together. Now, before you lose your shit about that, I didn't have much of a choice, unless you want to let everyone in here know about a trip to the strip club a few months ago."

He has a point there. "I'm pretty sure you didn't want her calling you Kyle and most importantly, no one here knows about her penchant for stripping. I'm pretty sure she'd like to keep it that way. Feel me?"

"Yeah, I feel you."

"You don't even have to talk to her if you don't want to."

Just then, the door opens and in walks a tall, gorgeous dark-haired beauty. If Liam hadn't warned me, I wouldn't have even recognized her. The blonde hair is gone and is replaced by a gorgeous blue-black color, her sparking blue-green eyes wide and worried. She's wearing a pair of tight fitting jeans and a nice, low cut, black V-neck shirt. Her hair falls in waves over her shoulders and down her back.

I'm staring at her when her eyes meet mine. I give her a smile and a wink. She gives me a small smile back and proceeds to find her friend.

I watch the interaction between her and her redheaded friend, who seems surprised to see her. My curiosity surrounding their exchange only grows further when the redhead is whisked away to the back room for some sort of surprise I heard about, something about a gender reveal. It seems appropriate since both the redhead and Cami are pregnant. Cami disappears with Ireland and Dyson, a friend of Cami and Tristan's, continues talking to the girl. Sorcha, Becca, Livia – whatever her name is.

Thinking about all the different names she's used makes me wonder what I should actually call her, provided I get the nerve to step away from the wall and approach her. It's not that I can't talk to women, because I most certainly can, but I'm struggling with the reality that I first met her in a strip club and she was on stage, not in the audience. I shake my head at the idea of the field day reporters will have with that one.

*If it bothers you so much, why can't you take your eyes off her?*

That painful inner voice is back again, and of course, it's right.

"What's wrong, lad?" I close my eyes, breaking the visual of her standing there smiling at Dyson as they chat, and I turn to Liam.

I nod my head in her direction. "What's her story?"

He shakes his head. "Not my story to tell. It's something you need to ask her."

I huff, "Yeah, because we met on such good terms the first time around. I recall a gun in your back at that one." I cock a questioning eyebrow at him. "How long have you known her?"

He leans against the wall beside me before answering, "Known her, known her? Not long. I first met her as a child, a young child. Then several years later, I ran into while I was working undercover in New York."

I nod in understanding. While I don't know anything about the job Liam did, I'm well aware of his undercover career while he was with the FBI. "Is she the reason you got hurt?"

He snorts, "No."

Liam was injured a few years ago. His injury put him at a desk job for the Bureau, or rather, they gave him the choice. He took the out. That's how he ended up with me. "So why is she so angry with you?" I ask.

"Because the last time I saw her, she thought I was working for someone else. Someone who, to this very day, may still want to get his hands on her."

"So why is she unprotected?"

"I didn't say that was the case."

"Ha! You keep telling yourself that, but you know as well as I do she wouldn't have been dancing in that club if she was protected. That much I know to be true."

Liam looks at me with a look of pleading, almost as if his

concern is too much for him to handle. "What's your deal with her?" he asks me point blank.

I shrug my shoulders and take a long drink of my neglected beer. "She's gorgeous."

"She's a stripper."

I glare at him. "So you keep reminding me."

*Becca*

"Congratulations," I say to Dyson and Ireland as Ireland wraps her arms around me after the big gender reveal.

"Thank you." She's beaming with pride as she looks up at Dyson. "You look amazing," she tells me as she reaches up and touches a strand of my hair. "I like this much better." She smiles.

"Much more fitting." Dyson winks. "Can I get you a drink?"

I nod. "The usual."

He leaves me and Ireland alone and heads to the bar. "How are you?" she asks as soon as Dyson is out of earshot.

I nod and give her a small smile. "I'm good, been busy working. Being on my own is kind of the pits," I chortle.

She gives me a sad smile. "We still have the apartment, if..."

"No, it's fine, you can't afford to pay for it."

"I wouldn't say that." She winks and leads me toward a table and we sit. "A lot has happened over the last few months.

I smirk and look at her small belly. "That's obvious."

She smiles wide as her hand slides over her slightly distended stomach. "Well, this is just one thing in a list of many that have changed, but enough about me." She leans

in closer then jerks her head toward the door. The gesture is meant to be subtle and to anyone else, it was. But to me, she's obviously pointing at the man who hasn't pulled his eyes off me since I walked in the door. "Have you met Bryan yet?"

For the first time in my life, I genuinely blush. "Yeah, we met a couple months ago." I don't launch into details about how I met him, but I'd seen him in the bar, then Leo or Liam, whatever his name is now, accosting me in my hotel room. "He was here during the Lee Brice concert."

"You haven't slept with him, have you?" Her eyes grow wide.

"Jesus, Vy, no," I say quickly. When Ireland first introduced herself to me, she said her name was Vyolet. I later learned that it was actually her middle name, but the name she preferred. Ireland isn't exactly suited for nicknames.

"I'm sorry, I...shit, Becca, I didn't mean anything."

"It's alright. I can understand why you would ask me something like that. I don't exactly have the best reputation, especially when coming here."

She shakes her head. "No, you don't. But you do know who he is, right?"

I nod, trying not to be over-excited since he's one of my favorite country singers and his music provided the soundtrack for the majority of my dances when I worked at the club. "I didn't know that when I'd seen him though. It took me a while to put two and two together." This isn't a lie, in fact it wasn't until his leech told me just a little while ago in the parking lot.

"Listen, I need to go talk to someone, but...can we get together? Soon? I miss you." Her voice turns solemn and for the first time in almost ten years, I feel tears prickling the backs of my eyes at the idea that someone misses me.

"I miss you too," I tell her, and it's the truth. "We really need to talk."

"About what?" She cocks her head at me.

"Well, I'd like to apologize for the way things went down back in February, and..." I take a deep breath before I can finish. "I think it's time I finally answered all your questions."

She gives me a sad smile. "Then expect to have dinner sooner rather than later. You can't lay that on me and then..."

"I know, listen, give me a week or so, let me..." I pause when I see Bryan pull away from the wall as he's talking to someone and they're making their way toward us.

Ireland touches my arm. "Call me when you're ready, okay?" She gives me a reassuring smile and I smile back at her.

I nod. "Okay, soon, I promise."

"Good." We get up from the table and she wraps her arms around me. "I'm here for you. Always have been, always will be, no matter what."

We'll see about that. I keep my cynicism to myself as I release her and she smiles at me. "You're not leaving, are you?"

I smile at her. "Not tonight."

She gives me a sad smile and a nod as she moves off to talk to someone. When she passes Dyson, they have a quiet exchange and she swipes a tear from her cheek before Dyson kisses her gently on the temple and comes to deliver my drink.

At the same time, Bryan, along with someone else I know, but I'm not sure who he is, approaches the table where Dyson and I are enjoying our drinks.

"It's not watered down." Dyson winks at me.

I chuckle. The tension leaves my body. "I'll behave tonight, promise."

"Good," Dyson says. "Are you alright?"

I give him my best fake smile. "I'm good. I didn't mean to make her cry."

"I know, she just misses you and her hormones are all over the place," he tells me.

"I promised her we'd talk. I owe her answers and she deserves all of them, but not tonight," I tell him.

"Good, she needs them. She does miss you and she wants her friend back in her life." His response doesn't surprise me. Ireland and I have always been like two peas in a pod and I've broken our happy little shell and I need to find a way to mend what damage I've done and the only way I know how to do that is to tell her the truth. All of it.

The two of us talk for another minute before Dyson is called away by Ireland, who gives me a reassuring smile. I am left face to face with Bryan Hayes, country superstar and a man I've given a lap dance to for money, along with a vaguely familiar man.

"Have you met Calvin or Mouse?"

Recognition rattles around in my brain and my eyes scan the room. Suddenly it all clicks into place. The band, 69 Bottles. Mouse, lead guitarist. I extend my hand to him. "I'm Becca."

Calvin takes my hand. "Pleasure to meet you, Becca." And the nickname rings true. I was always curious why his nickname was Mouse. Now I know. His voice is soft and mouse-like, yet there is a strange confidence that comes with it. "How do you know Cami?"

I look over to the petite, multi-color haired, nearly as pregnant as Ireland, owner of Blu Phoenix. "Indirectly really.

Though this is my favorite bar and I've met her a few times. She and Tristan see fit to take care of me while I'm here."

"They're good people," Bryan adds, but his eyes haven't left my face the entire time he's been here and I can feel his presence despite the comfortable distance between us.

"I'm assuming Cami is a friend of yours?" I ask Mouse.

He smiles, "she is, though she owns the company that handles all matters for the band."

I give him a wink, "my favorite band. I saw you guys play here in Phoenix last year. Ireland too, we went together."

"Small world," Mouse chuckles, "I was there too."

The three of us break into a comfortable laughter before Peacock joins us. Through our conversation I learn Calvin and Peacock, also known as Eric, are together, and despite no one actually saying the words, their love for each other is evident in their eyes. We stay chatting about the band, their upcoming tour and life on the road until Talon, the band's lead singer, pulls them away to set up.

"A private show?" I ask Bryan as the guys disappear out the back door and onto the patio.

"More like a jam session." He smiles at me and for the first time, I really look at the man who's been flirting with me for the last ten minutes.

His hair is a cut short on the sides, a little longer on the top and darker dirty blonde, almost brown in color. His eyes are greener than most I've seen before and while I'm considered tall at five foot eight inches, he's still significantly taller than I am. At least six three, if not six four. He has wide shoulders and while he could be intimidating if he wanted to be, he doesn't scare me. In fact, it's the opposite. He's a man I could see as a protector. And that scares me.

"Sounds like fun." I smile back at him and my cheeks heat

with a blush as the desire to kiss him grows hot in my veins. His eyes never leave my lips.

"Bryan?" someone calls from the other side of the room and he breaks out of our trance by looking toward the sound of the voice. "We're ready."

Bryan nods to the man who called for him; it's not a voice I recognize so I know it's not Liam interrupting us. Thank god. I sigh.

"Come on," he breathes as he reaches for my hand. The moment his fingers brush mine there is an electric shock between us and my heart skips a beat. The tingling sensation doesn't subside as he pulls me through the back doors and onto the patio.

# CHAPTER FIVE
## FINDING PERFECTION ISN'T EASY.

*Bryan*

I DON'T know whether it's the desire to learn her secrets or the fact that I'm genuinely attracted to her that's driving everything I've been doing tonight.

Hanging out on the back patio of Blu in June comes with its own brand of heat, but couple it with the sparks flying between me and Becca and I'm overheating. She's beautiful in every sense of the word. I knew the night I saw her at the strip club there was something about her. Her body language said something to me about her true desires and they did not include the stripping job she was working. She was great at putting on the front required, but there was something deeper in the depths of her blue-green eyes that spoke volumes about who she is underneath it all.

The reminder of where we first met brings me back to the present and reality. Is this a path I want to go down? Dating a stripper? No, it most certainly is not.

She slides between my legs while I sit on the bar stool and my cock stretches a little further inside my jeans and the painful ache reminds me he may have other ideas about the woman who's captured my attention as we watch 69 Bottles jam on the makeshift stage. The same one Lee Brice played that night back in February.

It took all of five minutes after coming out here to realize this is the girl Tristan was telling me about, the one who likes Piña coladas and they all take care of. Tonight seems to be different and that's a good thing. Neither me nor Liam will let her get too far out of hand. I think it helps that were surrounded by friends and not strangers. I hold back a chuckle when I realize that aside from the security staff, Becca and I are the only single ones here.

*Oh, the irony.*

69 Bottles finishes their latest song and Talon says something to everyone, no microphone needed tonight. There is only about thirty people here, most of which I know, but few Becca knows.

"Bryan?" Addison says as she approaches Becca and me sitting in front of the bar.

"Yeah, doll?"

Addison smiles, "They want to know if you want to, well, rather, if you want to join me?"

I smile wider and Becca squirms as she turns around. "You're gonna sing?"

I look at her wide eyes filled with excitement and joy, "I'd love to," I say, never pulling my eyes away from Becca as I answer.

She squeals and pulls back from me as she starts bouncing up and down.

"Well, then," Addison laughs as she makes her way back to Kyle. That's a relationship I'm not sure I understand, but the three of them are very much in love with each other, it's almost inspiring.

When I met Addison the first time, it was at First Avenue in Minneapolis. 69 Bottles was playing a show there and I was in town for my own tour. I stayed an extra day just to see the band, but it wasn't the band I was after. I'd seen the videos of Addison performing with 69 Bottles and I was enamored with her voice. She's anything but a country singer, but I knew I needed to duet with her. And I was right. The song we did turned out amazing and has been one of my biggest hits since its release.

When I met her, I was attracted to her. How could anyone not be? She's tall, has gorgeous eyes and a body that screams

to every man, and I'm sure some women, too. I made no secret of my attraction to her, but she gracefully turned me down. It was about a month or so later I learned the reason, or rather, reasons why. Not only had she and Talon, 69 Bottles' lead singer hooked up, but she was the center of a triad. Addison, Talon and Kyle, all three together and it's amazing to see.

"Any special requests?" I ask Becca as I wrap my arm around her waist.

"Anything." Her voice comes out breathy and wanton. My cock throbs.

"You got it," I tell her before planting a gentle kiss at her temple and leaving her to fend for herself. I find Addison and the guys near the stage and turn back to see Becca standing near the redhead, Ireland, and her boyfriend Dyson. The glow hasn't left Becca's cheeks as she looks at me through the group of people. I smile at her.

"How do you know her?" Addison asks me.

My smile fades a little at the question. "I don't, actually. I met her a couple months ago when I was in town, but this is the first time I've seen or talked to her since then. Why?"

Addison smirks, "Oh nothing."

I roll my eyes at her. "Do you know her?" I ask.

She shakes her head. "No, haven't even really met her tonight. I just know she's a good friend of Ireland's and Dyson is a good friend of Cami and Tristan."

So I've heard. "Are they industry tied?" I ask.

Addison shakes her head. "No, Dyson owns a company here in Phoenix, but I'm pretty sure they have little to do with the industry at all. Though I think there might be some type of relationship between Ireland and Cami that goes beyond friendship."

"What do you say that?" I ask.

Addison smiles, "take a real good look at Cami, then take a real good look at Ireland. If I didn't know better, they could very easily be sisters." I don't want to get into the fact that Cami only has a brother, but looking at both of them now, I see what Addison is talking about. There are some very subtle similarities. Not to mention the fact that I've seen Cami with super curly hair, like Ireland's, before. I have no clue what Cami's natural hair color is because it's always colored, but Ireland's tight curls remind me of Cami's.

"Huh," I say with a nod as Talon approaches us.

"You guys wanna do your duet?" he asks me and Addison.

Addison lights up as she looks to me. I give her a small nod and she bounces much the same way Becca did a little while ago. "You know it?" I ask Talon.

He smiles and nods. "I do. Acoustic?"

I nod and we go to the stage.

*Becca*

"Bryan?" Ireland raises a questioning eyebrow at me.

I shrug. I'm not sure I want to go into details about how he makes me feel. Feelings are not something I'm used to and to be completely honest, that urge to run is getting stronger by the minute. I feel so out of control with him and I don't like it.

"I think he likes you," she adds when I don't reply or offer up any commentary on her question. "Do you like him?" she asks, prompting me to pull my eyes away from the stage where they're moving some things around for whatever they're about to do next.

"Yes," I breathe.

Ireland's face lights up with excitement at my answer. "As in, like him like him?" I can't stop the blush of my cheeks and the smile that plays at my lips. "You do!" she exclaims quietly.

I shush her. "Do you want everyone to hear you?"

She giggles, "Yes. I think this has to be a first for you, Becca."

For some unknown reason the name irritates me tonight. Since Leo/Liam accosted me, it's brought back a lot of old memories and a lot of irritation with the fact that I'm hiding so many secrets from the people closest to me. Ireland's line of questions doesn't help matters any. Becca can like Bryan Hayes all she wants, but Livia? No, she can't. I can't let myself get caught up in the limelight that is a musician's life.

"Maybe," I answer her, trying to pull my attention away from her and back to the stage without giving away the fact that yes, liking Bryan is a first for me. But there's a cure for that and I intend to do just that.

She leans into me. "Good," she whispers as Talon, 69 Bottles' lead singer strums his guitar. I look at the stage and it's just Addison, Talon and Bryan sitting on stools, looking comfortable and casual. I know exactly what's coming and my heart skips a beat as Bryan starts the song he recorded with Addison earlier this year.

Bryan's eyes never leave mine as he sings the love ballad to the crowd.

I take in my surroundings and realize I don't belong amongst these people and my insecurities start to take over. You have celebrities in Tristan and Travis, then you have Cami, while not a movie star herself, she's the owner of the company that controls their lives. Follow them up with the entire 69 Bottles band and their wives or girlfriends, and then lastly, Bryan Hayes. Where Dyson and Ireland fit into this

mix is beyond me, but what doesn't surprise me is Ireland looks right at home. There are a couple of other couples whom I have no idea who they are, but they are either friends with the band, because I've seen them all talking, or they are friends of Tristan or Cami. The atmosphere is more family than it is friends and the reality makes me a little uncomfortable as Bryan and Addison finish their song and the group starts whooping and hollering at them.

Bryan cocks his head at me, as if he's analyzing my mood and it sends a chill up my spine. I hate it when people try to read me.

I break eye contact. I need a drink.

I turn around and head toward the bar. There are no bartenders tonight, it's open and Mouse and Peacock are standing there talking, drinking beers.

"Becca, did you meet Eric?" Calvin asks me.

I shake my head and extend my hand to him. "Pleasure to meet you, Peacock."

He smiles sweetly at me. "Likewise. I hear you're a fan?"

I snort, "Is it that obvious?"

His sweet smile turns into a full-on grin. "Not really. Are you having fun tonight?"

I nod, unsure how to answer that question.

"It's a bit overwhelming, isn't it?" Calvin asks.

"What is?" I counter.

"Having all these people here so casually."

I look around the patio, taking in the amount of celebrity and money standing on the concrete slab and my nerves kick back into overdrive. "Yeah, it is." I finally concede. "You know celebrities are human too, but when you see them, they have a super human vibe regardless," I add.

Both guys laugh. "You can say that again," Calvin chuckles. "When I first met Tristan, I stuttered like an idiot."

"Yes, he did," Eric adds with a loving smile to his partner. I remember feeling devastated when I'd heard the news that Eric was taken. He's gorgeous, but the two of them are obviously right for each other.

I laugh, "Good to know I'm not the only one. Though I've only casually known Tristan and Cami since they opened the bar. My nights spent here are as far as that relationship extends." I fill a glass with ice and pour some amaretto over it before grabbing the soda nozzle for a little splash of Sprite to add to the glass.

"It's a great place. We love coming here when we're in town," Dex adds as he joins our small group.

"You guys should play here sometime."

Dex smiles at me. "We do, just not publicly."

"That's what I mean. You guys would fill this place up to bursting," I say before taking a sip of my drink. "But I wouldn't plan it. I would just show up and start jamming."

"Not a bad idea, darlin'," Eric says to me.

"You'll still fill the joint." I laugh, "It takes all of thirty minutes to get here from the majority of the Valley."

Music starts playing again. Bryan sits on a bar stool with an acoustic guitar in his lap. His fingers strum gently against the strings and I quickly recognize the song. It's my song, the one I was dancing to at the club, but a stripped down version of it.

I war with myself. The part of me that gets irritated easily wants to run screaming from the patio. How dare he? But the longer I watch him, the more entranced I become. His soulful voice fills the patio, the guitar a gentle strum in the background and the deeper into the song he gets, the more I

realize this man will always be a part of me.

In just a short amount of time he's managed to sear his way into my brain and brand himself on my heart.

"WHAT do you say we get out of here?" Bryan drawls in my ear as I'm back standing between his legs. His impromptu, acoustic set was something I will never forget for as long as I live.

I turn in his arms and wrap my own around his neck. "And just where do you suppose we go?"

"How about your place?"

I shake my head. "Yours."

He laughs, "Mine is a hotel room."

"Even better."

He shakes his head slightly, but the smile on his face contradicts the disapproval at my request. Regardless, if this is going to happen, his hotel room is the best place.

We decide to leave separately after I get caught up talking to Eric and Calvin for a few minutes. I tell Ireland and Dyson good-bye before I leave. The promise of a conversation lingers between us. It's not going to be pretty, but it needs to be done. The result will mean one of two things. First, I move. Leave Arizona for good or second, we go about life as if nothing has changed. Though I am hoping for the latter option, I doubt that will be the case. My secrets are impossible for me to share. I can't imagine her wanting to hold on to them too.

When I leave the bar, Bryan and Liam are in a heated discussion near a black Escalade. The look on Liam's face isn't a pretty one and I get the impression their conversation isn't going well, but they both catch sight of me and stop.

"Whatever you two are discussing, continue. I'm leaving."

"Becca, don't," Bryan pleads with me. His eyes begging me

in a way that makes me weak in the knees.

"Good night," I tell both of them and side step them toward my car.

Bryan grabs my arm as I pass. "Take me with you."

I snort, "Why, so your bodyguard over there can have a conniption fit? No thanks." I pull my arm free. "Maybe one day he'll get his head out of his ass when it comes to me, but I highly doubt that day is today. In the meantime, maybe he'll explain to you why he doesn't want me to go with you. I'm sure he's only out to protect your reputation." I glare at Liam. "I'm pretty sure he doesn't want his detail to fuck a whore," I snap and turn toward my car again.

"You're not a whore," Liam says.

I laugh a humorless laugh, "Funny, you thought I was a few hours ago."

"What the fuck, Liam?" Bryan snaps.

"Oh, so you haven't explained to him how you know me?" I turn toward the two of them and Liam's face is filled with panic. Bryan's is full of confusion as he turns from Liam to me and back again. "Let me enlighten you, Bryan. I met Liam as Leo when he was working undercover inside the Ricci crime family in New York." My heart freezes in my chest. "In a whore house," I add. Bryan's eyes go wide, confusion and disbelief color his features. "Your friend over there was supposed to protect me, but instead he disappeared on me. Only to show back up years later with nothing but contempt for my chosen lifestyle. Which is why he doesn't want his prized client around me. So, I'll make it easier for both of you."

Anger races through my veins as I unlock my car door and pull it open. Neither one of them has said a word. I risk a glance at Bryan and there's nothing but pity in his eyes. I

growl in frustration as I climb into my car and turn over the engine.

"Livia, wait," Liam calls and I pull the car forward, rolling down my window.

"Don't call me that," I snap at him before rolling up my window again.

"You're not a whore," he yells as I step on the gas, only to slam on the breaks and throw the car into park before climbing out and getting in Liam's face.

"Why don't you say that a little louder? I'm pretty sure the entire bar didn't just hear you. You're right, Liam, I am not a whore. I am a woman who, no thanks to you, was forced into something no girl should ever be forced to do, and rather than respect me for surviving then and for surviving now, you choose to remind me of something I had absolutely no control over. When you get your head out of your ass and open your fucking eyes, maybe you'll see that."

"I'm trying," Liam breathes softly.

"Try. Harder," I growl.

I turn toward my car to find Bryan standing in my way. "Move," I demand.

He shakes his head. "Not unless you'll take me with you."

I look at him. His eyes are full of emotion unlike anything I've seen before and I can't tell if he truly wants to come with me or if he is doing his best to piss Liam off. I don't care.

"You're friend's right." My voice softens. "Go home, Bryan. Your secret is safe with me." I side step him again, but he steps in front of me and before I know it, his hands are cupping my cheeks and his lips are pressed against mine. The zing I felt before fires off again, this time straight to my clit. Sending my pussy pulsing, desperate for something to grab on to. I melt into him as he lowers his hands from my cheeks

to my neck and to my shoulders, pulling me closer to him. I wrap my arms around him. No matter how hard I squeeze, I can't get him close enough to me.

His tongue slides along my bottom lip, asking for permission. I grant him the access he wants and his tongue slides along mine and I moan into his mouth. My breathing hitches in my throat and my head starts to spin. Realizing what's happening, he reluctantly pulls back and begs, "Take me with you."

The space gives me a moment of clarity, but his warm body is pressed against mine and I can't stop what comes out of my mouth next. "Yes."

## *Bryan*

I realized the moment she walked away from me and got into her car that I couldn't let her go, not like this.

The moment my lips touched hers, I understood in that instant I can never let her go.

Liam seems intent on letting her past color whatever future she may have or whatever the woman is she's become and I won't have that.

"Get in," she tells me and I walk around her car quickly, afraid she's going to take off on me again. When I reach the passenger door, I look at Liam who appears to feel betrayed by my choice to leave. I don't know as if I've ever seen him in so much pain before, but he finds it in himself to nod slightly, telling me it's alright. Though I don't need his permission to do anything, seeing that nod tells me he understands and in his own Scottish way that he's sorry. I nod back and climb in.

"Where you staying?" she asks.

"The Biltmore," I tell her and she puts the car in drive. She

doesn't look at me as she pulls out of the parking lot. "Tell me about it?"

Her eyes meet mine briefly before returning to the road. "About what?"

"How you met Liam?"

"Just like I said earlier," she states firmly but doesn't offer anything further.

"How'd you end up there? In the house."

Again, she looks at me, but this time her eyes, while brief, are pleading with me. "That's not a conversation for a car ride. And probably more information than you want to know right now," she says before returning her eyes to the road.

"Will you tell me someday?"

She shrugs. "Perhaps."

I should argue with her a little more, but I'm not going to push her for more information when she clearly doesn't want to talk about it. "Okay, will you answer something else?"

"Sure," she says nonchalantly.

"What would you prefer I call you?"

Her eyes meet mine briefly before she looks back to the road. "What do you want to call me?"

"By your name."

"Well, then my name is Becca."

"Alright, Becca, tell me something else. Do you actually like that name?" I ask.

"No," she says, deadpan.

"Then why use it?"

She shrugs. "Because that's...you know, you really are nosy," she snaps and my cock stirs a little more in my jeans at her sassiness.

"I love your sassy mouth," I smirk at her. I lean in close and whisper in her ear, "I prefer Livia."

She sighs, but doesn't say anything as she drives down the streets of Phoenix toward my hotel.

After another ten minutes in the car, we pull up in front of the Biltmore Hotel and the valet is there before she even manages to turn off the car. Within a few short minutes, we're inside the hotel headed toward the elevator and my room. She's obviously been here before as she leads me in the right direction and I slide my fingers between hers as we walk. That electric charge that was there the moment I touched her and more so the minute I kissed her zings between us.

I notice her jaw goes slack as the sensation hits her too and my mind races with what this could mean for the two of us. I've never felt this way about anyone before and there is a part of me that starts feeling guilty for inviting her back to my hotel. This is only going to lead in one direction and one direction only.

My rock hard cock begs to say otherwise.

She presses the up arrow on the elevator panel. I chuckle, "How do you know I'm not staying in the basement?"

She smiles and looks at me. "Because there is no basement." She winks at me as the elevator signals its arrival and we step inside. "You got your key out?"

I laugh again, "And what makes you assume I need a key?"

For a brief moment, she looks offended by my question, but then her lips twitch in a playful smile. "Because Bryan Hayes doesn't stay below the penthouse."

"Well played, sweetheart, well played." She freezes on me. "What did I say?"

She turns and presses our bodies together. "If you want

to keep your dick, I suggest you lose that word from your vocabulary."

I cock my head at her, noting how tense she is. "My apologies, Livi."

"I'm sorry," she says sheepishly as she looks away and backs away from me. I take the chance to insert my key into the reader and press the button for the top floor.

"You're forgiven, and you are correct. Nothing but the best." I wink at her and she softens. "I will do my best to forget the word, but please know I'm only human."

She pushes a stray strand of hair behind her ear, making her look impossibly younger than she is. "I know, I shouldn't have..."

"Shh," I silence her with my finger and bring her chin up so her eyes are looking into mine. "It's alright."

Looking into her eyes sends a thrill through me and the air between us becomes charged with sexual, pent up, tension and I know the moment she feels it too. Her mouth falls slack and her body leans into mine. My cock, already straining past the point of comfortably hard, hardens further. Sending a shot of pain and desire racing through my body and I slam my lips into hers as I turn her back toward the wall of the elevator. Holding her still, I let my tongue do all the walking.

She opens for me easily and her breathing changes immediately. Her body writhes beneath mine. My free hand roams her body from her hip, along her side until I'm cupping her breast in my hand. I find her already hard nipple and roll it between my fingers. She moans into my mouth and I press my rock hard cock against her pelvic bone.

I feel her hips flick and grind, looking for some relief and I smile against her lips as I roll her nipple between my fingers

again. My smile breaks our kiss and the ding of the elevator pulls my hand from her breast. I lace with my fingers with hers as I pull her from the elevator.

There are only two doors on this floor and I slide my keycard into the one that's mine and the beep signals the door is unlocked.

It feels like slow motion as I turn the handle and push the door open, but we are inside quickly and this time, she pins me up against the wall.

Her lips claim mine and her hands begin to roam up my body. Her fingers tracing my stomach muscles as she brings her hands lower, searching for access. She pulls my shirt from my jeans and slides her hands around my back, pulling my shirt up as she goes.

She pulls her lips from mine but she kisses her way down my jaw to my neck until she reaches the collar of my shirt and pulls back. Her hands return to the front of my shirt and the buttons that stand in her way of skin on skin contact.

Her hands are quick, unbuttoning my shirt as quickly as she can before pushing it off my shoulders. She returns to my t-shirt, sliding her hands underneath it and tracing my abs as she slides my shirt up and over my head.

"My turn," I growl as I push her toward the other wall and she doesn't resist. I press myself into her, trapping her there while I reciprocate the process of lifting her shirt over her head.

I am greeted with a sheer black bra and the sight of her dark brown nipples peeping through. They're as hard as pebbles and the size of erasers perched atop her gorgeous tits and my mouth waters.

I lean down and blow hot air across one of her nipples before sliding my tongue up the shear fabric and catching

a nipple between my teeth. She moans and slides her hand into my hair, holding me to her. I pull her bra down and tuck it under her breast, giving me full access to the tasty treat. I wrap my mouth around her nipple and suck it into my mouth hard. She groans and tightens her grip on my hair.

I moan, sending a vibrating hum around her nipple and her eyes roll up.

I let my hands roam around to her back to find the clasp of her bra. I undo the clasp and release her nipple. She slides the flimsy fabric off her shoulders to the floor. I lead her backwards to the bedroom. I can't take my eyes off her.

*Becca*

WITH my hand in his, we head toward the bedroom. I've never in my life wanted someone more than I want him. It's the way he kisses me, worships me, and watches me as we walk toward his bed. Desire runs through my veins and judging by the heat in his eyes, he feels it in kind.

I've only felt true desire once before in my life, but even that pales in comparison to what I'm feeling for this man right now. That electric spark is ever present between us. It gets harder to ignore with each passing step.

For the first time in my life, I have absolutely no hesitation about what I'm about to do. His eyes never leave my body as I seductively remove my jeans with deliberate movements and a few well-timed shimmies.

I ignore the nagging thoughts in the back of my mind reminding me that he's seen all this before. If I let that thought consume me, the call girl in me will come out and she needs to stay far away from this.

My panties match my bra and leave little to the imagination. He licks his lips.

I saunter over to him and grab the waistband of his pants. I unbutton them and reach inside to wrap my hand around his shaft.

My breathing hitches when I grasp him in my hand. He's huge. Well, at the very least, wide. I lick my lips, wanting to taste him and I use the leverage I have inside his pants with my other hand on the outside to push his pants down his legs. When his cock springs free, I can't stop my eyes from wandering south and taking in the full package.

His hair is trimmed short and his cock is- "Wow," I breathe.

He pushes a stray hair behind my ear and smiles. "The same is said about you." His hand trails down my neck, over my collarbone and the swell of my breast while gently brushing his fingers over my nipple. The sensation sends goose bumps flying across my skin and both nipples harden.

The sensation sends new determination through me and I quickly lose control. My body drives what happens next as I lower myself to my knees and look at him through my eyelashes while I push his jeans down farther. He toes off his shoes then steps out of his jeans. He's standing before me naked. His body is gorgeous, accented by a couple of tattoos along his left thigh. I run my hands up his thighs while keeping my eyes on his.

His eyes roll up the second my hands wrap around his cock and stroke upward. His breathing hitches when I flick my tongue across the tip and his hands slide into my hair, holding me in place. His fingers tighten on my scalp and I lean forward, licking his cock, stroking it up and down while I wrap my mouth around the head.

He hisses through his teeth. "You're driving me crazy," he breathes and I smile as I swallow him as far as he'll go. Once there, I move my tongue and swallow farther, bringing him to the point of choking me before I pull back. I gasp for air before taking him back down my throat. "Fuck," he groans and his hips start moving forward, his cock sliding in and out of my mouth in short little spurts.

My pussy throbs.

I take him all the way in again, holding my breath and swallowing him a couple of times before releasing him with a gasp. "Fuck me," I moan.

He tugs gently on my hair, coaxing me to stand. Once there, his lips slam against mine and my desire for him sky rockets. My pussy is soaking wet, clutching desperately

for something that isn't there and I want to cry out in frustration. It's like he senses my need for him because suddenly his hand is in between my legs sliding through my slit. I moan into his mouth as he pushes me backwards, searching blindly for the bed.

My legs hit the bed and he pushes me down, breaking our kiss and all contact with my body. I reach for his cock, but he pulls away before lowering himself on his knees, between my legs.

I'm spread wide and his hot tongue is sears into my slit and my clit throbs as his tongue flicks relentlessly over the sensitive bundle of nerves. My legs begin to twitch with the pressure and motion of his tongue. His hand comes between my legs and starts tracing the seam of my folds before sliding a finger inside of me. I cry out. My orgasm builds faster than I anticipated. "More. God, please, I need more."

He adds a second finger inside me, scissoring them, spreading me open, stretching me before he slides them all the way in. I feel the flicker of his fingertips against my g-spot and my back arches off the bed. My hands cup my breasts and roll my nipples between my fingers. The new wave of pleasure shoots through me and I explode all over his fingers. My orgasm takes me higher than I've ever been before. My body starts to tremble as he pushes me up the bed and climbs between my legs.

I open my eyes to see him tear open a condom wrapper with his teeth before pulling the rubber disc from its casing. I watch with rapt attention as he rolls the rubber down his shaft. I lift myself to my elbows, desperate to watch him slide inside me.

He slides the head of his cock up and down my slit, coating the tip with my juices before he starts to push inside me. My eyes roll up and a tingling sensation I've never felt

before radiates throughout my body as he slowly claims me.

He slides all the way to the hilt. His pelvic bone presses against my hypersensitive clit, making my eyes close and my arms give out. He grabs me behind the knees, lifting my legs up so he has better, deeper access and he pushes in deeper as my body shifts.

"Oh God," I moan when he pulls back just a little. The ridge of the head brushes along my g-spot. The sensation is so intense, another orgasm balances just below the surface.

"Play with those tits for me," he grunts as he pulls out and slams back into me.

I oblige him. The sensation makes my body tremble again as he withdraws from my depths and pushes back inside, this time harder and faster.

His pace quickens and my orgasm is right on the verge. The edge so close I can taste it. He knows it too because he starts pinching my clit. Stars explode behind my eyes as my orgasm takes me over the edge.

He doesn't stop. His pace slows and his hips become more fluid in their motion as he works my orgasm from my body. Drawing it out in a way I've never known before this. Everything is new and different. I open my eyes to meet his lust filled orbs. It's like finding light in the darkness. For the first time in my life, I feel safe and adored by a man I barely know.

The realization sends a shiver through me and his pace increases again. "Come for me, please," I beg him.

His thumb starts to circle my clit as his pace increases. His movements become jerky and uncoordinated and his eyes roll up and his head lulls back as the sensation of my pussy grasping at his cock, milking him, registers and his thumb picks up its pace. My third orgasm sits on a fine ledge, ready

for him to come with me. I reach my hands up and run them along his chest and pinch his nipples between my fingers.

He grunts, and slams into me, hard. Then pulls out and slams in again. He's growling like an animal as his orgasm consumes him, tipping me over the edge for the third time.

* * *

"Where are you going?" Sleepy eyes meet mine as I sit on the side of the bed after gathering my clothes to get dressed to leave.

I reach over and cup his cheek before leaning down and kissing him softly. "Home," I breathe.

His arms wrap around my waist not wanting to let me go. "It's three in the morning," he groans. I don't want to leave, but I know if I don't, this isn't going to be pretty. "Stay with me."

I smile at him. "I can't."

"Why not?" he asks. His voice is soft, sleepy.

"Because..." I don't finish the sentence. I don't know how to tell him I have no idea how to sleep with a man. That I have no idea what it's like to wake up next to someone in the morning.

He releases me before sliding to the opposite side of the bed and climbing off. I look away from him, not wanting to see the disappointment in his eyes because I'm leaving. I pull my jeans on before putting my bra back on. I purposefully left my panties on the floor. I don't know why, but I felt compelled to leave something for him. I pull my shirt over my head and slip back into my heels.

"Running solves nothing, you know?" His voice is soft and

distant. He's on the other side of the room and I stand up to face him. He's back in his jeans.

"I'm not running. I have to go."

"No, Livi, you don't."

There's that nickname again. "My name is Becca."

"Go ahead, lie to yourself all you want, but tell me, Livi, do you want to leave?"

He's baiting me, I know he is. "Yes," I state before folding my arms across my chest. "You know why I came here tonight."

He gives me a humorless chuckle before stepping out of the shadows. "No, darlin', I don't know why you came here tonight."

I try not to let the tone of his voice get to me, but the backs of my eyes start to prickle. "Bryan...I..." I can't find any words to say to him. I've never felt passion or desire like I have with this man and I want nothing more than to have it again, but I can't. That's not how this works. At least not for me. "It was good to see you again," I say before moving toward the door. He steps between me and my exit. His proximity sends a spark of awareness through me. My body hums with the desire to touch him, lick his chest...

"I'm not a john, Livi."

My eyes meet his, and I don't hide the pain I feel at his words. "Why in the fuck would you think that?"

"Because you're leaving, you're running, just like I'm sure you do with every man you've ever been with. I am not one of them."

"I never said..."

His lips press against mine and my train of thought is lost the instant our lips touch. My resolve falters a little more.

I can't stay.

I pull away from him, fighting hard to maintain the guise that his kiss didn't affect me and fail. "Keep lying to yourself." His eyes narrow at me.

"You know nothing about me," I snap at him.

"I know that running away is the only way you think you can handle this. The only way you can justify it to yourself. You think by running out the door that you can put me behind you like you have every other man you've ever slept with."

Anger boils in my blood and I narrow my eyes back at him. "If you were any other man, you'd be paying me."

He reaches into his back pocket and produces a wad of cash. "That can be arranged."

My reaction surprises both of us when I slap him across the face. The action forces him to move out of the way of the door and I open it. I get three steps before he grabs my wrist, spins me around and slaps something in my hand before slamming the door in my face. I look down and see the cash in my hand. "You son of a bitch!" I shout before throwing the entire stack of money, a good four or five grand, against his door. A small thud follows and the money goes flying everywhere before I turn on my heel and leave his hotel room, slamming it shut on my way out.

I run straight into Liam's chest and I start fighting him. Throwing my fists at his chest, tears streaming down my face, the works. "Let me go," I scream.

"Calm the fuck down, Livia."

"Go to hell." I connect my knee to his balls and he releases me. I press the elevator down button and it's there for me immediately and I step inside.

Liam's pain filled eyes meet mine and I want to apologize

to him, but I can't and then the door closes.

"Bryan!" I shout as I step into the hotel room. I don't hear anything as I walk into the living room area of the suite, but I see money scattered on the floor near the door of his bedroom. "Bryan!" I shout again.

The door flies open. "What?" he snaps.

"What the fuck happened in here?" He looks around the floor at his feet at the money.

"Fuck," he groans before running his hand through his hair. A sign he's frustrated and not one he uses often. Now I know something happened in that room.

"Talk to me?"

"I overreacted."

"That's obvious, lad, but why?"

He shrugs his shoulders. "She was leaving, it pissed me off."

"So you tried to pay her off?"

"She was treating me like one of her johns. So..."

"You treated her like a whore," His eyes meet mine and the unspoken words are there in the pain I can see. "That girl has a lot of baggage. Are you sure it's worth all this?" I ask him sincerely.

"Considering I haven't stopped thinking about her since we were here in February? Or taking into account the fact that I've never felt like this before? Yeah, Liam, it's worth it."

"Then stop her."

He snorts a laugh, "How?"

"Valet."

I watch as recognition lights his eyes and he runs into his room for the phone. I lean over, putting my hands on my knees as I work through processing the burning in my balls from her knee to my dick.

"They're delaying her," he tells me as he races past me then skids to a stop. "What's wrong with you?"

"There was once a point in knowing her that I doubted her ability to take care of herself. Between the gun in my back and the knee to my nuts, I'm pretty sure she's covered."

"She..." he bursts out laughing. "I knew I needed this woman in my life," he says as he leaves the suite. I head for the shower in my room and my bed.

## *Bryan*

Of all the idiotic fucking things I've done in my life, this is by far the stupidest thing I've ever done. Hoping to stop her from leaving is the second idiotic thing I've done.

I don't know why I got so hot when she wanted to leave. I should have known she would, but I guess somewhere along the line we went from being two people meeting and hooking up to being an unattached one night stand.

This doesn't work for me.

The elevator finally arrives on the lobby level and I race toward the automatic doors and out into the warm June night, sans shoes, but I did pull on a t-shirt before leaving the suite.

As soon as I'm clear of the doors I start searching for her, looking from side to side, but I don't see her, I don't see anyone.

I run to the valet stand to my right and find no one is at the window. I step around the corner to see her standing there impatiently waiting for her car. She drops a cigarette on

the ground and stomps it out.

"I didn't take you as a smoker," I say as I approach her.

She whips around to look at me standing there, disheveled and desperate. Her eyes roam up and down my body. "You should go put some shoes on. You'll cut your feet."

I shake my head. "You should come back upstairs so we can talk."

"Is this your doing?"

"What?" I ask when she spreads her arms out in a gesture of 'look around, moron'. I blush a little at her accurate accusation. I shrug. "Maybe. I wanted a chance to apologize."

"You're a man of resources, Mr. Hayes. I'd imagine between you and Liam, you'll have me tracked down in no time."

"Aye, Liam is good at finding people, especially those who don't want to be found." I cock an eyebrow at her. "Though you seem to be the elusive one in that group."

"Good," she states simply before turning to face me head on. "I like it that way."

"For reasons you're still not going to explain to me?" I ask.

"Nope, again, you're a man of resources, I'm sure you can figure it out faster than I can tell you about it." She takes a few steps toward me and remembering how Liam ended up, I fight the urge to cover my crotch, but the idea of pissing her off isn't at the top of my to-do list right now. I've already done enough damage. "You wanted to apologize, so apologize." Her tone is cold, hard, and unforgiving.

"Upstairs," I counter.

She shakes her head. "No, then I'll be right back down here and the poor valet man will have to go hunting for my car again. Though I don't imagine it's this difficult to find."

I shrug. "He's probably taking a break around the corner." I

give her a playful smirk.

"Well then, Mr. Hayes, I'm waiting."

"Will my apology mean anything?"

She shrugs and takes another step forward. "Perhaps." There is a mischievous grin playing at her lips. "Then again, I am just a whore after all."

"Livi, don't."

She takes the last three steps she needs to be standing close to me. Her scent assaults me. The smell of Becca and vanilla and sex fills my nostrils and my mind races back to my bedroom. "You, Mr. Hayes, have not earned the right to call me that."

I give her a smirk. "Maybe, but I'm pretty sure I'm the only one who wants to use it. So, where were we?"

"Nowhere," she smirks then snakes her arm around my neck, pulling me down to her mouth. She flicks her tongue across my lips before planting a warm, passion-fueled kiss against my lips and my breathing goes ragged.

The kiss lasts but a moment before her car comes around the corner and I feel her body shift into position and I put my hands down, blocking her knee to the groin and knocking her off balance. I manage to wrap my arms around her waist before she falls to the ground. "Next time you want to knee someone in the balls, don't get his friend first." I give her an evil grin. "Now, about that apology." I straighten up, but I don't let her go. I simply wrap my arms around her, holding her to me.

To anyone else, we look like lovers saying good-bye. Anyone standing close enough to hear us will think we're insane. "You, Livia, are not a whore. Nor will I ever treat you as such."

"Too late, big buy, you already have. Now, let me go before

I cause a scene."

"No, I didn't. You treated me like every other john, every other man you've ever been with. The only difference here, Livia, is that I actually care about you."

"You don't even know me."

"I know enough to know I care about you, I care about what happens to you, and most importantly, I want to see nothing bad happen to you, ever."

"You're barking up the wrong tree, Mr. Hayes. No one cares about me." She pries herself from my arms and beelines toward her car as the valet tosses her keys to her like it's a well-coordinated effort before she speeds off.

Reality dawns on me.

Nothing about tonight was special between the two of us. She's been here before, she's... "God damn it!"

"Can I help you, sir?" the valet guy says.

"No, no you can't." I turn to go back inside and spin back around. "Wait, maybe you can. Her..." I nod my head toward where the car was parked. "How often does she come here?"

"A couple nights a week, sometimes more. Why?" His voice is devoid of any emotions whatsoever and my heart turns to ice in my chest.

"Thanks," I mutter and turn to head back inside.

"If it helps, I haven't seen her here in quite a while."

I turn back toward the kid and stare him down. "Define 'quite a while'?"

He shrugs. "I don't know. It was cooler, maybe back in January or February." His eyes roll up in his head as he thinks. "She had a room here for a few nights, something about her roommate was pissing her off. I remember her coming back late one Saturday and someone was following

her. She'd said something about going to a concert, some country guy at a bar on the west side."

"Lee Brice?" I ask.

"Yeah, that's him. Sorry I don't listen to that shi... stuff."

I roll my eyes and shake my head. "You haven't seen her since then?"

"No, sir, and I always work the weekends."

"Thank you," I tell him before I go inside and back to my room.

Once inside my room, I call out to Liam and he appears in the doorway. He's changed into a pair of shorts and a t-shirt; his typical sleeping attire. My eyes land on his missing leg and no matter how many times I see it, I can't help but be reminded of how we met all those years ago. "You feeling alright?" I ask him.

"Yeah, I'm good, was gonna crawl into bed. Did you catch her?"

I nod. "It was pointless," I share. My voice dejected.

"Wanna talk about it?"

I give him a humorless laugh. "Not really. I'd like to go home though."

"I'll call the airline."

I shake my head. "Go to bed, we can call in the morning."

He gives me a smile. "It is morning."

My eyes move from him to the windows and sure enough, you can see the sun rising over the mountains to the east.

"Well, later, after we get some sleep."

"Alright. Anything else?"

I shake my head. "Good night, Liam."

"G'night, lad. He uses the knob of the door to brace himself before he hops forward and closes the door.

No matter how much I work him, no matter how fast he has to move, Liam is an oak. Solid and stable. If it wasn't for the fact that I met him in a bar shortly after his accident, I would never know he'd lost his leg. He doesn't walk with a limp, he doesn't give the impression he's incapable of doing anything and I'd be surprised if Cami or any of the other security guys from last night even know.

I climb into bed, the bed that smells of sex and Livia, and curl myself around the pillow she was laying on before I let the memory of Liam and I meeting fill my mind as I fall asleep.

*Walking into a New York City bar is just what I need right now. The last few weeks have been completely insane. One thing after another has happened that I could have only dreamed about.*

*I grab a stool at the bar and pull my baseball cap and sunglasses off my face, setting them down on the bar before the bartender comes over and asks what I want. I point at the guy sitting a few stools down from me. "Whatever he's having."*

*The bartender looks sad for minute but he pours my drink. It's a Tuesday night in Manhattan and it's a quiet, hole in the wall pub across the street from my hotel. It had some Irish name on the outside and it's tucked between two tourist shops. It seemed like a good place to duck inside for a while and grab a drink.*

*The man whose drink I copied raises his glass in a toast when Brian, the bartender hands me my drink. I return the gesture and slam back the drink without actually tasting it. The burn is almost too much and I sputter a little bit. The*

*guy I copied chuckles as he gets up and moves closer to me.
I notice then that he's limping and he looks like he's in pain.*

*He takes a seat on the stool next to me and extends his
hand. "Liam," he smiles, but there is a real pain in his eyes
as he does.*

*I take his hand. "A Scott in an Irish Pub?" I cock an eye-
brow at him and Brian, the bartender, laughs.*

*"This fool's been coming here for years." They both
chuckle over what appears to be an inside joke.*

*"Name's Bryan," I tell Liam before releasing his hand.*

*"Well, that should be easy enough. What brings you to
the Big Apple?"*

*I point to my glass and Liam's indicating to Brian, the
bartender, the next round is on me. "Business."*

*"Ahh," Liam exclaims as if that explains everything.
"Good business?"*

*I nod. "Very good business."*

*"Well, then we have a reason to celebrate," Liam says as
Brian sets down new glasses in front of us and we both grab
them, this time clinking them together. "To good business."*

*"Aye." I smile and this time I don't down the glass, but
rather take a sip of the single malt. "So, why you in here
drinking on a Tuesday?"*

*"Lost my job," he states honestly.*

*"Ah, shit, I'm sorry. What did you do?" I ask.*

*Liam chuckles, "If I tell you, I'll have to kill you."*

*Something in his voice says he's serious yet the humor is
underlying and Brian laughs. "Federal agent?" I ask.*

*Liam smiles, "FBI."*

*"Nice, why'd they let you go?"*

*"Lost my leg a few months back." His answers are short and I can tell he doesn't want to talk about it anymore.*

*"Sorry to hear that, but I hardly see that as grounds for termination."*

*"That, my friend, is the million dollar question. They didn't like it too much when I said the same thing, but the truth is, I was miserable at a desk job, they gave me the option to stay in that position or leave, I left, so it's a win-win."*

*"What do you plan to do now?" I follow up before taking another sip of my whiskey.*

*"Don't know. Warm this stool for a while then go from there."*

The night progressed until we were both completely hammered, but we exchanged numbers before the night was out. The next morning, I called him and offered him a job as my bodyguard. He was reluctant to step into that kind of role, especially considering he still had a long time in rehab to get through. I told him I would pay for his rehab and asked him to move to Nashville with me. Before the year was out, he'd moved in and settled into his role with an ease I wish I could have had with my newfound fame.

That night in the bar, was fate intervening on a life altering event in both our lives. Liam never talks about his days with the Bureau and, up until Livia, I never bothered to ask.

Neither one of us sleep much before we're on our way to the airport to catch our flight. Leaving the hotel is bittersweet in a way I don't expect. I don't even have her number and leaving means the only place she could possibly contact me is now gone.

"Can you do me a favor?" I ask Liam as we board the plane to head back to Nashville, my home.

"Always, lad. You know this."

"Find her for me."

"If that is so important to you, why are we leaving?"

"Because the only way is if I find her, she won't come looking for me," I tell him as we take our seats.

"You can't know that."

"Ahh, but I can. You didn't see her resolve last night. She's protecting herself."

"Something that girl has done since she was sixteen years old," he says morosely.

"Tell me about it?" I meant to be more demanding of him, but it came out as a question instead.

He settles in, buckling up and stretching out. "What do you want to know?"

"Everything."

"Aye, but I won't tell you that, and you know that. But part of what was said last night is true. I found her in a whore house run by Vito Ricci in New York."

"So they do exist?"

"What? The Mafia?" I nod in answer to his question. "They do, unfortunately." He runs his hand in an absentminded gesture over his knee on the leg he had amputated.

"So if you won't spill the details on Livia, tell me about that."

"This?" He points to his leg, I nod again and he sighs. "Honestly? It's still a blur, but it was during a bust on one of Ricci's joints. We had some bad intel on what was going on at the warehouse we were raiding. We were under the impression it was a drug house and it wasn't. It was an ammunition holding facility owned by Ricci. So I'll let you draw your own conclusions on that one. I was lucky all I lost

was the lower half quarter of my leg. The Bureau lost four men that day." He falls silent again.

"And Ricci?"

There is an almost evil grin that spreads across Liam's face. "That warehouse was the key to finishing off the Ricci organization. Over the course of the next three weeks the Bureau, along with the CIA and NYPD managed to take out the rest of the family and the remaining moles they had in place in various organizations. That warehouse held the servers Ricci stored all his information on. It was the holy grail of the organization." His evil smile turns into a smirk as he's transported back to that time in his mind.

"I vaguely remember reading or hearing something about the big takedown," I tell him.

"I'm sure you did. Everyone knows about it."

"And you played a part in that. That's pretty epic." I stroke his ego a little over that one. He just smiles and looks at me.

"It was, but it was also tragic."

"Yeah, it was, but it wasn't in vain," I tell him.

"No, that it was not."

We fall silent as the plane slowly fills with passengers before pulling away from the gate and taking off toward Nashville. Meanwhile my mind wanders back to the woman who's crept her way into my heart. I can't even begin to imagine all the pain she's endured in her life, but I'm going to make it my goal to find out and then erase her pain.

*Livia*

"Can I help you?" the man behind the registration desk asks me as I approach.

"Can you call up to the penthouse for me?"

"I'm sorry, ma'am, but there is no one in the penthouse. They checked out about an hour ago."

Fuck. "Were they scheduled to leave this morning?"

"No, ma'am, they cancelled the rest of their reservation. Is there something else I can help you with?"

My heart sinks into my stomach. "No, thanks." I step away from the desk and back toward the doors to leave.

If only I'd gotten here sooner.

If only I hadn't spent an hour pacing my tiny apartment debating on whether or not this was the right thing to do. Debating why I felt so compelled to come back here after the way he treated me last night. It's still not something I can comprehend because right now, it makes no fucking sense whatsoever.

Once outside I pull my phone from my back pocket. I don't carry a purse; they just get in the way. I pull up Ireland's number. I haven't used it in months and that's not her fault. It's mine. I press the call button and slowly put the phone to my ear.

"Becca, you alright?"

"Yes, no...I don't know."

"Talk to me? What's going on?" she says and I can hear her concern through the phone.

"I need a favor," I tell her.

"Anything."

"You seem to be pretty close with Cami now..."

"Yeah, that's something we need to talk about." Her voice is softer, concerned and maybe even a little heartbroken.

"We will, I promise, I just need some time."

"Understood." Her voice has a softer, defeated tone to it, but she circles back to the reason for my call. "So what about Cami?"

"She's Bryan's agent, right?"

"No, but her company represents him. Cami delegates."

"Can she get in touch with him?" I ask after a beat of awkward silence.

"Uh...what's going on, Bee?"

The nickname brings me back to when we first met back in college. A chore I didn't want to take on, but I did it. Got myself a useless degree under the name of Becca Carpenter. A name that, if my discussion with Ireland goes south, will no longer matter. When our names were placed on our door, she was listed as Ireland McK and I was listed as Bee Carp. It was dumb, but that's how it started. I gave her hell for having the name of a country as her first name, and she never stopped calling me Bee. I smile at the memory and wipe a stray tear from my cheek.

"Nothing," I finally manage to answer. "I...this is so stupid."

She chuckles into the phone. "You slept with him, didn't you?"

"What makes you say that?" I snap.

"Becca, come on, I know you. But I also know that if you slept with him, you wouldn't want to call him again, unless..." she trails off, "Unless you're actually falling for him."

"Good god, no, nothing like that..."

"Yup, okay, fine, be that way."

"What way?"

She laughs, "It's okay to have feelings for someone, you know?"

"Can Cami help me or not?" I ask, redirecting the subject from Bryan and me to why I need her to contact Cami.

She laughs and I can picture her shaking her head. "It's gonna cost you."

"What?" I smile into the phone. This is our little game.

"Dinner?"

"I told-"

"I'll make chili," she interjects.

"Dude," I laugh, "It's a bazillion degrees outside. I don't want chili."

"Liar." She has a point. Ireland's chili, no matter the temperature, is amazing.

"When?"

"Tonight?"

I sigh, "I can't, I have to work."

"Tomorrow?"

"Will you call Cami before then and if she gives you a way to contact him, will you call me?"

"Of course I will, but I'll still hold you to dinner."

"Alright. I'm off Tuesday. Can it at least wait until then?"

"Sure. I'll let you know what I hear back from Cami, alright?"

"Thank you, Vy, you're the best."

"Uh huh, remember that," she laughs. "Everything else alright?"

I sigh into the phone and lean against my car. "Yeah, I'm good."

"Promise?" she counters.

"Pinky." I smile.

"Good, I'll call you a little later."

"Thanks, Vy."

"Anytime."

We hang up and I climb into my car and turn on the A/C but I don't pull out of the parking lot. A part of me wonders if the guy at the desk was just pulling my leg. I call the hotel for good measure and someone, a female, answers the phone. "Biltmore Hotel, this is Angie, how can I help you?"

"Bryan Hayes, please," I say into the phone.

"What room?"

"The penthouse."

I hear some computer keys clicking before she answers me, "I'm sorry, ma'am, Mr. Hayes check out this morning. Is there anything else I can do for you?" My heart sinks into my stomach as I hang up the phone.

I'm such an idiot.

*Livia*

"I HAVEN'T been completely honest with you." I finally manage to get the words out to my best friend. It's only taken three glasses of wine to get to this point. We spent the better part of an hour discussing Ireland's latest news. Between the baby coming, where she ran off to, why she ran off and most importantly, her father is alive, but he's not the man she originally thought he was. The whole thing is so convoluted and fucked up that it would take an entire book to tell the story.

Now, it's my turn.

It's been over a week since I went back to the hotel in search of Bryan, and in that time I haven't heard anything from him. Cami was all too willing to hand over his number to Ireland, but it was for Ireland's use only. Not that Cami doesn't like me or trust me, it's a celebrity thing and while I bought it for a little while, it pissed me off after that. Ireland, being the best friend she is, dutifully passed my number along to Bryan, but alas, I haven't heard a peep.

"About what?" Ireland interrupts my musings about Bryan's lack of phone calls.

I wring my hands and debate on where to start.

"Whatever it is, Becca, you can tell me. You know this."

I start to pace her living room. She invited me over for dinner and while Dyson was with us to eat, he's left us alone so we can talk. "I know, but this..." I pull a deep breath into my lungs, hold it for a moment then let it out. "This isn't just me copying your homework."

She sits up a little straighter and I continue to pace the room. "Are you in trouble?"

I stop and look at her. She's always been the intuitive one.

"Not really," I hesitate, "Well, not that I know of. That's part of why I wanted to get in touch with Bryan. Liam and I, we... we have a history."

She cocks her head to the side. Her vibrant red curls fall over her shoulders, her eyes grow concerned. "What kind of history?"

"Uh...he used to be an undercover FBI agent."

She straightens and raises an eyebrow. "What exactly did you do to come in contact with a...Becca?"

"Oh god, this is harder than I thought it would be. I don't know if I can do this, Vy."

"Becca, I..."

I cut her off. "My name isn't Becca."

"What do you mean?" She's clearly shocked, judging by her tone, but she's not pissed off.

"That's probably not the best place to start," I mutter.

"Then why don't you start from the beginning," she offers.

"That makes this a really long story."

She sits back, getting comfortable on the couch, and I notice as she leans back that her baby bump is more pronounced. "I've got all night," she encourages

"When I was a little girl, my mother was killed. But you already know that part. The part you don't know is that my father was a cop with the NYPD."

"You never told me that."

"I know. There's a lot of this story I haven't told you. Call it embarrassment or whatever, I just..." I pause and stop pacing. "My father being a cop isn't exactly something I'm proud of. You would think, as his daughter, I would be honored by him serving, especially because he was a 9/11 responder."

"Oh, Bec-" She stops herself.

"Livia, my real name is Livia."

A smile spreads across Ireland's face. "That's a beautiful name."

I can't help returning her smile with a small one of my own. "That's all you have to say on that subject?"

She sits forward with her elbows on her knees. "I'm guessing that whatever you're trying to tell me has to do with why you no longer use that name, so until I have the full story, I refuse to pass judgement."

"Jesus, Ireland, you're like a damn saint, you know that?"

She smiles and shrugs. "I wouldn't go that far, but I want to hear the rest of your story."

I nod and go back to finding my place in the story. "When I was fifteen, my father was killed. But rather than being killed in the line of duty, he was killed because he was a dirty cop." She gasps, but I ignore her and continue, "I don't know the whole story because I wasn't there when it happened. All I knew at the time was he'd disappeared, but then...then they came after me. They tried to use me as leverage to get my father to talk."

"The cops?"

I shake my head. "No, worse."

"Go on," she says as she leans back again.

"I was pulled off the streets in broad daylight as I walked home from school. From there I was taken somewhere and... the details of that are unimportant, but let's just say it wasn't a vacation. When they realized I wasn't the leverage they needed over my father, they tortured him and ruined me before they killed him in front of me."

She gasps, but I can't look at her. I don't want to see the

pain and pity in her eyes. "After that, I became the property of Vito Ricci and the Ricci family. They were a living, breathing Italian Mafia in New York and because my father couldn't pay his debts, I was forced to do that for him."

"With what, exactly?" Her voice is soft, hesitant, as if she doesn't want to know the answer.

I look straight at her, hoping she'll read the unspoken words in my eyes before I go on with my history. "When I first met Liam, Bryan's bodyguard, I met him as Leo. He dyed his hair black so he would fit in. Italian mobsters are not big fans of the Scottish. He infiltrated the highest rings of the Ricci family by working his way up the ranks on an undercover mission that had been going on for years. Anyway, Vito, or one of his upper hands, had ordered Liam to oversee the inner workings of one of the Ricci family's primary sources of income." I turn and look at her again, silently pleading with her to understand so I don't have to go into details.

"Which was?" she prompts.

"Sex trafficking."

Ireland's eyes well with tears and she covers her mouth. Her silent sobs shake her chest. I close my eyes, fighting my own tears. "I've never told anyone any of this. So please..." The emotion is thick in my voice. "Please don't." I brush tears away from my eyes. "Liam found me in a house in Brooklyn where some of the girls, me included, were held. I learned later that Liam's role at the house was because Fat Tony was skimming money from Ricci. Ricci sent Liam to find out what was going on. Liam and I became close, he became a handler of sorts for me and he used the information I gave him to take back to Ricci, or so I'd thought. Then, one day, the house was raided. Fat Tony and his goons were taken into custody and all the girls were processed and released,

except for me." I go back to pacing. "Someone had tipped them off that I was the head girl, been around the longest and they quickly figured out I have a photographic memory. So, for four days they questioned me, grilled me even, for all the information I had on Fat Tony, his accomplices and then finally what I knew about the chain of command within the organization. I spilled my guts on the promise I would be protected."

"So that's where Becca came from?" she asks.

I shrug. "More or less. I was handed a new passport and identification and sent to California. Only once I got there, I was basically on my own. So, I did what I had to do in order to survive. I did the only thing I knew how to do."

"You became a prostitute?"

"No, I was already one of those. At least in the eyes of the Feds who were more intent on taking down the biggest Italian crime family in New York than they were about taking care of one of their whores. I did the only thing I knew how to do. The only difference is I knew the business, I knew how it worked and I was able to handle myself."

"As the years in California progressed, I heard less and less from anyone in New York, but the name I was given was racking up an arrest record that would destroy any chance of moving on with my life. I used the only card I had left to gain a whole new identity."

"What was the card?"

"My father's murder. He was, after all, an NYPD Detective who had turned up dead in an alley somewhere in New York. By that point, the case was cold and they had stopped investigating his murder. I handed them the murderer."

"Who was it?"

"Vito Ricci."

Saying his name out loud sends my mind racing back to the day I played all the cards I had left in my arsenal.

*My hands shake as I dial the number.*

*"McMurray," a familiar male voice answers the call.*

*"I have information on a homicide."*

*"Then you need to call nine-one-one."*

*"It's a cold case," I say into the phone.*

*"Then you need...."*

*I cut him off, "It's about the murder of NYPD Detective Mercutio Fazio."*

*The line goes silent for a few moments before he responds. "Don't bother trying to trace it, I'm going to tell you who I am, where I am and how I know this information."*

*"What's your name?" McMurray inquires.*

*"Livia Fazio."*

*He sucks in a deep breath. "His daughter? His daughter is dead."*

*"On paper, but you, Agent McMurray, are the one who made me look that way before sending me packing to California."*

*"Why are you just now coming to me with this?" He sounds irritated.*

*"Because, I need something from you and then I will hand you your killer on a silver platter," I answer into the phone.*

*"What do you need from me, Alison?" He uses my new given name. I look like an Alison, apparently.*

*"A new identity."*

*"Your identity hasn't been compromised."*

*"How would you know?"*

*"Because the case is still under investigation. We would know if they knew about you. Though, like I told you then, they don't care about you."*

*"I wouldn't be so sure about that, and given that I'm the only witness to my father's murder who is going to talk to you, I assure you, you'll need my testimony."*

*"We have more than enough..."*

*"That will put them in jail for what? Twenty years? Thirty, maybe? Wouldn't you rather put them on death row for killing a New York City Detective?"*

*He sighs.*

*"That's what I thought. Now, will you deal?"*

*He covers the mouthpiece and speaks to someone before returning to me. "We'll deal. But I need details, full and complete details."*

*"I'll even lead you to the missing money."*

*"What money?"*

*"I'll call back soon. Make sure you have the case file, Agent McMurray; you're going to need it. Pictures and all." I hang up the phone. My heart pounds in my chest at the gravity of the information I'm going to unleash on them. Hopefully it will finally set me free.*

"Becca," Ireland brings me out of my daydream, "You alright?"

She looks concerned so I give her hand a squeeze and muster up a small smile. "Yeah, I just...I've tried so hard to put that out of my mind, but lately it's all coming back to me."

I continue pacing the room, unsure of where to go next with the story. "I think the name Becca was the FBI Agent's way of getting back at me for making him work so hard," I snort.

Ireland doesn't laugh but adds, "Becca is a pretty name. It just…
well, when you were a blonde, it fit, but now, with your dark hair, not so
much." She runs her hand through her hair before she stands up. "Why?
Why after all this time are you telling me this?"

"Because, I'm tired of the lies, I'm tired of the games. I want this all to
be over and I can't do that if I'm not honest with you."

She stares at me, her mouth agape. "How much more have you lied to
me about?" she manages to ask.

"Nothing, just my name, where I came from, though California isn't
exactly a lie, just not where I grew up. When you went to New York back
in February, a part of me freaked out that you'd learned the truth. With
Dyson's resources, I…"

"Oh god, no, Becca…sorry, it's going to take some getting used to."

I give her a small, pathetic smile. "You actually want to get used to it?"

She cocks her head at me, "It's not easy knowing you've been lying
to me all these years, but under the circumstances, I think it may have
been warranted. You are who you are, Livia, a name isn't going to change
that."

"There's more," I breathe.

"More, what? Lies?"

I give her a non-committal nod. "Up until February, when I told you I
was working at the restaurant?"

"Yeah," she says slowly.

"It wasn't a restaurant. I purposefully told you a place that would be
nearly impossible for you to get to without a car and one that was far
enough away that you wouldn't take a cab ride to come see me because I
didn't work there. I was working at CatTails, as a dancer."

"Str-stripping?" she stutters.

"I was doing what I needed to do…"

"By stripping?"

Jesus, she's going to be okay with the fact that I'm not the person I said I was, but she's going to blow her lid at my job? Seriously? "How do you think I paid for college?"

"Loans, grants, things like that."

"Yes, but those were never anywhere near enough money to cover the full cost of my tuition. Working at Dunkin' Donuts isn't exactly a million dollar a year job."

"No, but your degree would get you somewhere that would be better money than stripping and yet you're not doing anything with that."

"Honestly, Ireland, the only reason I stayed in school was because of you. Because you let me see things differently than I ever had before, and I knew if I dropped out, we'd grow apart. For the first time in my life, I'd found someone I could depend on, someone who was there for me when I needed them and who didn't judge me. You never asked too many questions and we just clicked. After having been alone for pretty much my entire life, I savored what we had as friends. I didn't want to ruin what we had because I needed to make money, a lot of it, and make it in as little amount of time as possible. Stripping and whoring are the only two ways I know how to do that."

"Prostitution too?"

Her surprise is blatantly clear. "When I had to," I breathe.

"Still?" she asks.

The memory of Bryan handing me a wad of cash slides through my mind. Then I remember throwing it at his door before walking about. "No."

"How am I supposed to believe you?" So much for the supportive best friend.

"What difference does it make now, Ireland? You're pregnant, practically married and living in a house bigger than the entire apartment complex I grew up in. You weren't in any position to help me out, so I did what I had to do."

"Why tell me?"

"Because, I believed you were truly my friend and if you were truly that person, what I've done in my past shouldn't matter to you, but I can clearly see it does."

"Breathe, Jesus," Ireland snaps. She takes a deep breath. "You have to see this from where I'm coming from on all this before you go off half-cocked." She looks me square in the eye. "Your past? I understand that. I understand why you've changed your name, why you feel the need to run, but I can't for the life of me wrap my mind around why you felt you needed to…"

"Become a whore?" I spit.

She nods. "But I wouldn't put it that way, exactly."

"But it's the truth. And honestly, I don't know and I have no clue how to explain it to you. I just, fuck, Ireland, it's all I know."

"But you're not anymore?"

"I haven't since February. I have no plans to go back to it either," I tell her. It's the truth. It's about time I grew up, got a real job, did real things. In order to do that, I've had to come clean with my best friend. Her acceptance or denial of who I am determines what happens next.

"I don't know what to say," she finally says.

"There's nothing to say. I needed you to know, now you know. What you decide to do with this information is a decision only you can make," I tell her.

"I need some time," she whispers.

I nod and grab my keys from the counter. "I'm sorry to disappoint you," I quip before I go down the stairs and out the front door. I climb into my car and slam the door shut before screaming at the top of my lungs.

Ireland: I don't know what happened between the two of you, but she doesn't deserve your silence.

Bryan: It was one night.

Ireland: Keep telling yourself that. Call her, text her, something.

Bryan: Why is this so important to you?

Ireland: She's broken.

Bryan: That's obvious but I can't fix that. She made it very clear where she stands.

Ireland: Did it ever occur to you that maybe she was wrong? (623)555-0159 – Call her.

Broken? Duh.

Apologetic? Highly unlikely.

"You ready?" Liam asks from my office doorway.

I nod. Despite my desperate attempts at putting her out of my mind over the last couple of months, I've failed miserably. Today, I will tell the world. "It's now or never," I respond.

I grab my bag off the hook near the door and follow Liam out of the house and into my SUV.

That night in Phoenix replays in my head on a constant loop. It's like a broken record and I can't, no matter what I do, wash her from my mind.

The last couple of months have been busy with my new album and some last-minute studio work. Tonight is the launch of my newest single. I've given full access to one of the satellite stations because one night, back in June, while in the car with the girl that would inspire me in ways I never imagined possible, I noticed she had the station programmed in her car. Now the catch is, getting her in the car.

Once Liam has us on our way to the studio on Lower Broadway in Nashville, I pull up my phone and for the first time ever I anonymously text a number I swore I would never use.

"Less than an hour to go before country music's biggest superstar will be sitting in our studio and we couldn't be more thrilled to have him in studio with us. Are you ready for the nationwide release of his newest single? I know we are." The DJ's voice fades to nothing when the next song starts playing on the radio.

It's been two months and still nothing from him. No phone calls, no text, no nothing. No matter how hard I've tried to move on and ignore it, the feelings I managed to develop for him have only grown deeper. Taking root in my heart in a way I never imagined I could feel. I've been on my own for so long, forced into a lifestyle I never would have chosen for myself. Not having a choice in the matter has altered everything I know about relationships.

I used to tell myself that had my father died without me having to be involved in the whole shit-show, I may have ended up there anyway. I was, after all, only fifteen at the time.

Then the fantasy side of my brain kicks in with ideas of grandeur and the possibility of being adopted or taken in by a family that would have nurtured me in ways a teenage girl should have been. That fantasy always fades when the reality would have been a group home or some other living situation barely above poverty and being on the streets. Had I ended up on the streets and alone, I often wonder if I would have turned to drugs, alcohol and prostitution on my own just to survive.

Had my father not died because of his own idiocy things would have gone on much the same as they always had. A man married to his job and a slave to it. When he was alive, I barely saw him. I heard him coming in at all hours of the night and leaving at all hours of the morning. From the time I was nine years old, I've been responsible for myself and it would have continued that way, I have no doubt.

I recognize that had the things that happened to me not actually happened, I would have never ended up in California and more than likely never ended up in Phoenix where I met Ireland.

It took a few days, but Ireland gradually came around and we spent the following Saturday curled up on the couch watching movies and hanging out like we used to do. It was a little awkward at first, but eventually we settled in and had a good time. So much has changed in her life since her mother passed away and it made me feel guilty for being such a bitch to her.

We also talked about her relationship with Dyson and to say I was envious is an understatement. Pea-green with envy might be a better phrase for it, but I am happy she's found happiness. I'm just sorry it took ten years for them to find each other again. Her life is heading in the right direction and now if I could get mine going that way, I think I would be much happier.

Since that day, I've seen Dyson and Ireland more and more and it's obvious he adores her and she him. It's the stuff of romance novels. Seeing them together and seeing the love they have for each other and the graceful way they are handling the unexpected gives new meaning to my desperation and desire for something I'm not sure I can have. But I'm damn sure going to try.

"It's almost time, ladies and gents. We are happy to report

that the one and only Bryan Hayes has entered the building."

I chuckle at the radio. That kind of announcement needs to be made in front of a live audience. It would have a much better effect on the masses. I look up the spire sitting in front of me and I can only imagine what's going on inside, up toward the top, as the radio station I'm listening to prepares for the biggest, best kept secret to be revealed while I sit in my car, fifty feet below them biding my time. Usually, new singles can be found all over the internet before they're actually released, but not this one, not this time. As of twenty minutes ago, it wasn't even available to download, despite the reveal in less than an hour.

A small crowd forms, surrounding the entrance to the spire. It's significantly smaller than I'd expected it to be. I mean, it is Bryan Hayes after all.

His stubborn ass refuses to call me.

My stubborn ass realized I owe him an apology and I'm determined to give him one. In person.

> Ireland: Are you listening?
>
> Livia: I am.
>
> Ireland: Did you make it?
>
> Livia: I did. I'm here. Outside the radio station.
>
> Ireland: Stalker.

I laugh.

> Livia: Well, considering all station listeners know he's here, I'd hardly call that stalking.
>
> Ireland: Truth. Keep me posted.
>
> Livia: Will do.
>
> Livia: Thanks.

Ireland: For?

Livia: Always being there.

Ireland: That's what friends are for. *smooches*


A Keith Urban song plays on the radio as I wait in my car. It's a favorite song of mine that reminds me of my life. Then again, I think most of his songs do that. I'm singing along when I'm interrupted by a loud knock on my window. I squeal and jump before turning to see who's outside my car. All I can see is black pants, a black belt, and a gun. "Livia, get out."

"Shit."

Liam chuckles as I open the door I turn up the radio before I climb out. Can't miss my song.

"How the fuck did you know I was here?" I glare at him.

He laughs, "I saw you when we pulled in. What are you doing here?"

"What do you think?"

"He doesn't want to talk to you." His voice is deadpan.

"Bullshit," I snap. "Are you the reason he hasn't called me?"

My phone chimes in my hand. It's a text from a private number.

"No, Livia, I'm not. He's an adult."

"Why are you so against me being with him?" I ask as I unlock my phone.

"I'm not. Despite your beliefs, I worry what this kind of lifestyle would mean for you."

"Meaning what, exactly?" I look at him while I wait for my messaging app to load.

"That," he says as he points toward the spire where

Bryan is and the many faces pressed to the glass along with more than fifteen different cameras all waiting for a shot, a glimpse, of the man himself. There's everything from video to still cameras. My heart sinks. "Is that what you want? Your face plastered everywhere? People talking about you? Your past getting brought up? People digging into everything you've worked so hard to suppress, not to mention Ricci or one of his goons could see you, find you. Do you want that?"

I look him square in the eyes and tell him with conviction, "If it means I can stop running, then yes. I want that."

My phone beeps again and the radio switches to the DJ as I look at my phone.

Private Number: Turn on your radio.

"Livia, you're never going to be able to stop running."

"Then maybe it's time to face the music," I admit.

"How you doing, Bryan?" the DJ asks.

"I'm good, doing good. Really excited to be here tonight," he drawls in his sexy southern accent.

"He's nervous, isn't he?" I ask Liam.

He snorts, "Petrified."

"Why?" I raise an eyebrow at him.

"You'll see." We stand there listening to Bryan and the DJ, Dewie, talking about miscellaneous stuff for a few minutes. "Would you rather listen from your car or inside?"

I look at him, my eyes wide with fear, a fear I didn't know I had inside of me and Liam leans into me. "I will protect you, no matter what," he whispers. "That was the vow I made to your father all those years ago. I failed you by letting Ricci get his hands on you, but I can assure you that I will never

ever let that happen again."

"So, the new album, tell us a little about it?" Dewie asks Bryan through the radio.

"Well, it's number six."

Dewie laughs, but it's obvious that Bryan is nervous, which is unusual for him. "Number six in just under eight years. That's a lot of albums," Dewie adds.

"It is, but I've got a lot of songs to sing. Working with songwriters is probably my favorite part of doing what I do and this album? It's, well, Dewie, it's probably my favorite. It's full of heart, emotion and there's a little heart on your sleeve mentality to it."

"You can say that again. I should tell you, Bryan, this album is, it's simply incredible. The stories you tell are amazing and there's just so much raw heart and emotion behind it. Where did you get all that?"

I look at Liam, silently seeking answers while we wait for Bryan's answer to the question.

"I found it in Phoenix, Arizona," he says and Liam gives me a smile unlike anything I've ever seen from him before.

"That is why he hasn't called you and that is why you have that text message. He's been planning this whole thing for the last couple months. The only factor he didn't consider is that you'd show up here."

"What did you find in Phoenix?" Dewie asks Bryan.

"Something I never expected to find and that I hope to one day see again."

"So is there a woman in county music's biggest superstar's life?"

My heart freezes. What if he found someone else? Panic courses through my body and my heart picks up to double

time. The look on my face alerts Liam to my distress. "Relax," he says softly.

"That, Dewie, is a question that will be answered in time."

"Fair enough. So what do you say we get to it? How about we give the fans a little tease of the upcoming album with the title track. Now, this was originally supposed to be the first single off the album. What made you change your mind?"

"I wanted to change it up a little. I love this song and the writers behind this song have been incredible to work with, it just doesn't seem like that right time to premiere it as a single."

"But you're gonna let us play the title track here today?"

"I am, Dewie, and I think my fans will really love the song. It was the song that kicked off the album writing process and it's been a true labor of love."

"Want to introduce it for us?"

"It's called 'Bring on Tomorrow'."

The voices disappear and there are a couple guitar chords before the music kicks up and Bryan's gorgeous voice comes through my radio and the first song from his upcoming album is playing on the radio. It's not the big reveal, but usually when they do these release launches, they'll play a couple songs from the new album. I'm excited to hear the first single.

I knew I needed to be here for it. Something kept telling me I needed to hear this song. What he's told Dewie so far about changing up the single song at the last minute just reiterates why I drove all this way.

"You ready to go inside?" Liam asks. I got so engrossed in listening to them talking on the radio I almost forgot he was here.

"Is that really a good idea?"

Liam smiles at me. "I think so. Right now, they are moving downstairs where they do the live sessions. If you don't want him to know you're here, you can blend in down there."

Without thinking about it, I climb back into my car, turn the car off and climb back out, locking the car. "I guess it's better than acting like a crazed fan when he tries to leave."

Liam winks at me. "Now you're learning. Come on."

I follow Liam toward the tower and my heart picks up its pace with each step I take. The closer we get, the more my breathing becomes labored, not from walking, but from freaking out. I drove all this way on the hope that maybe I would be able to get his attention when he went to leave. If that didn't work, I wasn't opposed to stalking him.

"What were you gonna do if he didn't see you?" Liam asks like he has a line to my thoughts.

I snort, "Follow you."

"Bit stalker-ish, don'tcha think?" Liam says with humor in his voice.

"Well, all my other attempts to reach him have failed," I tell him. It's the truth. I respected Ireland for keeping the number from me. She understood I wasn't just a fan looking for a number. It wouldn't have looked very good on Cami or Bold's part if they handed out one of their biggest client's phone numbers to someone they didn't know.

"Aye, but listen, lass. Part of him not reaching out to you is self-preservation." He turns toward me.

"What's that supposed to mean exactly?"

"It means he met you in a strip club. Now, whether you still work there or not is a moot point."

"He also met me in a bar at a friend's birthday party and

the name Becca Carpenter is not associated with anything stripper related. If you run a background check on me, which I'm sure you have, then you'd know that Becca worked only at Dunkin' Donuts."

"Smart lass," he smirks before turning and opening the door.

Between the door and the makeshift stage area there are several dozen people and I sneak behind them while Liam goes in the opposite direction. I can easily see him over the crowd and while my five foot eight frame isn't tiny, the tallest people in the room are in the back. I find a place to squeeze in and I peer between the shoulders of two men, giving me a great view of Bryan and Dewie, the station's DJ, as they continue talking about the album. I drown them out and focus on Bryan. He's sitting on a stool with his guitar strung across his lap.

If I thought Bryan was sexy before, seeing him like this now is way better than even my biggest fantasy could conjure up. His long legs allow one foot to rest on the floor and the other, the one with the guitar on it, is sitting on a rung of the stool. He's wearing a baseball cap, and t-shirt that has some writing on it, but I can't quite tell what it is. The shirt is tight on him, showing off his muscles.

He's unshaven. Scruffy. Like he's been hiding in the dark for the last few weeks. Put the whole package together and there isn't a woman in the world who wouldn't do anything to be with him. Women who would do far more than I ever could or did by driving across the country.

Watching him and seeing him makes me wonder if I've made a huge mistake.

Then my mind wanders back to the random text message I got.

I pull my phone from my pocket and read it again.

Private Number: Turn on your radio.

Private number? Bryan? Liam? Who would text me...?

"Ladies and gentleman, the premiere of 'Fate Has a Reason' by Bryan Hayes."

I hold my breath in anticipation.

Bryan starts to strum his guitar. The melody is soft, slow, and deliberate. The acoustic sound carries throughout the room as Bryan leans into the microphone and starts to sing.

*Met you in a club.*
*Saw you dancing there...*
*Your body like an unanswered prayer*

I pull in a sharp breath through my teeth as he continues singing.

*Then you gave me the reason I needed*
*The hope that had faded*
*Became fate that had a reason.*

*Fate has a reason*
*For bringing me to you.*
*Fate has a reason*
*For all that we do.*
*Fate has a reason*
*For showing me you.*

Before I know what's happening, I'm trying to push my way toward the front of the crowd without making a scene. I need him to see me, I want him to see me.

I only make it a row in before a hand wraps around my arm. I turn to punch out the person who's touching me only to realize it's Liam. He puts his finger to his lips, indicating I need to be quiet then points his thumb over his shoulder and he brings me along. Once we're in the back of the crowd, he releases me and I follow him off to the side, right into Bryan's line of sight. And our eyes meet.

*Bryan*

IT takes everything I have to keep singing when my eyes land on the gorgeous eyes that have been invading my dreams and consuming my life since I left Phoenix a couple months ago.

All the strength I'd thought I'd had performing this song slides out of my body. Considering her full, beautiful, emotion filled eyes is almost my undoing.

One final chorus.

I can do this.

*Fate has a reason*

*For bringing me to you.*

*Fate has a reason*

*For all that we do.*

*Fate has a reason*

*For showing me you.*

The audience erupts in cheers.

"There you have it, folks, the world premiere of Bryan Hayes's newest single, 'Fate Has a Reason', live. We'll be back after these songs for more with Bryan Hayes."

Then the music cuts in and the crowd keeps cheering, but I hear none of it. I only have eyes for her.

Dewie, the station's DJ, comes over and congratulates me on another hit. We chat for a few moments before we return to the airwaves.

Livia never strays too far from me. I can't begin to imagine

what it is she's doing here, but judging from the unshed tears in her eyes, I'm not the only one who's been a wreck these last two months.

Before I'm escorted back upstairs to the studio, I walk over to her, our gazes locked on each other the whole time.

"Stay?" I ask since she can't accompany me upstairs.

"I will."

"Good," I tell her as I'm whisked back upstairs.

My radio spot lasts another twenty minutes with questions and some calls from listeners. So far the feedback has been amazing and while the song is deeply personal for me, I'm glad people are catching the true meaning behind the song.

Liam meets me outside the studio and we head down in the elevator together. While we were upstairs the lobby was supposed to be cleared of people. "She still here?"

"Aye," he tells me.

"Did you know she was coming?"

He snorts, "How would I know that?"

"I don't know. You have a knack for knowing all sorts of shit. I figured you knew she was coming."

"No, but when we pulled in I saw her in her car. That was where I found her before bringing her inside."

"That nearly killed me," I breathe.

He chuckles, "I know, lad."

The elevator doors open and the only person in the lobby, besides the security staff, is her. She looks at me as the doors open and she smiles a bright smile and my heart melts a little more.

"Hi," she breathes as I come to stand next to her.

"What are you doing here?"

Her smile fades. "You asked me to stay," she counters, but her voice betrays her confusion.

"No, I mean here in Nashville," I clarify.

"I never heard from you."

"That's not true. I texted you about forty minutes ago," I smirk.

"From a private number, not exactly conducive for texting back."

"So you drove across the country in the hopes of seeing me?" I ask. I know why she's here and I'm glad she's here, but I need to hear her say it.

"Well, I figured one of two things would happen. Either you'd acknowledge my existence or you'd ignore me completely. One way or another I would have my answers."

"To what, exactly?"

"Is this really the best place to have this conversation?" she asks. She has a valid point, it's most certainly not.

"Where are you staying?"

"With you," she answers quickly and unabashedly.

"That's awfully presumptuous of you, sweetheart."

Her eyes narrow at me, her cheeks flare red briefly before her jaw ticks. "Don't call me that," she says through clenched teeth.

"You're like an angry cat ready to pounce, aren't you?"

She releases the air she was holding and relaxes. "This was a mistake." She moves to walk away. "Congrats on the new single. It's amazing, Bryan."

She walks quickly, passing through the doors before I can register what's happened in the last ten seconds.

"Livia, wait." She doesn't stop, she keeps walking toward

the parking lot and the doors slide close behind her.

"What the hell, Bryan?" Liam snaps at me.

"Shit." I take off after her, charging quickly through the doors. "Livia, wait."

She still doesn't answer, doesn't even flinch. She just keeps charging toward her destination. Likely her car.

"Dammit, Becca, wait."

She skids to a stop before turning back to me. "You're a cocksucker, you know that?"

"And you're fucking gorgeous when you're angry."

We slam into each other. I wrap my hand around the back of her neck, holding her to me. She's pushing back and I don't blame her, but I don't care. I crush my lips to hers. My breathing is ragged from running after her but it gets worse the moment our lips touch. Her breathing hitches and she moans into my mouth. Her body falls lax in my arms and she stops struggling. I slide my tongue against her lips before she gives me the access I need and I slide my tongue in along hers. Her breathing quickens and I can feel her heartbeat increasing under my fingers on her neck.

I pull back, gasping for air, but I don't release her. "Stay with me."

She looks at me as if I've just lost my mind. I probably have. "I should go back home."

"Oh, for Pete's sake, would you knock off this tough girl attitude?"

She pushes me, freeing herself from my hold. "Why? So, I can be open, honest and vulnerable to you again? No, thank you."

"Look, I didn't mean to come off as a dick, alright? I'm just..." I take a deep breath. "What do you want from this,

Becca?"

"Livia," she corrects me.

I cock an eyebrow at her. "Okay, Livia, what do you want from this?"

She folds her arms over her chest, taking a defensive position as she curls in on herself. "I want the chance to start over. To see where this is going, okay? Is that so wrong?"

I smile at her. "I thought you'd never ask." I straighten. "Now, where's your car?"

She hitches her thumb over her shoulder. "Over there."

My smile fades into a mischievous grin. "Lead the way, princess."

"I'm no princess," she retorts.

"No, darlin', that you are not."

She scowls at me, "Well, fuck you too. Asshole."

I laugh, "Come on, let's go." I wrap my arm around her shoulders, holding her close to me as we walk toward her car. I catch Liam in my peripheral and nod toward her car. He gives me a chin lift in acknowledgement and heads toward the SUV.

"Where are we going?" she asks.

"My place."

"How far is it?" Something in her tone causes some concern.

"About forty minutes, why?"

"Uh, I need gas."

I stop walking as I reach into my pocket for my phone. I pull up Liam's number and call him. It rings half a ring before he answers. "Yeah?"

"Come swap cars with us."

"Aye," he disconnects to call.

"What are you doing?" Her eyes are filled with concern.

"This is where I pull the celebrity card."

"What do you mean by that?" she says as we approach her car.

"I mean that without Liam, I don't like to make unscheduled stops."

"So we schedule a stop..."

"No, he can take your car, fill it up and meet us back at the house."

"Oh," she says as she understands. "Alright."

Liam pulls up with the SUV and hops out, leaving it running. "Fill it up and we'll see you at home."

"Aye, lad," he says with a smile and he takes her keys from her. I open her door for her and once she's seated in the SUV, I kiss her nose and close the door.

*Livia*

"DOES he normally do whatever you ask of him? Or rather, tell him?" I ask Bryan as he pulls the SUV onto the street. Liam is following us in my car.

"Yes, it's what he's paid to do," he tells me, straight-faced.

"True, but wouldn't it be nicer if you asked him?" He looks at me briefly before returning his eyes to the road. "What if he had plans when you guys got home?"

He snorts but then sobers a little. "Stopping for gas will only add ten minutes to his drive, if that. I highly doubt he has something that pressing going on."

"But you don't know that because you didn't ask." I'm just giving him shit and I love how flustered he's getting.

"And what do you want me to do about it now? It will take more time to pull over and swap cars again than it will for him to stop and get gas." He pulls up to a stoplight and looks at me. I have a shit-eating grin on my face and he catches it immediately. "Why are you giving me a hard time?"

"Paybacks, Mr. Hayes."

"For what, exactly?"

"For being a dick." I sober. "If you can kiss me like that, you could have just texted me, you know that, right?"

"But then I wouldn't be able to do this." He reaches over the center console and puts his hand on my thigh, then slowly slides it toward my crotch. My breathing hitches and a horn blows behind us.

"You apparently can't do that and drive at the same time," I snicker as he steps on the gas.

"Oh, I assure you I can do a lot more while driving." He gives me a sideways glance and a wink.

"Road head is not my specialty, Mr. Hayes."

He laughs, "Good to know. Now, I need to you answer me something."

I hesitate, only because I don't want to get into an overly in-depth conversation with him in the car. Though I plan to sit him down and tell him everything he needs to know before we can take this any further, the car isn't the ideal place to start. "Okay." My voice is cause for alarm as he looks at me quickly.

"It's a simple question. I promise. I'll save the harder stuff for when we get home."

"Alcohol might be a good idea for that conversation," I mutter.

"I had a feeling it might. So, tell me, what am I supposed to call you? You ignored Livia, but turned when I called you Becca. You asked me to call you Livia, but I get the feeling you're uncomfortable with that name."

"I'm uncomfortable with that name because it's a name I haven't used in nearly eight years, that's all. I'm not used to people calling me by that name. I am slowly getting used to it, it's still not exactly normal for me." That's the truth.

I decided on my drive to Nashville that if I got this chance, got to talk to him, that I would tell him everything. He needs to know.

"Understood, but you do realize that if we pursue a relationship..."

"Don't jump that gun too fast. You need to know everything before you can make that decision," I urge him.

"And how long am I going to have to wait for that?"

"Until we get to your place. Unfortunately, I cannot tell you alone. Liam needs to be there too." I stop looking at him

and move to looking out the front of the SUV, watching the closeness of the buildings start spacing out the farther we get away from Lower Broadway.

"I don't care about your past, Livia."

I can't look at him. "But you have to care about it, Bryan. My past is not exactly conducive to a public life. There are going to be risks to being seen in public with you and I need you to know and understand all the risks. Once you know, you and Liam can decide for yourselves what it is you want to do. He will be able to tell you what exactly I'm up against. If you decide you don't want to have that kind of influence in your life, your career and most importantly, your reputation, I will understand and walk away."

No need to add that I will disappear completely. From Ireland's life and from Bryan and Liam's life. I've done it before, and I will do it again.

"I have no intentions of walking away."

"You say that now, but you don't even know the half of it," I tell him.

We spend the rest of the ride in silence while I mull over what I need to say, what I need to tell them.

Just when I'm figuring it all out, we pull into a gated driveway. I can't see anything beyond the gate and some large trees, but the big iron gate is a huge indication that I'm meddling somewhere I don't belong.

Being in a hotel room in Phoenix, be it the penthouse or not, doesn't allow someone the inclination of what their life is like. This is his home. Where he spends his time when he's not on the road. It would only make sense that it's huge.

We round a corner on the driveway and the trees give way to open land. A lot of open land. Though there are trees surrounding the property, the house that sits in the middle

is not what I was expecting to see. It's a ranch house. Albeit, a very long, ranch house. Much of the house is two stories, except on the ends it drops down to one story for about the length of a normal house. "Wow," I breathe.

"You like it?"

"It's gorgeous, Bryan," I tell him.

The house is white, with black shutters on either side of all the windows. The roof is a steep A-line that dips low, and there are pillars on either side of the doorway.

Bryan pulls off to the left, into a barn that's been turned into a garage. "Holy shit," I squeak as my eyes roam around the open area of the garage barn. There are four cars that line the sides of the barn and another everyday kind of car in the center where we pull in.

My eyes land on the Aston Martin parked toward the back then follow to the other side of the garage where there is a... "Is that a sixty-seven?"

He turns his head to look at me, his eyes wide with surprise. "You know your cars?"

"Hell yeah," I tell him with a grin on my face. "Growing up in New York, cars were something you didn't need or didn't have, but it made for a great obsession. The cars you did see were usually high-end. So, it became a fun little game for me to figure out the makes and models of cars as I walked past them on the streets."

Bryan laughs, "That's one way to become obsessed. Come on, come look." He smiles as he opens his door and climbs out. I follow him with excitement and bound over to a Corvette.

"She's gorgeous," I say as I take in the sleek curves of the most gorgeous car I've ever seen in person. It's shiny cherry red and perfect. "Did you do any work to her or did you just

buy her this way?"

"I mostly bought her this way. I did do some work and had her repainted. Unfortunately, the engine was in perfect condition, but the previous owner didn't take a lot of pride in her exterior and the interior was worn pretty well."

"How many miles are on her?"

He smiles wider. "Only about sixty thousand."

"Damn, she's worth a pretty penny."

"Wanna drive her?"

I stare at him without blinking. "Uh, no."

"She purrs like a kitten." The spark in his eye as he talks about his car is something I've only seen when he looks at me and it sends my heart racing in my chest.

"I bet she does, but I would never forgive myself if I scratched her or worse," I admit truthfully.

"Then I'll take you for a ride sometime."

"I'd like that very much," I respond softly and he comes over to tuck a stray strand of hair behind my ear.

"Good. Wanna look at anything else?"

I shake my head and look at him through hooded eyes. His proximity and the adrenaline from the car have my blood racing in my ears. The only thing I hear is the sound of my own heartbeat. That is until another car pulls into the garage and breaking the trance. Liam is back.

I cringe. "You should park that p.o.s. in the street."

"Hardly." He reaches for my hand and leads me toward the opening of the garage. We walk past a series of bikes, six in all. Two Harleys and a couple others I can't identify. Bikes aren't my thing, but I don't mind riding on them. The vehicle opposite the bikes is a Tesla, the expensive one. The car we parked behind is a Nissan Moreno, not something I would

expect amongst the Escalade SUV and everything else, but I wonder idly if it's Liam's.

Liam climbs out of my car and hands me the keys. "She's all filled up."

"Thanks, how much do I owe you?"

He shrugs it off, "No worries."

I roll my eyes but let it go. I can tell an argument will be futile and not worth it.

"She wants to talk, to both of us," Bryan shares with Liam.

"I had a feeling she might," Liam says looking at me. The look is oddly reassuring and I give him a small, worried smile.

"Are you busy?" I ask Liam.

"Not at all, lass." He smiles at me, again reassuring me.

"Let's go inside," Bryan says. "I'll give you the nickel tour."

He leads the way toward the house and I look around the open property. There are a couple horses in the distance.

"You ride?" Bryan asks me.

I shake my head. "Never have, but I think they're beautiful animals."

"I'll take you sometime."

"You're sure making promises for a future with me..." I whisper before he cuts me off.

"Because, it doesn't matter to me what your past holds, but I need you to know that you can tell me anything. I won't have secrets between us, Livia."

"We'll see about that," I mutter remembering Ireland's reaction. I'd known her for years and she still needed time to come to grips with what I'd told her about my past and the things I've done to keep my life moving forward. Yes,

she's come back around, and we've talked since then, but that initial rejection still stings, hard.

Bryan opens the door to his home and ushers me inside. Liam follows us inside and Bryan punches some numbers into a keypad near the door, deactivating the alarm.

"You two hungry?"

"No," I say.

"Yes," Bryan says at the same time.

Liam chuckles, "I'll work on some food while you show her around the house." He disappears down the hallway.

The house is wide open. You can see from one side of the house to the other on the lower level. The décor is everything you'd expect in a country home. It reminds me more of a log cabin with rich wood floors and wooden accents. The furniture is sparse, but what is there looks masculine and inviting.

On one end of the lower level of his house are three bedrooms and four bathrooms. One common one and each bedroom has its own. The rooms downstairs are obviously guest rooms or never used because they're quite stale when compared to the rest of the house.

On the other side of the house is a 'playroom' with bar décor, a pool table and a built-in bar. The room is bigger the apartment I shared with Ireland. It's obvious this room gets used quite a bit and it makes me smile. It means he's capable of letting loose occasionally. Reminds me that the superstar is human.

Beyond the playroom is another door. Bryan points out that it's Liam's area. It's basically his own apartment within the house. It has a bathroom, a kitchen and a second small bedroom. Then the house turns to the left, toward the backyard.

"This is where I spend much of my time," he says as way of introduction before ushering me forward. And the house changes, taking on an entirely different demeanor as I step from hardwood to tile floor. There is a door ahead of us but there are also two more doors on either side of the hallway.

"This," he opens the door on the left, "is a spare bedroom." I look inside and see the bed is a mess, like it was slept in last night. "I sleep here a lot when I'm working. Sometimes it's just too far to walk upstairs," he explains before closing the door and turning and opening the door on the right. "This is my office," he smiles as he ushers me inside.

I step inside and while it's messy, typical male, it's nonetheless a gorgeous office. It's long and narrow, but still spacious. There is wood paneling on the walls that match the rest of the house. At one end of the room is a sitting area with several pieces of paper scattered on the coffee table. Up on the wall are a series of six flat screens. Most of which are on. The top three have various news outlets playing, though there is no sound. Below them, in the bottom row, one screen is running a screensaver like it's tied to a computer, the other has something I can't quite make out and the last one is off.

I point to the one I don't understand, the one in the middle. "What's that one doing?"

He smiles at my curiosity. "It's monitoring social media," he explains as he walks toward it. "It runs twenty-four seven so I can see various things that are happening." He gets a little closer. "Come here," he says with excitement.

I walk to him, skirting the coffee table and I see there are four different things on the screen, one for each of the major social media outlets, and he points to the side of a couple of the panels. "These are trending lists," he explains. "Look at the top of the list," he tells me.

I do, and I see two at the top of each list, one is Bryan

Hayes and the other is 'Fate Has a Reason'. "Wow, congrats, Bryan. That's awesome."

"That didn't take long," he mutters as he touches the screen and the screen changes, pulling up one of the media outlets and he starts scanning the messages.

"And what's the verdict?" I ask him. Unsure if I want to know. He doesn't seem all too thrilled with whatever he's looking at.

Then a smile as wide as Texas spreads across his face. "Well, there is one way to know for sure," he says as he reaches over to the monitor that's turned off. It flickers to life and looks a lot like the one we're standing in front of.

"What's that one?"

"This one is always off. If I leave it on, I'll stand here and stare at it forever."

"Why?"

He chuckles, "Because this is the one that shows sales. This one tells me how many sales have happened, both in pre-orders for the new album, single sales and then previous album sales. From here I can see where my songs rank on the various charts for sales outlets." He looks at it a little closer. "Here," he points to something on the screen, then his finger traces to the other side. "These are the two major outlets for digital album sales and their charts. Look." There is a little more excitement in his voice as I look at the charts.

"Number one? On both?" I say, shocked.

"Uh huh," he says in such a way that tells me he's not sure how to put it into words.

"Congratulations, the song is really awesome."

His eyes meet mine. That look of pure happiness in his eyes once again. "I wrote it for you."

I blush as red as a cherry. I can feel the heat in my cheeks as he looks at me. "I know," I breathe. I can't let him see how much that song truly affected me. If I do that, I'll never be able to walk away from him when I tell him everything.

"Come on," he says, taking my hand. "I have one more room to show you."

I nod, but don't say anything. And I don't remind him that he hasn't shown me upstairs yet. Maybe it's better if I don't see upstairs, at least not right now.

Bryan leads me by the hand through the doorway and back into the hallway. He takes me to the door at the end of the long hallway that is his house. He opens the door and my jaw drops. Beyond the door is a mixing room and beyond that room is a small recording studio. "You record here?" I ask.

"Some stuff. I usually use it to play around, check the sound on some songs, things like that. I do a lot of practicing in here because it's quiet and soundproof."

"Wow." That's all I've got. I step into the room, looking over all the equipment he has inside. I haven't a clue what any of it is or what it means, but it is no less impressive. The door between the mixing room and the studio is open. I step inside.

There are several guitars on stands, a grand piano, a few stools and no less than six microphones on various stands and one hanging from the ceiling. I approach the piano and my fingers play along the keys.

"You play?"

I'm glad he can't see my face. "I used to."

"Play something?"

I shake my head. "Bryan, I haven't played since I was a teenager. I wouldn't even..."

"You might be surprised." He comes up behind me, wrapping his arm around my waist, and I feel something gentle brush along my hair. Either a kiss or just reassurance that I'm standing here.

"Maybe another time." Embarrassment colors my tone.

"Alright," he says softly. I can tell he's disappointed but the truth is I don't even know if I could play anything anymore. Seeing the piano brings back many memories I've worked hard to suppress over the years.

*"Livi-belle, come on," my dad says from the living room.*

*"I don't want to," I whine back.*

*"Yes, you do, come here, let me hear what you learned today."*

*My dad's sudden interest in my piano playing piques my curiosity. It's not something he's taken an interest in over the last five or so years that I've been taking lessons. Sometimes I think he made me take lessons just so he could keep me out of the house during the day while he slept. One way or another, I grew to love playing piano. Per Mrs. Larson, I'm good at it.*

*I leave my room and walk into the living room. My dad is sitting in his recliner rocking aimlessly back and forth. Something's off about him tonight and I don't understand it.*

*"Alright, dad. One song. Okay?"*

*"Sure, whatever you want, baby girl."*

*I sit down at the upright piano we've had since I was a little girl and I test the keys. I don't play at home very often because the walls are thin and I usually manage to piss off my neighbors. But it's late afternoon, most people aren't home from work yet.*

*Satisfied that the keys are the way I want them, I start*

*playing Beethoven's Moonlight Sonata. As a fifteen year old*
*who's only been playing for four years, this song is pretty*
*complicated, but my fingers fly over the keys with ease.*

I slip back to the present and I find myself sitting at
Bryan's piano. My fingers glide over the keys with an
unforgotten ease and my mind is lost to that night. A tear
streaks down my cheek as my fingers continue to move along
the keys. Bryan sits next to me.

"Why are you crying?"

My fingers slow against the ivory as I find my voice. "The
last time I played this was for my father, the night before I
was taken off the street and away from the only life I knew,"
I breathe.

Bryan takes my hands in his. "You ready to talk?" he asks.

"No, but I don't have a choice."

"Let's find Liam." His voice is soft, sober and
understanding.

*Bryan*

WE find Liam in the kitchen setting out food. "Just in time," he smiles at both of us. I return the smile but I can see Livia has tensed up dramatically since leaving the studio. "Why the long face?" Liam asks her, beating me to the punch.

"I don't want to do this." Her voice is barely above a whisper as she speaks.

"You don't have to," I tell her. Her eyes meet mine and they are pleading, but whether it is for an out or because she knows she has no choice, I don't know.

"I'd like Liam to start." Her voice is soft, a bit unsure and unsteady, something I've not seen from her before and I don't I like it.

"What would you like me to start with, lass?"

"Everything you know, leading up to when you found me."

Liam nods. "Alright, but we might want to take a seat for this." He gestures for both of us to take a seat at the breakfast bar. Livia sits first and I follow while Liam hands us each a glass of wine.

Liam takes a deep breath to settle himself before he begins a tale that will blow me out of the water.

"Vittorio Ricci, an Italian immigrant, came to the United States in the early nineteen hundreds..."

"Do we really have to go back this far?" I interrupt.

"Aye, we do. It's relevant, I assure you."

"It is. I've heard this story before, and in order for you to understand how I got to where I did, you need to hear the whole story," Livia adds.

"Continue, my friend."

Liam nods and continues, "He was young, maybe fourteen or fifteen years old. His parents had sent him with other male members of his family, but no one over the age of twenty and no one younger than fourteen. The idea had been to send them here to find good work that would bring the rest of the family over. When the boys, and I say boys because that's exactly what they were, arrived in New York, there were nine of them left. Having lost one, the youngest at barely fourteen, during the journey over. By the time they'd found a permanent place of residence, Vittorio was one of three remaining Ricci males in the U.S., well, that were still in New York." Liam takes a drink from his glass, though he's not drinking wine. He chose something stronger, whiskey. He stares blankly into space as he continues his story.

"The boys settled into a life of work, sleep, shit and work some more. But Vittorio started to hate the mundane tasks of everyday boring life. The males barely had enough to scrape by, let alone bring their family to America. He wanted more and he missed his parents. So he started picking up odd jobs here and there for different businesses within the city. Doing so not only granted him more money, but the ability to meet people he would have never normally come across. He started working as a courier for what he'd originally thought was a printing house. The longer he worked there, the more he figured out what the business was doing. And it was illegal. He discovered the company was a front for something else. Being young and naïve, it took him a long time to realize he was moving money, weapons, drugs – though not like the ones we know of today. The long part of this story summed up is that Vittorio Ricci was a smart kid. Too smart. He started tapping into the company's suppliers, offering them deals and obtaining his own product. Once he'd managed to obtain enough of it, he went around to his normal delivery distributors and offered them the same product, only cheaper.

"It was smart business because each one of the 'clients' he targeted took his offers. In short, he swiped the business right out from under his employers and the clients just assumed they were getting a better deal from the same company. At this point Vittorio brought his family on board and they were helping him maintain the new family business.

"By the time the gang found out about it, there was little they could do to set it right. Vittorio had managed to corner the supply lines and triple the amount of business in less than two years. The suppliers were dry because of Vittorio's business.

"Nineteen-Nineteen hit and Vittorio was the only one left of his family. His brothers and cousins had all been killed by the violence in New York or by various diseases and his business had pulled away from the drug market, and into alcohol supply lines. It was amazing business for about a year. Then prohibition hit and it hit Vittorio hard.

"The Ricci family had expanded. He'd brought his father, mother, three brothers – who were younger than he was – and two eldest sisters to America. His father didn't handle the journey well and died shortly after coming to America. His mother followed shortly thereafter from a broken heart. At least that's how the story goes. This put Vittorio in charge of his brothers and sisters. His brothers were all too eager to join the new family business, while the sisters disappeared." His voice trails off as he stares out the window behind us.

"When prohibition ended, Vittorio Ricci came out the other side completely unscathed. He came out of prohibition with his family and his businesses intact and until the early nineties, no one could figure out how. Their name was no longer associated with the drug scene, and although the weapon trafficking had never stopped, it was hardly enough to keep the family afloat.

"Over the course of the eighties and nineties, illegal gambling rings, drugs, and eventually prostitution were all tied back to the Ricci family, but cops never had enough information to take down the entire family. Individuals went to jail, did their time, got out and moved on. Spending time in jail was a badge of honor for most of those men and it always proved to Ricci who his most loyal members were. The ones who never squealed got their lives back in the circle as if nothing ever happened to them. Those who squealed usually never made it out of jail.

"The NYPD," Liam looks very pointedly at Livia, who nods before he continues, "realized quickly there were moles within the police force. For years, they fought the uphill battle of trying to figure out who Ricci's men were. Sometimes they were planted men and other times they were well-paid men. Ricci was always one step ahead of law enforcement, which is where I came into play.

"The FBI had to step in because there was very little the NYPD could do. There were moles inside the FBI, there were far fewer than the NYPD. A small group of men were brought in from various other branches of the FBI and a few CIA because the Ricci family was making bigger waves than we could keep up with.

"It was around this time we figured out how after all these years the Ricci family maintained their business." He stops, looking at Livia.

"Human smuggling, human trafficking and sex trafficking," Livia breathes.

"So where do you fit into all of this?" I ask Livia.

"My father was a mole."

Terror grips me at what that could mean and I look from Livia to Liam, who nods somberly, and then back to Livia. She stands up, slams back her entire glass of wine and starts

to pace the kitchen.

"I don't know the exact history of how my father got involved with the Ricci family." Her voice is still soft, and there's an edge of fear to her tone.

"I can answer that, lass."

"Please do, I've been dying to know."

"You might want to sit back down," Liam encourages her.

She shakes her head and remains standing. "Believe me, nothing you tell me now will change the past. He's dead, been dead, for years."

"Aye, he has, but it doesn't mean it won't fuck with your head." Liam's accent grows thicker the longer he talks.

"I don't care," Livia says as she continues to pace the length of the kitchen.

"What do you know about your mother?"

Livia freezes in her tracks and slowly turns toward Liam, glaring at him. "What does she have to do with any of this?"

"Everything," Liam answers.

"How so?"

"Your mother was born Elisabetta Maria Ricci. Great-granddaughter of Vittorio Ricci and sister to none other than Vittorio Ricci the fourth."

Livia's eyes go blank, her body ridged, her skin pale. "No!" she wails before collapsing onto the tile floor of my kitchen. I rush to her and pull her close against my chest while she sobs in my arms.

"Sorry, lad."

I look to Liam for help, silently begging him to help me pull her from the emotional storm, but it's no use. She's completely broken.

*Livia*

As I sob in Bryan's arms, a memory begins to play in my mind.

*"She's gone. What do you expect me to do now?" It's my father's voice, but I don't recall this memory of him. He looks much younger than I remember and the apartment has a lot of stuff in it I don't remember. It looks like a woman has lived here. Is he talking about my mother?*

*"The same thing you've always done."*

*"That's not easy for me to do, Liam. They've got me by the fucking balls. He's always been there to bail me out when I've needed it."*

*"Well, you have two choices. You can either bite the bullet or you can do as they ask of you. You knew when you married her that you'd have no choice. The only reason Vito allowed you to marry her is so he would have another inside mole. He'll expect nothing less of you now. You don't just walk away from a man like Ricci. The only way you get out is by death and that little girl in there deserves so much better than that. If you die, what's to stop him from turning her into one of them? You being alive is the only thing that will save her. You die..."*

I gasp for air and sit straight up, my heart pounding in my chest.

Warmth, something warm.

I try and calm myself by breathing through my nose.

It's him. It's Bryan.

His kitchen.

His house.

Liam.

My mother.

My mother is Vito Ricci's sister...

I pull away from my warm, protective barrier and look blankly around the room for something familiar to grab on to, something to bring me back to the present. Anything.

My eyes land on Liam.

My breathing gradually slows back to normal, but my mind races a million miles a minute. "I'm his niece?" I breathe.

"Aye, lass."

"How? How could he do that to his own flesh and blood?" I ask.

"Remember his sisters?" I nod absently. "They were the first of the Ricci family prostitutes."

I gasp and put my hand to my throat. I'm fighting to keep my breathing even when long, strong arms wrap around me from behind. My back presses to Bryan's front and his warmth consumes me, grounds me.

"I'll never be free of him, will I?" I ask in a whisper.

"You're free of him now, Livia. You have nothing to fear from Vito Ricci or anyone in his establishment. They're gone, done for, dead or locked away."

"But they always get out," I breathe.

"Not this time they won't. Vito is locked away in a federal prison, as far as he or anyone else knows, you're dead," Liam says in a reassuring tone.

"I have to go." I try to free myself from Bryan's arms. He holds on tighter.

"I'm not going to let you run away again." His voice is in my ear, a soft whisper and yet it holds all the power.

"I can't be with you," I mumble.

"Says who?" I'm surprised when it's Liam's voice I hear asking and not Bryan's.

"Says the fact that I can never be seen in public with him. Says the fact that our relationship is built on the knowledge I could be killed or captured at any moment..."

"You're not listening to him, Livia. Hear him out. Please," Bryan pleads. Spinning me around to face him as he continues, "If what Liam says is true, that Ricci is gone for good, then you have nothing to worry about."

"But I'm his niece."

"And the only people who know that are in this room," Liam says.

"No, they're not. Vito knows."

"But Vito thinks you're dead. You need to understand something, Livia." Liam's voice is stern. It's breaking through the fog of disbelief and fear that clouds my thoughts and feelings right now; I'm scared out of my mind. If Liam can find me, without even looking for me, who else can find me if they're trying? "Vito is in a federal prison. His phone calls and mail are scanned and scrutinized because the FBI is still trying to uncover more dirt on him. He's in isolation and there are no known associates of the Ricci family in the prison he's in. Believe me, the FBI knew what they were doing when they went after him."

My heart rate finally starts to slow to a normal rhythm and my breathing returns to normal. Bryan's eyes are on me, watching me for any signs I'm going to freak out again.

"I meant what I said earlier. Nothing and no one will ever hurt you again," Liam reminds me as Bryan gently strokes my

back.

"You say this like you have control over that. You can't be around me twenty-four-seven."

"Says who?" Bryan counters.

I stare at him a moment before responding. "That implies that either he leaves you or I never leave..."

He gives me a very pointed look and I pull away from him, but I don't break our eye contact. His face is passive, not revealing anything about what he's thinking. "You don't even know me," I breathe.

"I know no matter how hard I try, I can't wash you from my mind. I know if I don't at least give this a chance, I will spend the rest of my life wondering what could have been. I've done enough of that in my life, I'm not prepared to do it again," he says warmly with a confidence I wish I could feel about this whole situation.

"I haven't even told you everything," I breathe, trying my hardest to back out of this. It falls on deaf ears.

"Tell me if I have this correct because I've been listening this whole time." He nods, asking for permission to continue and I nod back, giving him his chance to analyze my situation. "Somehow you ended up in the hands of Vito Ricci and he did what he does best, buried you inside one of his many whorehouses. From there you were forced into prostitution, and god only knows what else. Am I close?"

Staring blankly at him, I nod. "They ripped me off the streets, hauled me to some warehouse where they beat me, tortured me and raped me, repeatedly." The horror of my circumstances washes over his features. "From there, they made my father watch me being raped before I had to watch them kill my father because he was playing both sides of the fence. He was doing Ricci's bidding in the police department

at the same time reporting it to whoever would listen."

Liam's breathing changes behind me. I turn to him. "You didn't know that, did you?"

"I knew he was killed, that's...that's how I knew to go looking for you and when I couldn't find you, I figured Ricci had gotten his claws in you."

"You can say that again. The only reason I know is because they made me watch them torture and kill my father. His death came only after he divulged the names of the cops he was working with."

"That was a bad year for the NYPD. They lost four more officers after your father's death. They could never tie them to Ricci," Liam says looking between Bryan and me.

"Did you ever tell anyone this?" Bryan asks, bringing me back around to face him.

"Which part?"

"Any of it?" Bryan asks.

"I used my father's death as leverage to get my Becca identity. I needed a change and to do that I had to ditch the other name. I told them who killed my father and led them to something they didn't even know they were missing," I explain.

"Are you talking about the box, the one they found in the subway?" Liam asks.

"How'd you know about that?" I ask him.

"It's a long story, but the short of it is that McMurray – I think that was his name – made no secret of the fact he'd 'figured out something no one else could'." Liam rolls his eyes. "More or less, he took credit for it."

"Whatever," I grumble.

"What was in the box? And how did you know about it?"

Bryan looks at me for a response.

I look to Liam for guidance on whether I should share or not. He gives me a slight nod. "It was the black book of women. It had detailed accounts of all the women trafficked into the US from all over the world. It contained passports, photos, birth certificates, their new identities and then whether they were alive, incarcerated or dead," I tell them both.

"They used the information contained within to further their case against Ricci and those who ran the trafficking side of the business. They also used it to solve missing persons cases going back more than forty years. Law enforcement was finally able to give more than four hundred families the closure they needed," Liam adds.

"Jesus Christ," Bryan spats. "How in the hell did you know about that box?"

"That's another long story, but the bottom line is I spent way too much time coherent around my captors. I never drank, did drugs, hell, I barely took Tylenol while I was in their possession. I didn't need anything clouding my judgement." A shiver creeps up my spine and I shudder at the memories of being in that house. "Living in that hell hole was bad enough; I didn't need to wake up not remembering what happened the night before. Because of that, I overheard a lot. Mostly between Fat Tony and his idiot goons. Sometimes Ricci himself, though that was a rare occurrence. I was a good girl. I did what I was told, never gave the guys trouble and I earned their leniency. I was a free-roaming prisoner."

Without realizing I'm doing it, my hand runs along the back of my neck as I feel the scars that are there. I remember the days of being tracked like an animal.

"You alright?" Bryan asks.

"Huh? Yeah." I look at him.

"You got kind of pale on me."

I frown. "Sorry. I..." I lift my hair off my neck and turn around, showing him the scars. Liam grumbles something under his breath about humans not being animals. I give him a small smile as Bryan looks at my neck.

"What happened there?"

I snort, "Each night I was chosen, I would be escorted, usually by two different men, to wherever it was I was supposed to go for the evening. Then, most nights when it was over, I would get picked up at the same location. As time went on and I proved my loyalty to Tony and Ricci, I was given leniency to return to the house on my own."

"Why didn't you run?" Bryan asks.

I drop my hair. "Those scars are why. I was tagged." I turn back around to face them. "If we got picked up by the cops, which happened often enough, and we didn't return home, they'd know where we were. It took me a long time to figure out how they knew where we were. I always figured someone inside the police department contacted someone who called someone, so on and so forth. While that may have been the case, the chips were a surefire way to make certain they knew where we were at all times."

Bryan's eyes take on a heated look as anger coats his features and Liam is cursing left and right behind me. "Look you two, it's in the past. I can't fucking change it and neither can you."

"It doesn't mean I don't fucking feel guilty for not getting you out of there faster," Liam barks.

"Liam, stop. You did what you could. You had a cover to maintain, I understand that now. But what I don't understand is why, if you were an undercover agent, I never saw you

again," I shout. "You promised me you'd protect me and then I was interrogated for days on end with no sight of you. How do I know you're not still working for Ricci?"

I step away from both of them.

Bryan goes to say something but Liam cuts him off and speaks.

"Do you remember the day of the raid on the house?"

"Vividly," I snap.

"What you may or may not know is there were nine other raids happening in the city at that exact same time. It was a total sting operation. Between the FBI, CIA, ATF, and NYPD, we took down Ricci's entire organization that day. After the tactical part of the raid was over, I left. I had to in order for the techs to get in there and comb the place for any information they could find. I was sent to another building, another raid." Liam moves around the counter toward me. He stops a few feet in front of me. "That raid was organized based on misinformation. We were under the impression it was a drug warehouse. A simple in and out." Anger builds in his face as he continues his story. "We were very wrong. Instead of a warehouse full of drugs, we found a building full of weapons- everything from guns, to missiles, to rockets, explosives, to you fucking name it. If it was shot or launched, it was in this warehouse. It was also one of Ricci's most protected buildings. This meant we charged in and we were in for the fight of our lives."

Tears begin to streak down Liam's cheeks, but he continues, "We lost a total of eleven officers that day. Eight of them in that warehouse alone." He leans down and lifts his pant leg.

Slowly I'm able to make out what I'm looking at. Liam has a prosthetic leg. "Oh god," I sob.

"I wasn't there for you because I was in the hospital."

"I had no idea," I breathe.

He gives me a sad smile as he drops his pant leg back down. "Not many people do, lass. Just you, Bryan and my old partner. I'm sure there are more. But I was one of twenty-two injuries in that building. By the time I was well enough, you'd already been shipped off to California. Due to my undercover gig, I was not privy to your name or your location."

"I'LL be honest, I knew it was bad, but..." I say aloud before thinking about what I'm saying.

"I'm sorry, I just needed you to know."

"Oh, it doesn't change anything," I reassure her because it's the truth. I do my best to show how sincere my words are and say, "What happened to you is something that should never happen to anyone, and I cannot express to you just how sorry I am that it happened to you. But, it's in the past, Livia, just as you said. There is nothing you, Liam, or I can do to change it."

"I have demons, Bryan. Very deep, dark demons."

I snort humorlessly, "I would be more concerned if you didn't have them."

"Have you ever sought out counseling?" Liam asks Livia.

"No," she states very matter of fact. "Until this year, I've avoided talking to anyone about my past. But somewhere in the middle of an outlet store in Phoenix I realized I needed to stop running from my past."

"An outlet store?" I question.

She laughs a little. "Ireland," she says by way of explanation and I raise an eyebrow, prompting her to continue. She swallows before answering me, "I don't let myself get attached to anyone, except for Ireland, so when she and Dyson were in the process of trying to figure their shit out I became a bit of a bitch. I was being catty and stupid. I felt like I was losing my best friend." She folds her arms over her chest and asks, "Can I have some more wine?"

"Of course," Liam answers and steps behind the island to retrieve the bottle.

"I would have never guessed," she says shyly as she watches him walk.

"If it wouldn't have explained where I was, then I probably wouldn't have shown you either. The only reason Bryan knows is because I met him in a bar and my limp was much more pronounced back then. I don't make a habit of telling people, so I've worked very hard to cover it up as best I can," he tells her and it's true.

"It shows." She smiles at him as he hands her another glass of wine. She takes it and swallows half of it down before setting the glass back down on the island.

"She cornered me in the dressing room over why I don't really show emotion and why I can't be more open with her. I saw the hurt in her eyes when she understood I wouldn't be sharing anything. It bothered me." She chuckles, "It was just a few days before you came into CatTails. The irony is I was already making changes in my life."

"How so?" I ask.

"Around the time Ireland and I were getting ready to move in with each other, I'd decided it would be easier for me to give up stripping so I wouldn't have to explain to her where I was all hours of the night. But then," Sadness moves over her features, "her mom died unexpectedly." She wipes a tear from her cheek. "She was so torn up. I didn't know what to do and it started bringing back memories of the past that I had long forgotten, or thought I had. Then after she got home from Missouri, she found Dyson. Her life changed and she started opening up to me. I realized there was so much more to life than stripping in a dingy club and whoring myself out. I shut down my website, but it didn't stop my usual tricks at the bar." She looks at Liam very pointedly.

"What's that all about?" I ask.

Liam looks at me and inquires, "Do you remember that

night we went to Blu, after the strip club?"

"Yes," I say hesitantly.

"Well, I followed her out of the bar. She was with someone, and I was curious what she was up to and while I couldn't hear too much of their conversation, I caught on to what she was doing. I waited outside the guy's house and followed her to where I thought was home, but it turned out she was staying in the same hotel as you were. It wasn't my proudest moment," he says sheepishly.

"No, it wasn't," Livia adds. "But it made me wake up and realize I needed to get my shit together. I needed to come clean with my best friend and most importantly, I needed to open myself up more."

"And did you?"

She looks at me. "Did I...?"

"Come clean to your friend?"

She nods her head. "Yes, I did. It wasn't pretty, but I did. I hurt her. She was so mad at me, but the twist to it was the fact that she was mad at me for stripping and prostituting myself because she knew I was so much better than that and she's right."

"Yes, you are," Liam and I say in unison.

"So, what now?" Livia asks before turning to me. She ignores Liam and she says to me, "I drove all this way for the chance to apologize to you for running out on you that night."

I shake my head back and forth. "You have nothing to apologize for, Livia."

"But I do. I wanted what happened that night to be special, to be different, and it was so much better than I could have imagined. I panicked."

"I didn't treat you very fairly that night. I got angry because I didn't want you to leave. I was afraid if you walked out that door, I'd never see you again."

"I'm here now." She smiles at me. "But we still have some problems." She turns back to Liam. "If we're going to do this, the press is going to have a field day with my past. Becca Carpenter was a stripper and a prostitute, though never arrested as such, but she still has a record." Her voice portrays her embarrassment. "Livia Fazio is dead. So, what do we do?"

I look to Liam as this is his area of expertise, but I add what I find most important, "To me, she's Livia, no matter what."

Liam nods his understanding. "My concern is your friends, Ireland, Dyson, and the fact that the Michaels know who you are. This wouldn't be the first alias Cami has ever dealt with and that girl has her own skeletons in the closet, but I think we can make something work."

"Good," she says then turns back to me. "Now, where were we?" She smiles an impish smile.

I wrap my arms around her and kiss the top of her head. "Starting over."

*Livia*

BRYAN'S declaration brings new hope that this just might work between us. All my cards are on the table, I have very little left to hide when it comes to my past. If he's accepting this, then we have a chance to move forward.

The darkness settles in outside as we sit down to eat. My nerves are shot from the conversation and it's making eating difficult. Liam's cooking skills surprise me. He's good at it.

Our conversation flows effortlessly from serious to free and fun.

Bryan reluctantly answers a phone call about two-thirds of the way through dinner that he couldn't ignore anymore. When I asked Liam about the call, he said that its business and he explained that Bryan is adamant about leaving business at the door when it comes to meals, but it doesn't always work out that way. No matter how hard Bryan tries to put work away during certain activities, it's a constant reminder that his job takes precedence.

"What do you want me to do?" Liam asks me when Bryan leaves the room.

"About?"

"You, your identity."

"I'm wondering if this is a conversation for right now. I'm getting ahead of myself assuming he wants to take our relationship public. We barely know each other," I admit. And it's true, we don't know each other. However, any man who can accept me for who I am, flaws and baggage included, deserves a chance. "I'd hate to see you go through the hassle and this turn out to be nothing."

Liam snorts. "If you think he's going to let you go, for-get-it," he emphasizes. "He's been a mess since we left Phoenix.

I don't remember the last time he slept in his own bed. He's spent hours upon hours in that studio and tonight is the first time I've seen him relax in months."

Liam's forthcoming attitude warms my heart. My gaze travels to the door Bryan left through and I wonder if he's feeling what I'm feeling. Is it possible? I've met the man twice. The first time I danced naked for him. And I slept with him the second time. That doesn't have to mean the attraction I felt from the moment I laid eyes on him isn't real. I'm a firm believer that there are people who come into your life that you just know are meant for you. Ireland was the first person to be that way for me. Thinking about that now, I realize I was more ready for a relationship than I realized. The idea of a relationship sends my heart into triple time.

"Think about that night at the party, lass. Everything that transpired before you left the bar. You might not remember it the way I do, but the two of you were inseparable. Add in the fact that you literally drove across the country for a chance to apologize. Tell me you didn't expect this to happen?"

I can only blink at him. He's right, of course. I have no intention of going anywhere until Bryan tells me to get lost. "I had hope," I state simply. "Things could have gone terribly wrong." I take a deep breath and explain, "Honestly, had this not gone so well, I would have disappeared."

"Running isn't the answer," Liam says with sadness in his voice.

"It's the only thing I know to do."

Liam nods in understanding. "Not anymore. I assure you, you're safe."

"For now."

"Listen, you need to understand that the Ricci crime family is dead. Those who could possibly have had any beef

against you are either dead or in jail for the rest of their lives and that's based on what they've already been convicted of. That's not counting the mounting case in the trafficking portion of the investigation. When that comes to fruition, there are going to be a lot of domestic and international arrests made. I assure you, those people are so far removed from you that you shouldn't even consider they'd come after you. No one, and I do mean no one, knows you're the one who lead the Bureau to the box. Trust me when I tell you that McMurray made that his personal find and he took all the credit for it."

"How do you know my name isn't in some file somewhere?"

He nods and reaches into his pocket for something, his phone. He presses a couple of buttons and then there's ringing. It takes two before someone comes on the line. "Declan," the voice answers.

"Dec, it's Liam."

"Hey man, what's going on?"

"You busy?"

Declan snorts into the phone, "Always, but what can I do for you?"

"McMurray..."

"That fuck-tard, what's he done now?"

Liam indicates toward the phone with a smirk. "The box."

"Oh, for the love of, what the hell are you bringing that up for?" Declan demands and Liam smiles.

"How'd he find it?"

A gruff laugh comes through the phone before Declan responds. "He found it, according to him, along with other documents. But honestly, I'm pretty sure someone,

somewhere, tipped him off. That man is the dullest tool in the shed."

"Say someone did tip him off?" I look at Liam with wide eyes. I'm not sure I want to know where he's going with this. "Would he have documented it?"

Another laugh comes through the phone. "Believe me when I tell you that I've combed through every report, every file, every scrap of reporting and scrape of evidence and there is absolutely nothing in there about where he got his tip from."

"If you asked him, as his superior, would he tell you?" Liam counters.

"Fuck no. He's hell bent on maintaining he found that shit on his own. Not even to me." There is a brief pause, "why are you asking me this shit?"

"Because, Declan, he didn't find it. That shit was handed to him on a silver platter."

"No kidding, but who?"

I shake my head vehemently, indicating I don't want him to tell his friend. "That was the point, Dec. You're not supposed to know; you don't know and I'm not going to tell you."

"Yeah, alright. Regardless, McMurray covered his tracks pretty well when it came to that damn thing. Whoever told him has a secret safer than Fort Knox. Hell, I'd be surprised if McMurray even remembers where he got the intel," Declan shares.

I give Liam a small smile of satisfaction and gratitude. Knowing this information makes me feel more secure.

"Good, thanks man."

"Aye, no problem. Listen, you planning on coming up

anytime soon?"

Liam takes the phone off speaker. "Maybe. The schedule's pretty up in the air right now. I'll keep you posted."

I don't hear Declan's response, but Liam's demeanor changes and he looks at me. "Aye, she's safe."

Liam leans onto the counter and the phone is loud enough for me to hear Declan. "How do you know? You're back in Nashville, aren't you?"

"Aye, but Declan?"

"Yeah?"

"Let's just say I have inside information." He winks at me.

"Yeah, whatever. You need anything, call me."

Liam stands up. "Aye, come down sometime. There's someone I want you to meet."

I miss Declan's response, but Liam gives me another wink. "No, lad, she's not mine."

Declan says something to Liam that evokes a smile and he replies, "Alright. I'll let Bryan know....okay...later." Liam ends the call, looks to me and says, "Feel better now?"

I shrug. "A little. You can't fault me for being paranoid."

"No, that I most certainly can't do, but I assure you, if there is any mention of Livia Fazio from Vito Ricci or any of his cohorts, we'll know about it."

"I want to see him."

"Who?" Liam asks with a crease in his brow.

"Vito."

"Why in the hell would you want to do that?" Liam's shock is evident.

"Or rather, I want to stand in front of him when they put the needle in his arm. I want him to see me and realize as

he's about to die that I'm the reason his world fell apart."

"Who's world?" Bryan says as he comes back into the room.

"Vito," Liam answers.

"What about his world falling apart?"

"I just told Liam I would like to be standing in front of Vito when they put the needle in his arm, so that just before his lights go out, he'll realize it was me who brought him down," I explain to Bryan. He looks confused. I swallow and elaborate, "I didn't know it at the time, because he never shared that he was undercover." I give Liam a pointed look. "But after he showed at the house and earned Fat Tony's trust, he started taking me to 'appointments' but those appointments weren't normal appointments. There was usually an undercover agent who wanted information from me. At first I was reluctant to give it up, but eventually I realized it was my chance to get out of my situation. I started giving them some information about the house I lived in, who lived there, how many girls were there, things like that." I sigh. "In hindsight, I gave them the information they needed to raid the house."

"Among other things," Liam adds. "The only difference was I was usually in the room next door listening and watching. I was able to fill in some of the blanks."

I stare blankly at Liam, still trying to wrap my head around the fact he was one of them. "Why didn't you ever tell me?"

He gives me a resigned smile. "I was supposed to. It was going to be me who questioned you after the fact, but I was otherwise indisposed."

"I know, I just...I guess a part of me would have been a little more open, more forthcoming and, I don't know, maybe things would have turned out differently if you'd been there."

The regret is evident in my voice.

Bryan wraps his arms around me and holds me gently to his chest. My back to his front. I feel warmth unlike anything I've ever felt before and it brings me comfort. "I guess in a way, I knew," I add.

"How so?" Bryan asks.

"Because he was different toward me, toward all the girls. Fat Tony and his goons treated us like trash, but he didn't. He had respect for us, he treated us kindly. Almost as if he felt guilty." I look again at Liam and my statement is confirmed by the sorrow in his features.

"My guilt had more to do with you than those other girls. I didn't know who they were or even where they came from, but you..." His eyes well with tears. "You're my best friend's daughter." He looks away from me. "I knew when they found his body that it was Ricci's work. The investigation team didn't want to believe it, but I knew and more importantly, I knew with Mercutio gone, Ricci had gotten his hands on you. The longer you stayed gone, the more I knew. I was supposed to be pulled from the Ricci project but I made them keep me in. Finding you was my driving motivation for getting into Vito's inner circle. It wasn't easy, but I managed to do it."

He looks off into space, remembering something I can only imagine. "A little over a year after his death, I'd heard some of the guys talking about the cop job. It killed me to keep my emotions in check they talked about how the cops had given up ever finding out who killed him. But that wasn't what gutted me. When they started talking about his 'smoking hot' daughter, I broke their noses." He flexes his right fist, remembering the crunch of their faces under his knuckles. "I got what information out of them that I could and that was when I learned you were still alive, but neither one of them knew where you were." He turns back to us. Bryan gently

strokes his thumbs in slow circles along my arms, giving me comfort as we listen to Liam's tale. "I'd pissed Ricci off with my stunt, but neither one of them were willing to tell Ricci why I busted their noses. I told Ricci they were being idiots, so I set them straight. It was what got me deeper into the Ricci sanctum. After that, I kept my eyes and ears open for any signs of you, any acknowledgement from Ricci about your whereabouts. But, like most things with Ricci, you were never mentioned."

He lowers his head, but doesn't stop. "I got so angry with him because you were his niece, but that didn't matter to him. As much as Ricci claimed to be about family, he didn't care unless you were one of his brothers or his son. Women were nothing but decorations to him. His wife was walking, talking, breathing proof of that."

"I didn't even know he was married," I add to his statement.

Liam snorts and Bryan gently kisses the top of my head. "No one did, really. She was never allowed around business dealings and the only time anyone saw her was at a rare party for one thing or another. Hell, I only saw the woman twice and talked to her, once. I knew getting anything out of her was a waste of time because she was so devoted to Vito. She didn't care what he did." He sighs, "Anyway, eventually I put two and two together and assumed he'd taken you into one of his whorehouses. So, I started pressing Ricci for the other side of the business, the side no one ever talked about. That's how I got assigned to Tony's house. Ricci wanted me to learn how things are run and I did."

"I'll say," Bryan states. His voice vibrating his chest against my back, reminding me of the ever-present spark between us.

"Like I did with Ricci, I earned Tony's trust and he let me start carting the girls around."

"Did anyone else squeal?" I ask.

Liam shakes his head. "No, most of those girls were scared out of their minds. Whether from immigration or from the things Tony and his goons made them do, I'm not sure. Once I found you, I knew you were the only hope the Bureau had at breaking up Ricci's trafficking business. When I found you sober, alive and for all intents and purposes, healthy, I knew you would give them what they needed."

"I was ready to run. I was just waiting for the day I got picked up again. I wanted that out but I couldn't go to the cops on my own. If they tracked me, I would have been killed. I had to wait for the right opportunity. This came when I thought I was going to get picked up again. What was that guy's name?"

"Who, lass?"

"The one who was always in the room? O'Brien, or something like that."

"Yup, that was him," Liam confirms.

"I was scared at first, but not of being arrested."

"Of what then?" Bryan asks, looking at me. My eyes meet his and they're filled with compassion and understanding.

"Of what Fat Tony would do when I got out." I shudder and Bryan's arms wrap tighter around me. "Getting arrested was always nice. I'd hoped the next time it happened, I'd get sent to jail."

"Why?" Bryan breathes.

"Because I'd be away from them, but somehow I always managed to avoid it." I look at Liam. "That wouldn't be your doing, would it?"

He puts his hands up in defense. "No, I had no clue you'd ever gotten picked up. Trust me, if I had, you would've been

out of there much faster."

I nod in understanding. "They'd run my prints and every single time, they let me go. Like they had no clue who I was. That's the part that always hurt me the most."

Liam sighs, "I'd imagine Ricci was behind all of your releases."

"So prostituting his niece was okay, but letting her rot in jail was not?" Bryan snaps, releasing me. "God, I want to get my hands on that..."

I grab his arm, pulling him back to me. "Ricci knew. He knew I would talk if given the chance. That's why he never let me have one. I knew too much to be left in custody too long. I knew he killed my father. Between that and what they did to me, it was enough to put Ricci away for life. He wasn't going to let me hang around a precinct for long."

Bryan cups my cheek with his hand. I lean into it, savoring the warmth and taking comfort in his touch. "Is there anything else I should know?" Bryan asks me, but he looks to Liam too.

"I don't think so," Liam says.

I look at Liam. "Thank you," I tell him.

"For what, lass?"

"For helping me tell Bryan, for filling in a lot of the blanks about how and why things happened the way they did. I've wondered for years about a lot of this stuff. It's nice to finally know," I share.

"I'm always here if you have more questions. There is one more thing I'd like to tell you about," he adds. I nod. "I cleaned out your father's apartment after he died. There is a storage unit in New York filled with the stuff I saved."

"I don't know that there's anything in there that I want.

I've been without for so long," I tell him.

"True," Bryan says, "But there might be some stuff in there you want. We can make a trip up there, clean it out."

I shake my head. "I don't think I can go back there," I admit.

"Understood, but we'll talk about it later. Okay?" Bryan asks and I nod.

"There is one more thing," Liam states and I look at him, puzzled. "Your father had a life insurance policy. You were listed as beneficiary. I pulled some strings after I found you and got the claim filed on your behalf."

I shake my head. "I don't know how I feel about that."

"Understood, but the money is yours."

"How much?" Bryan asks and Liam looks to me for permission to share; I nod.

"The policy was for two-hundred thousand. I imagine it's grown some over the years."

My jaw falls in shock. "Two-hundred grand? Seriously?"

"Aye, lass. Between his department insurance, accidental death coverage and his private policy, it totaled just under two-fifty when it went into the account. There's a P.O. Box in New York where I've had all the statements sent to."

"I..." I pull in a deep breath. "I don't even know what to say to all this," I whisper.

"Don't worry about it right now, Livia," Bryan smiles at me. "We can discuss it more later. Nothing needs to be decided tonight."

I nod and relax. "Why don't you two go, I'll clean up the kitchen," Liam says, effectively dismissing us.

Bryan grabs my hand and pulls me toward the door. I put my finger up, asking for a minute, and he nods as he

releases my hand. I move around the counter to approach Liam and our gazes meet. I can't stop the tears that fill my eyes. I wanted to say something, but it all dies on my lips so I wrap my arms around him and hope my hug can convey my feelings. He's surprised at first but he slowly wraps his arms around me. We don't say anything; we don't have to.

I LEAD Livia by the hand to my bedroom upstairs.

"Liam said you haven't been sleeping up here since you came home from Arizona?" The question throws me off a little and I want to curse Liam for sharing that with her.

"No, I haven't. I've been a little occupied."

She smiles sweetly at me. "So I heard."

"From Liam?" I ask, confused.

"No, on the radio." She winks at me. "He said you got home and threw yourself into writing that song."

"I did. I tend to get a little manic when I'm working on new material. The label gave me very little time to get it recorded if I wanted it on the album."

"Is that the only reason?" she asks. Her innocence is alluring.

"No, it most certainly was not." I smile at her. "It was all I could do to keep my mind off certain things." I wink at her. Writing the song let her live in my mind until such a point in time when I could reveal it to not only her, but the world. I wanted to show her that no matter who, what or where I was, she was on my mind.

"Good," she smirks. "Now I know you weren't trying to win me over with that song."

My jaw falls slack, but I recover quickly. "Well, did it work?"

She laces her fingers behind my neck and pulls me down to her level. "Yes," she breathes before capturing my mouth with hers.

You've read about it in books, seen it in movies; that special moment when the sparks fly, fireworks ignite, and

the world falls away. Until you feel it, you can only imagine its existence in reality. This is it, that perfect moment where everything in the world rights itself. Her lips are warm and soft pressed against mine and a piece to the puzzle of my life that I didn't know was missing clicks into place.

Her tongue slides along mine and my cock hardens in my jeans. Somewhere in my haze, I manage to open the door to my room and I push her into it. She giggles, breaking our kiss, but I don't let her go far before pressing her front to mine as I back her farther into the room. My goal is the bed. "I can't wait any longer," I breathe against her lips and she smiles.

"I have no idea what you're waiting for," she smirks.

"Without risking the mood, I have to ask."

"No, I'm not going to run."

"Promise?" I confirm.

She nods. Her eyes are hooded and full of the desire I'm feeling for her reflected back at me. "I can't promise this isn't going to be an uphill battle, but I promise I will do my best," she whispers.

"That's all I ask," I whisper back before claiming her lips once more. Pulling her body flush against mine. Feeling her warmth and hearing her whimpers forces my cock to strain harder against my jeans, but it is my goal to savor her tonight. To worship her body and the woman she is.

She squeaks when her legs find the bed and it breaks our kiss. I pull her shirt over her head. She doesn't stop kissing along my jaw and down my neck while she reaches for my shirt and pulls it free of my body. Her tongue darts out and flicks across a nipple and I hiss. I slide my hand into her hair, tilting her head back and looking into her eyes. "Take off your pants," I demand.

She smiles wide and reaches for the button of her jeans and unbuttons them, and then slowly she slides her zipper down to reveal a pair of red lace panties that match the bra she's wearing. My eyes roam over her perfect body. Her tits are trussed up in her bra, giving them a full look that has my mouth watering. I dip my head and slide my tongue along the upper swell. She shivers and her breathing fractures and falters. "Take 'em off," I say again and she leans forward, pushing me back as she slides her jeans down her legs and over her feet before kicking them aside. "On the bed," I order her and she sits down and starts to slide back, but I grab her thighs, stopping her. "Stay."

She smiles at me. "Bossy, aren't we?"

"Got a problem with that?" I ask.

"No, not at all." She smirks and reaches for the button of my jeans, but I back out of her reach.

"Oh no, it's my turn." I wink at her before lowering to my knees between her legs. She slides her hand into my hair to guide me and I take my cue, but I don't go straight for the apex of her thighs. I flick my tongue across the inside of her right thigh and her breathing hitches. I stare into her eyes as I do it again on the other leg. I go back and forth, climbing closer to my goal.

The sweet smell of her sex makes my head spin.

Her back arches off the bed and her eyes disappear from my line of sight and I feel slightly disappointed until she settles down. I spin slow circles with my tongue as I draw closer to the one place I know she wants me to be. I go from the crease of her thigh to her stomach on up to her hip. Kissing, licking, and blowing warm air over her skin causes goosebumps to rise across her flesh and she whimpers.

I use my teeth to pull her panties down and she smiles at me. I can't help my returning smile as she lifts her hips. I

reach underneath her ass to grab hold of the waistband and pull them down her legs. She helps by switching position and I pull them off with my teeth.

As soon as she's free of the barrier, I go straight for the source of the sweetest smell on the planet. Livia Fazio.

My sudden change of pace causes her to gasp in shock but she settles as my tongue slowly circles her sensitive clit. Her legs jerk slightly with each pass of my tongue and I know the sensation is getting to her. I smile before putting everything I have into pushing her toward an orgasm I know she desperately wants and needs.

Bryan has his face buried in my pussy. I slide my hand into his hair, holding him to me and his eyes never leave mine. He's watching me closely, but the sensation against my sex is making it difficult to keep my eyes from rolling up and closing.

My orgasm balances on the edge of a knife and I bite my tongue to hold it back. I'm not ready to have this end. His tongue feels amazing against my sensitive sex. I don't want him to move, ever.

As if he can read my mind, he picks up the pace, forcing my eyes to roll up into my head and my body to start quivering. I can't hold back anymore. I explode. Every nerve ending ignites with pleasure unlike anything I've experienced before.

Desire roars through my body as his tongue slows and his hands roam up my torso to reach the tight peaks of my nipples. He rolls them between his fingers and it sends a new wave of pleasure rocketing through me as he draws out my orgasm.

He begins to slow his tongue and his fingers loosen on my nipples as I come down.

After a few heartbeats my breathing returning to normal. He extracts himself from between my legs and stands up. His body is gorgeous, muscled and perfect in every way. Though it's obvious he works out, he doesn't go to extremes in doing so. He unbuttons his jeans and gives me a bit of a show that reveals a tiny, dark blond trial of hair disappearing beyond the waistband. I smirk at him. "What?" he says playfully.

"I just can't believe I'm looking at you again. This is a first. You do realize this, right?" I ask. I don't want to bring up my past, but I would be remiss if I didn't mention that I've never slept with the same man twice.

"What's that?" he asks.

"I've never slept with the same person twice," I tell him and he cocks an eyebrow at me.

Skeptically he asks, "Really?"

I nod. "Really."

He doesn't press for details, which is good since I'm not about to give them out, but he does slide his pants down his legs and takes his cock in his fist and begins sliding his hand up and down as he draws closer to me. I set my elbows in the mattress and slide deeper into the bed. He climbs between my legs and puts a foil packet between his teeth before propping my legs on his thighs.

For the first time in my life seeing a condom is disheartening. I've never slept with a man without one. I want to with him. I want him to claim me, to do things no one else has ever done to me before. He deserves it. If he's willing to accept me with all my baggage, then he deserves to claim me as his.

"What are you thinking about?" His eyes are gentle,

concerned even.

"I don't want to spoil the mood," I tell him and it's true.

"Rule number one for this relationship. Communication. It is required. So, what is on your mind?"

I frown. "We have rules?"

"Not exactly rules, just guidelines. There are, of course, the obvious ones, like no sleeping with anyone else, no more stripping and no more prostituting."

I roll my eyes. "That goes without saying, Bryan."

He smiles. "Good, now, back to what you were thinking about?"

"I don't want you to put that on." I share honestly.

He looks at the packet in his hand then back at me. There are unasked questions in his eyes and I expected them, so I answer them without him having to ask. "I'm clean, have always been clean. I've been tested every three months since being released from Ricci. I've never used drugs, so I've never shared needles with anyone and more importantly, my last test was a couple weeks ago. I've been given a clean bill of health and I'm on birth control."

"I've never..." He doesn't need to say anymore and he doesn't.

"Then the choice is up to you." I give him a reassuring smile, but he doesn't move. I'm concerned I've ruined the mood and I don't know how to fix it. "Communication, I think that's what you said rule number one was. What's wrong?" I ask.

His eyes meet mine and it's as if a light bulb has come on inside. He blinks, clearing his mind and says, "Honestly?"

"Always," I answer.

"I'd never even thought about it. I've always worn condoms

and somehow I knew all this. I guess it just took me by surprise to actually hear you say it."

I slide away from him, reaching for a pillow to cover myself. I feel exposed.

"I'm sorry, I just-" He sits back on his feet, adjusting his position to get more comfortable.

"This is why I didn't want to say anything. I'm sorry, I shouldn't have..."

"No, it's alright. I don't know what I'm thinking right now. I'm not sure it would matter to me, Livia. That's the part that scares me."

"What do you mean, it wouldn't matter to you?"

He sighs, "I mean I want to be with you so bad, condom or no condom, that I can't even think straight when I'm around you. It's...confusing."

I take the pillow away, putting it back where it was and I crawl, naked, across the bed to him. "I understand better than you think," I tell him as I get closer to him. I stand up enough that I can straddle his hips and I sit down on his lap, my legs on either side of him, his cock pressed between us. I ruined this moment and now I'm going to fix it. I have to fix it. "I need you," I breathe.

The remaining remnants of the fog that was clouding his vision clears the moment I flick my hips, pressing my clit against the head of his cock. "Put it on," I tell him. Taking his cue to be a little bit bossy.

He smirks at me, "I don't want to."

I reach between us and grab his erection and slide the head against my slick sex. "Then claim me," I breathe before claiming his lips in a soul-crushing, panty-melting kiss that has my head spinning within a heartbeat. I line him up, but I don't push down.

He wraps his arms around my back, takes hold of my shoulders and knocks me off balance onto my back. He slides his way between my legs, lining himself up my core. The head of his cock teases my entrance and his breathing takes on a more carnal rasp. "Jesus," he growls before pushing inside of me.

"Oh, God," I cry out as he pushes all the way in. He stills, giving me a moment to get used to the sensation of him buried inside me. The motion sends a warm tingling throughout my body and my eyelids flutter.

He pulls back until just the tip of his cock is inside and he teases my entrance. The motion sends a wave of pleasure pulsing through my sex. I moan.

"So tight, so wet." His voice is more of a moan and he pushes himself back inside me, but he doesn't stop. He immediately pulls out and back in and I cry out as the pleasure is too much to contain.

I can feel every pulse of his heart, every vein and bump of his cock as it moves inside of me. The sensation is overwhelming and my eyes close. He's never been this deep inside me before. He's crawling into my heart and taking over my soul with each thrust.

It doesn't take long for him to bring my orgasm to the brink. His thrusts become harder, more erratic and frantic. He's close. I'm close. "Don't stop," I moan and I find strength to open my eyes. His eyes are full of lust, desire and a happiness that can only be matched by what I'm feeling as my orgasm topples over the side. I cry out his name and my pussy clamps down on him. He thrusts two more times inside me before he empties inside me. He's claimed me. I am his and only his.

*Liam*

"WHAT do you need from me?"

"I don't know. It depends on what you want." Declan replies into the phone.

"I need a whole new identity, a background and everything that goes along with it. It has to be verifiable and fool proof," I tell him.

"What do you need that for?" His confusion is clear, which is good.

"It's not for me."

"I'm not an idiot, Callahan. But I'm going to need more to go on here."

"It's for Livia," I share reluctantly.

"What's she need a new identity for? What's wrong with the one she has now?"

I sigh. "I really don't want to discuss this over the phone."

"Well, you're there and I'm here, so how exactly are we supposed to discuss anything?"

"I'll come to New York, but will you do it?"

"She's going to have to come with you. We're going to have to do everything all over again and in order for me to do that, I need fresh fingerprints, a new DNA sample, you know the drill."

"That's not going to be an easy task. She won't go back to New York."

He snorts into the phone, "You can't blame the girl. She's been through hell in this city."

"We have other business to address up there. Maybe I can use that as an excuse to get her to go."

He laughs, "Good luck with that."

"Thanks so much," I mutter.

"Why does she need a new identity anyway?"

"She doesn't, but it just might be easier. Her life is about to become very public."

"That's not a good idea and you know it," Declan grumbles.

This time it's my turn to snort at him. "I'm pretty sure she's already made up her mind."

"How in the world did she and Bryan meet in the first place?"

"How'd you..."

"I'm an FBI Agent, remember? I didn't get here on my dashing good looks, though there was this one woman..." He trails off, no doubt thinking about some woman from the past. Declan Callahan, my brother, has always been a ladies' man.

"Yeah, whatever. Do you want the truth on how they met, or would you rather have the lie we plan to tell everyone?"

"Both."

I roll my eyes. "Truth, they met at strip club."

He laughs, "Now that's original."

"But it's the truth. Remember that night back in February when I called you about her whereabouts?"

"Aye," he says with some hesitation.

"I was standing in the middle of a strip club in Phoenix."

"No shit?"

"The public side of the story, which can be corroborated easily enough, is that they met at a party in Phoenix this last June."

"The strip club story is better."

"Not if she's the stripper."

"Oh hell, seriously? I thought she dumped all that shit when she got to California?"

"Apparently, whoever her handler was royally fucked up with her. They left her high and dry. She did the only thing she knew how to do to make money."

"Fuck," he growls. "I had no idea."

"How in the hell do you think McMurray got his intel?"

"Oh, fuck. You're fucking kidding me?"

"No, Dec, I'm not. She used it as leverage to gain the identity she has now. The one she was given was tainted by solicitation arrests. She wanted a fresh start so she played the last of her cards. Gave McMurray the undeserved promotion and she got a new identity, but when I run her background, it's full of holes. Hell, her date of birth is three different dates across the three credit bureaus. So, if you're going to do this, she needs a solid history, no holes. Social security, birth certificate, you name it, she must have it. Then she needs a plausibly identity with actual records and transcripts where necessary. It has got to look like she's lived this life her whole life."

"Fuck, that's a lot to ask of me, brother."

"I know, but you'll do it. You know as well as I do that she got a raw fucking deal. She's doing everything she can to set things straight. I need the public perception to be clean. For her sake and for Bryan's."

He's silent on the line for a few long moments before he finally sighs into the phone, "Alright, I'll do it, but you owe me."

I smile. "Name it."

"I'll let you know."

"You're a saint," I tell him.

"Yeah, yeah."

"I'll let you know when we're coming."

"I need at least a week, maybe a little more."

"You got it."

We hang up shortly after that. As for the plan to get Livia to New York? No fucking clue.

"Where are you going?"

"Shh, just to the bathroom," I tell Bryan. His concern is obvious. "Have you slept at all?" I ask him.

"Not really," he yawns.

"Why not?" I ask as I stand up off the bed. "I'm not going anywhere, Bryan," I assure him. I have no intention of running. "Besides, I'm not even sure I could find the front door," I tease as I step into the bathroom.

When I come out, he's sprawled across the bed, leaving me plenty of room and a great view of the erection tenting the sheets. I lick my lips and pad across the room to the bedside.

I pull back the bed sheet and he has one eye open, looking at me with his eyebrow raised. "No wonder you can't sleep," I smirk and climb onto the bed. I straddle him, putting his cock right at my entrance. "Someone's still horny."

He snorts, "You walked to the bathroom buck ass naked, what did you expect?"

I line him up with my entrance and slide the tip through

my wetness. I use little thrusts up and down to help coat his cock before he's all the way inside me. I reposition my legs, giving me better leverage. "So good," he breathes and I rock my hips, sucking him in deeper. The head of his cock rubs along my g-spot and my legs tremble with pleasure.

He slowly slides his hands up my thighs, over my hips and across my stomach until his hands are cupping my breasts. He rolls my nipples between his fingers and I groan. My back arches and my eyes roll up as pleasure explodes. I grind my hips against his, my clit rubbing along him, adding more pleasure to my all ready to explode body.

"You're so tight. God," Bryan groans as he throws his head back. I place my hands on his chest, giving me more stability as I slide up and down his cock. His little grunts and groans drive my orgasm higher but I want him with me. Concentrating on his pleasure helps stave off my own. My hips glide up and down a few times before I grind against him. Letting the head of his cock impale me deeper than before.

The muscles in his neck tense, his fingers roll my nipples again and my clit hits him in just the right spot. My orgasm explodes and I cry out his name. I flick my hips a couple more times and he too finds his release.

I collapse on his chest. His cock is still semi-hard inside me and our breathing is erratic and uneven. He wraps his arms around me and kisses me along my hairline. I sigh in contentment.

"I'll never sleep again if that's what's going to happen."

I lift my head to grace him with a satisfied smile on my lips. "Sleep. I will be here in the morning," I tell him.

No need to tell him that somewhere between his acceptance of my god-awful past and him claiming me, I've fallen in love with the man under me. Leaving him is no

longer an option. Doing so would be like cutting off the oxygen I need to breathe. No more fractured breaths. I can breathe easy feeling whole and complete in his arms.

*Livia*

WAKING up wrapped in Bryan's arms is the most delectable thing I've ever experienced in my life. Somewhere between our middle of the night session and this morning, I ended up on my side with him spooning me. He didn't let me go all night. We were always connected physically somehow.

I awakened to the most delicious pleasure I never knew existed. Morning sex.

I get the impression that no hard-on will ever be wasted in my presence and I like the sounds of that.

Doing what I did for all those years was never about sex. It was always about the money. When I started at the house, at only sixteen years old, I did it for survival. I did it because if I didn't come home with money from the John I was with, then I got my ass beat by Fat Tony and his goons. After getting screwed a couple times, I learned how to take care of myself when it came to getting the money I earned. From then on, Fat Tony never had to kick my ass for lack of money when I returned. He found other ways of keeping me in line and making me pay when I failed.

I shudder at a memory that's not worth repeating. Remembering how Fat Tony himself, or one of his hired hands, would remind me of the whore I had become.

I spent many nights sobbing myself to sleep because of what I was forced to do. Eventually the tears turned to anger. Anger at my situation, anger at myself because I couldn't, no, I wouldn't do anything about it. I was so afraid the police wouldn't believe me. As time progressed, I was terrified of walking into the police station and landing in the clutches of one of Ricci's lapdogs. My life would have been over, for sure. Over time, I came to accept my fate. I came to accept that I would be one of Ricci's whores for eternity. Or until

my beauty wore off and I was no longer a viable product for their business. I spent two years under Fat Tony's thumb, but I never saw anyone age out. Whoring doesn't exactly have a retirement plan.

Most of the girls indulged in drugs and alcohol to numb the pain. When Fat Tony wanted one of them gone, they'd mysteriously disappear from the house with no explanation. My guess is Fat Tony or one of his hired hands killed them, or they were sold to someone who eventually did.

Until I met Bryan, until I found myself driving across the country toward him, I didn't understand why I had such a will to live during that time. Maybe somewhere in the back of my mind I knew there was something better for me.

"Penny for your thoughts?" Bryan says as he returns to his room where I've been lying in bed while he took care of "country superstar" business.

I shake my head. "Nothing of importance," I tell him.

He subtly shakes his head. "You were zoned out for quite a few minutes, and I highly doubt it was nothing."

I sigh, resigned to telling him what's on my mind. Even when I don't want to. "I was just thinking about what happened to me."

"Which part?" he asks as he joins me on the bed.

I sit up, wrapping the sheet around me, keeping me covered. I know I'm about to expose a part of myself to him and having the sheet between us gives me a layer of comfort I need right now. I can't look at him while I talk to him. Instead, I fidget with the sheet next to me, smoothing it out repeatedly. "I was thinking about how in my two years under Ricci's control I never considered suicide," I confide.

"I'm glad you didn't," he whispers.

I give him a melancholy smile. "Until I met you, I wasn't

so sure about that." My heart squeezes as sadness fills his eyes.

"I'm no reason to live."

"That's not what I meant. I just meant that I think there was some sort of higher power at work. A reason for me to still be here. The reason I survived in Fat Tony's hands. The reason I became a girl the other girls looked to. Though that didn't stop them from overdosing or committing suicide, or giving Fat Tony a reason to 'make her disappear'," I say with one-handed air quotes.

"What those girls did is not your fault," he tells me softly.

I give him another small smile. "I know that. But the part about it that does bother me is the fact that I felt nothing when it would happen. I didn't fight Fat Tony or Deets or any one of his other guys when one of the girls died or 'disappeared'. I was so numb to it all and I hate myself for that," I tell him as a tear streaks down my cheek.

"And what would you have done? What would you have been able to do that wouldn't have gotten you into the same situation as them?" His eyes widen expectantly.

"It should have been me," I breathe.

"Why do you say that?"

"Because, I should have protected those girls. I should have done something more," I sob.

Bryan slides across the bed and scoops me into his arms. I let him.

Unable to help myself, I snuggle into him, breathing in his scent and letting it ground me. His hand strokes along my back, comforting me. "I tried to step between the girls and Fat Tony. I defended them when I could. I took some beatings on their behalf, but it never mattered. When Fat Tony or one of his goons got done with me, they turned on the girl

anyway."

"So then why are you beating yourself up over this?"

"I don't know," I cry. "In all these years, I've never let myself feel anything about what happened to me. I buried it as deep as I could and now, I can't stop it."

"Shh, breathe, baby," he coos.

I try to lock away the pain, but I can't. Pulling air into my lungs is hard enough to do while sobs wrack my body. I don't have the strength to fight anymore. Closing my eyes, I cry harder as the faces of so many young girls flash before my eyes. The girls I once knew in what feels like another lifetime.

All while I break down in Bryan's arms, Bryan whispers sweet nothings in my ear, and he comforts me until I cry myself to sleep in his arms.

## *Bryan*

Once I'm sure Livia is sound asleep in my bed, I seek out Liam in his room. I knock twice before he hollers, "Come in," from the other side.

"Hey," I tell him as enter. He's sitting on a bench at the end of his bed removing his leg.

"What's up?" he asks as he places his prosthetic next to the bench and looks up at me.

I shake my head. "It doesn't matter how many times I see you do that, it still takes me by surprise."

He frowns. "Sorry, lad."

"No, don't be sorry. I've seen you run. I've seen you do so many things that people with two legs can't do."

"When you found me in New York, I got determined. I wanted to prove, not only to you but to myself, I could do

anything I did before without hesitation," he tells me.

"It shows."

"Did you need something?" he asks me.

I nod. "I went back upstairs and found Livia zoned out. When I coaxed her into talking to me, she completely broke down on me. It took me by surprise, and I didn't expect the things that came out of her mouth," I share with him.

"Like what?"

"She is suffering from survivor's guilt in the worst possible way,"

"Explain?" he asks.

"She was beating herself up over the fact she couldn't save the other girls. She blames herself for not standing up against her captors in a way she thinks would have protected them."

He sighs.

"What I don't understand," I continue, "Is why now? Why after all this time?"

"Because she's forced herself to talk about it," he tells me. "Imagine something embarrassing that you've done." I nod. "Okay, now imagine telling people about it?"

I nod again. I think I understand what he's saying. "The difference," he raises an eyebrow, "is she has to relive a life she's fought to suppress for years. Even while it was happening to her."

"How do I help her?" I ask.

"Talk to her, let her keep talking. If she's comfortable enough to tell you about her past, let her tell you more about it. I can only tell you the things I witnessed and trust me, those are images you don't want in your head."

I sit down next to him on the bench. This is a lot to digest. "How do you handle it?"

He shrugs, "Some days are easier than others. But I also had a different perspective on it. Each time I saw Fat Tony, or Deets, or one of his other minions, beating on one of the girls or raping them, it was another notch in their charges. I pacified myself with that knowledge, but it killed me. Every. Damn. Day. But I had a job to do and I knew if I continued to do my job, then the end result would be exactly what it was."

"Did you ever..." I swallow hesitant to go on.

He sighs. "No, I didn't. Not with Livia or any of the other girls. I could usually tell when Tony was in one of his moods so I knew to stay clear. On the rare occasions I got caught up in Tony's mood swings, the other idiots were more than willing to hand out punishments." His voice is soft by the time he's done talking.

"I'm sorry, I didn't..."

"No, it's alright. Maybe she needs to see someone, a shrink? Someone who can help her with the past," he tells me.

I nod. "That might be a good idea. I'm a good sounding board, but I'm shit with advice."

He smiles. "Some people just need someone to listen. Sometimes they don't need advice. In her case, I think she needs to learn how to handle the guilt, the fear. Not just bury it again. That's what got her to this point to begin with."

I nod, understanding everything he's saying. "I just want to be able to help her."

"You've got a good heart, Bryan, and she deserves someone willing to help her through this."

"I just hope it's enough," I mutter.

"Only time will tell." Knowing he's right, I stand to leave, but he stops me. "There's something that the three of us should discuss. And soon."

"What about?" I ask, curious.

"Her identity," he states simply.

"What about it?"

"You need to decide if you want her to be given a new identity or if you're going to deal with the backlash when people find out you're dating a stripper. Or worse."

I sigh, "That doesn't bother me."

"No, I know it doesn't bother you, but it may bother them."

I scowl at him. "Do you really think I care what they think?"

"No, I don't, but the PR nightmare is going to fall on someone else's shoulders. So you need to either discuss it with Raine, or you need to offer up a new identity for her to take on. I've made some calls."

"I'm not sure how I feel about this," I tell him.

"It's not an easy decision to make and one you can't make for her. It would be a lot easier to tell the small handful of friends that she has about a new identity, than it will be to defend her past. She can't go out into the world on your arm as Livia Fazio." He speaks in a tone that I've come to recognize as concerned.

"No, she can't and she won't, but I don't understand what is wrong with the Becca identity."

He looks at me as if I've lost my marbles. "Becca Carpenter was a blonde-haired stripper. Not to mention the fact she was a prostitute, too."

"But did she ever get busted as such?"

"Not that I know of. But it would be easier to hide that part of her life. Do you really want men who've been charged for sex to come out to reporters and tabloids?"

"I get the impression she wasn't entirely forthcoming with the name Becca."

I shrug. "I guess we won't know until we talk to her about it. But what good will a new identity do for her? Reporters will dig, no matter what."

"Trust me, I've already thought about that. If we give her a real name, a real identity and a real social security number then reporters won't have too much to find. Trust me, we can and will make it look legit. We do it every day in witness protection. You can't send someone off into the world without a solid history. Employers will look at histories. Trust me; Declan knows what he's doing."

"I trust you."

"There is one problem."

"And that is what? If it's money..."

"No, it's not that. She will have to go to New York."

"No," I say vehemently. "Absolutely not. I will not make her go back there."

"I think that's a choice you need to let her make. She has other things to deal with up there too." He sighs. "Look, let's not make decisions for her. She's an adult. She can decide what she wants to do, but I assure you, no matter what, I will do everything in my power to protect her."

I nod absently, not sure what to say. He's right. Livia needs to decide for herself how she wants to do this. I refuse to have a woman who isn't capable of being with me for some of my most important events. I've been alone for far too long. I want someone to share those things with and I know she's that person. "We'll talk about it later."

"Aye," he smiles. "Cheer up, lad. It will all work out how it's supposed to. Besides, she hates the name Becca." He winks. I smile back and leave him in his room. This is not a conversation I'm looking forward to.

*Livia*

BRYAN'S forehead is pressed against mine. His breathing is as ragged as mine as I feel his cock soften and slip from my sex.

We'd started off talking and ended up fucking like animals. It's what we do. And I love it.

It's been like this for a week now. During the day, he works, usually in the studio or in his office. The amount of people that come and go from his house is astonishing, but I have to tell you, I'm not sure I've ever been happier.

"Is this what it's going to be like?" I ask.

"What do you mean?" he asks as he lifts his head from mine.

I laugh, "A simple conversation turning to sex?"

He laughs too, "I can't help myself." He groans as he rolls off me, but he takes me with him so we're facing each other. I curl my arms around my chest and he pulls the sheet up to cover our hips.

"I know you can't." I kiss the tip of his nose.

"Are you complaining?"

I give him an expression that displays mock shock. "Never," I breathe and smile at him. "I just don't remember what we were talking about," I laugh.

"It was nothing important, only that I want you to come out on tour with me."

I nod my head. "Ah yes, I remember, that was about the time you were coaxing me into coming with you by explaining what fun it would be to have me all to yourself on the bus."

"We can go back to that conversation." He winks.

"Mmm, maybe in a little bit. Do you really think it's a good idea if I come with you?" I raise an eyebrow.

"I don't think I can leave you behind for three months."

"Three months?" I prop myself on my elbow, staring down at him. Being the sex fiend that he is, he brings his hand up to brush my nipple with the backs of his fingers. I huff. "You're awful," I tease. "Seriously? Three months? It's bad enough I've been here for a week."

"Do you need to go home?"

"Oh yes, going home to a dead end job at Dunkin Donuts is really what I want to do," I mock. "But it is my home."

"What if I told you I wanted you to make this your home?" He gestures around the room.

"You can't be serious?"

"As a heart attack."

I sit up, pulling the sheet farther up and around my chest.

"Livi, what's wrong?"

I'm not sure I want to tell him that I never want to go back to Phoenix. Sure, I miss Ireland and yup, I can't think of much else. "I'm not sure I am the type of woman to be kept. It's been nice sitting around here doing nothing, but I feel useless and it's starting to make me restless," I admit.

"Well, then what would you like to do?"

I shrug. "Honestly? I have no clue. I feel like I should go get a job or something."

"I'm not going to stand in your way, but if you do that, then you can't go on tour with me."

I give him an exasperated look. "And what if you'd found me in Phoenix with a real career? Would you ask me to give that up to come on tour with you?"

He shrugs. "Maybe, I can't say for certain what I'd do. The circumstances here are much different." He starts tracing invisible lines on my back and it sends goosebumps flying across my flesh and my nipples harden.

"Okay, say I do go on tour with you. I can't and won't sit around on the bus all day doing nothing. I'm going to need something to do or I am going to go crazy."

"Talk to me, throw out some ideas for me. Let's see if we can't come up with a legitimate job for you to do." He sits up. "Get dressed. I can't talk about this while you're naked."

"Oh yes, because clothes are such a barrier for you," I tease and he laughs.

"Well played." He winks and climbs off the bed. I'm frozen in place as I watch his sculpted ass cross the room and go into his closet. A closet I now have half of. Though I don't have much in the way of clothes to fill it, a few things have shown up for me over the last week. I didn't protest at him buying me things because, well, I liked it. I'm not one of those girls who couldn't sit around and be housewife material with a husband who spoils her stupid. The fact that he thought enough about me to buy me something makes me happy in a way I never imagined possible. Maybe it's because I've had so little in my life that having finer things like designer jeans and shoes make me giddy. Not to mention the face I get from him when I show up in his office or studio wearing one of the outfits he picked for me.

He comes out of the closet wearing jeans, a black t-shirt and a pair of flip-flops on his feet. Naked Bryan is the best picture on earth, but Bryan in jeans, a tight t-shirt and flip-flops sends my pulse racing. Probably because I know what's underneath it all.

"Meet me in my office?"

I nod. "Be there in a few minutes."

He leans over me and kisses my forehead and his fingers find a nipple and roll it twice, just enough to put me back on edge and I groan. He smirks as he walks out of the room.

Once I'm alone, I throw off the sheet and head into the bathroom. I turn the water on in the spacious shower and while giving it a minute to warm, I look in the mirror.

My hair is disheveled, as always, my cheeks are still flush from the three orgasms he gave me before he gave up one for himself. My lips look swollen. I bite my lower lip thinking about Bryan's tongue. I shiver and pull myself away from the mirror and into the shower.

## Bryan

"I want her to come on the tour," I tell Liam.

"I figured you would," he replies. "Have you brought it up to her yet?"

"I did. She hasn't said no, but she hasn't exactly said yes. She said that she needs something to do, a job or something to help occupy her time."

Liam gives me a knowing grin. "You do realize that she has a marketing degree, right?"

I stare at him, blinking a few times. "Seriously? Why has she not said anything?"

"Maybe you're not asking the right questions," Liam suggests.

I sigh. "Well, I guess that might be a good place to start, but I don't want to step on Raine's toes either."

He shakes his head. "I'm pretty sure Raine wouldn't mind the help. Besides, you know Cami; she doesn't like to send you on tour without one of her own to tag along. Do you really think Raine wants to spend three months on a bus?"

I shake my head. "No, I doubt she would, but I know she would if its business."

"Well, what if Livia and Raine can work side by side?"

"Is there time enough for that?" I ask. "I'd imagine Cami will want a say in all this."

"A say in what?" Livia asks as she enters my office.

"Liam tells me that you have a degree in marketing?" I ask her.

"Pfft, I do, but I'm not sure it was the right choice of degrees."

"Why do you say that?"

She laughs, "Because I'm not that creative. Ireland got those genes. We graduated together. Though she went into advertising, I just hung out."

"Well, I may have a solution for you for work while on tour."

"Oh? Doing what?" She perks up a little and comes to stand behind the couch where Liam is sitting.

"Marketing," I smirk.

She groans, "Don't you already have people for that?"

I chuckle, "I do, but that would mean she'd have to go on tour with me."

Livia pales. "She?"

"You met her at Cami's party."

She scowls at me so I elaborate, "Raine, Dex Harris's girlfriend."

"No way? She's your marketing person?"

"Well, she's more of a public relations person. She handles the press, the news, more or less my image. But she's also responsible for a good part of my social media and things like that."

"She sounds like an assistant," Livia counters.

"Well, she handles all that because I don't have an assistant. I don't have someone to handle things like social media or whatever else I would need."

"Then who does it?" she asks.

"I do."

"So what, you'd want me to get you coffee and shit?" she says, skeptical.

"If that would make you happy, sure. But I assure you, I'm perfectly capable of getting my own coffee. But it would be nice to have someone who helps me with my schedule, helps keep me on track and on time, and then fills in the blanks with answering emails and dealing with things like social media."

"Doesn't Liam keep you on time?" She looks at the top of his head and he turns to her to answer.

"Aye, lass, but I can only keep him on time with the schedule he gives me. I don't schedule his appointments, nor do I make sure he's not double booking himself. He handles all that and I assure you, it's a mess," Liam teases with a wink at me.

"I've never done anything like that before."

"Would you want to?"

"As long as you promise to keep me busy, and you're not a dick, then yes, I'll do it."

"Oh, I'll keep you busy alright." I wiggle an eyebrow at her.

"Fiend," she teases with a laugh.

Liam stands from the couch and moves to leave. "That's my cue, lady and gent."

Livia and I both laugh, and Liam leaves us to it.

*Bryan*

"WE have no choice."

"I know, I just, this isn't going to be easy to discuss with her."

"What isn't easy to discuss?" Livia asks as she enters my office. It's been a little more than a week since I offered Livia a job, and in that time, she's taken on a lot and seems to be enjoying it.

"Sit down, lass."

"Uh, okay? Something wrong?"

She looks at me with worry in her eyes and I hate what I'm about to tell her. "We have to go to New York."

"So go."

"But you need to come with me."

"I don't have to do anything," she counters.

"Maybe this isn't the best way to start this conversation," Liam offers. "Livia, Bryan has some business to attend to in New York. This includes the tour kick off, among other things."

"I can't go back there," she breathes.

"I understand, but as I've said a million times before, you will be perfectly safe," Liam tells her.

"You can't know that," she argues.

"You're right, we don't know that, but there is nothing to fear," I add, trying to be reassuring.

"There is also another reason I need you in New York," Liam adds. This is about the conversation we had a couple weeks ago and it's still not one I'm prepared to have. Livia and I have been living in this perfect, happy, little bubble that

we built together, but that bubble is about to burst, and I'm not ready for that.

"There isn't a reason good enough to get me back in that state, let alone that damn city."

"A new identity."

"What?" she breathes, looking up at Liam.

Liam sighs as he sits on the other couch next to her. He looks her square in the eye and doesn't hold back from what he tells her. "You've said it before. You hate the name Becca, do you not?" She nods in response. "What if we could give you back a name similar to what you're used to. Something that wouldn't be so far from the truth if Bryan, or myself, call you Livia, then no one will think twice about it."

"What about my friends? They won't understand."

"I've taken care of most of that. Ireland already knows Becca is not your real name. She also knows that Livia is your real name, does she not?"

"She does," Livia says with hesitation.

"Then who else is there?" Liam asks.

Livia doesn't respond right away, but reality washes over her features. "No one, I guess. Well, the people who saw Bryan and me together at the party. I was introduced as Becca."

"There are two relatively simple explanations," I add. "The first being, Cami and Tristan know you as a bar patron, and although they know you as Becca, that doesn't mean giving them a different name will mean much to them. Second, the majority of those in attendance that night meet hundreds, if not thousands, of people, so remembering your name isn't going to be easy for them. Lastly, for all they know, Becca could be a nickname. A middle name..."

"And what, I just decided to start going by my first name again?"

"Or a middle," Liam interjects.

She looks confused as she switches between looking at Liam then at me. "Why do you want to cover up my name so bad?"

I sigh. "I don't. This is all Liam's doing. But from a PR standpoint, your past could paint a rather unflattering picture about the person you are or were. Do you want reporters digging up your past?"

"This is your chance to lose the prostitute label forever," Liam reminds her.

The bluntness of his response takes me by surprise and I scowl at him.

"You've said it yourself. You turned to Becca because you were tired of that lifestyle but when you found things to be too rough, you turned back to your old ways. Neither one of us fault you for that, Livia." I nod my head in agreement with what Liam is saying. "Neither one of us will ever hold your past against you or over your head. This would give you the chance to rid yourself of that past forever. No arrest records, no one seeing your name in the papers and coming forward about paying you for sex. This would eradicate that life altogether. Give you the fresh start you want."

"And save Bryan from a PR nightmare," she murmurs. I can tell by her slouched posture she's feeling embarrassed right now and I don't like it. I switch to her couch, sitting next to her.

"I am not ashamed of your past. It is who you are. It's what brought you to me. I will never be ashamed of that. I want you to do this so you can be happy with yourself. So you can finally feel like that part of your life is in the past." I take a

193

deep breath and continue, "You deserve to move on with your life and this is a way to do that." I take her hands in mine and force her to look at me. "I want you to be able to hold your head high and know that nothing from your past can ever harm you again."

"How can you be so sure they won't find out about my aliases? Reporters have a way of doing things like that," she questions.

"Declan is very good at what he does. Livia Fazio is dead and Becca Carpenter will just disappear. You have an advantage that many people in your situation often don't have. You have no family, Livia."

"Thanks for the reminder," she scoffs.

"I'm sorry, it wasn't meant that way," Liam apologizes. "But it's true. You also only have a limited number of friends who know your past."

She sighs, "I don't know if Ireland will understand the change."

I smile. "You'd be surprised, and not only that, but we could easily change your name to something like Olivia, making Livi and Livia easy nicknames. We could use Olivia as a middle name."

"The possibilities are endless," Liam adds.

"I want Livia back." Her voice is barely above a whisper, but there's conviction in her words.

"Then we will do everything we can to get back as much of your original name as possible," I tell her. "What's your middle name?"

She snorts a laugh. "That is so not happening," she tells me with the first smile I've seen since Liam started talking.

"Meadow," Liam declares with a smirk and she glares at

him.

"Traitor."

The three of us laugh. "Meadow? Really?" I ask, incredulous.

"Italian, remember?" she teases back.

"Isn't that the name of one of the wives or kids or something on that Italian mob show?" I say, jokingly.

"Wouldn't surprise me. It was a popular Italian name in the nineties," Liam adds.

The tension of the identity discussion seems to have vanished, if only for a minute. "So, why do I have to go to New York to do this?" she asks Liam.

"Because Declan needs to update prints, photographs and DNA records. The prints we already have, but fresh ones will be better and they don't have DNA for you. It wasn't exactly available when they gave you your first identity. It will ensure Declan can give you a solid background and history that, when verified, can be addressed by you publicly," Liam explains.

"Why can't I send him all this stuff?" she asks.

"Trust me. It will be easier to do it this way," Liam tells her.

She doesn't say anything for a few moments and I silence Liam. I want her to have time to mull this over in her mind. Only she can make this decision. It's not an easy one for her to make and I don't want to pressure her into it.

"Alright," she finally speaks. "I'll do it, I'll go."

"I'll make the arrangements."

"Isn't that supposed to be my job?" she retorts.

I smile at her. "It is, but I'll handle this one." I wink at her, then cup her face between my hands and pull her close to

me. "Thank you," I breathe.

"I just want to put my past behind me. If this is the only way to do it, I'll do it," she whispers back and I slant my lips over hers. Her lips against mine spark desire and my cock hardens.

"Good, we leave day after tomorrow," Liam says, interrupting my kissing of Livia and I smile against her lips as I glare at him. He puts his hands up in mock defense. "Now, the real question, commercial or private?"

I shake my head and release Livia from my grasp. "You're the worst cock-blocker ever," I laugh. Livia blushes. "She's going under one name and coming back under another. I would say private."

"Aren't we leaving on the bus?" she asks.

"No, not from New York. It's just the tour launch. There are several radio and television spots scheduled while we're there. When it's done, we come home for a couple days. The bus leaves from here."

"Here as in Nashville, or here as in the house?"

I smile. "The house. The house is monitored twenty-four seven, so we let the crew park here. It's just easier."

"How many people are we talking?"

Her questions make me smile. She's not dwelling on New York and I like that, though I get the feeling we have a rough forty-eight hours before we take off. "There are five band members, plus an additional six on the set up crew. There are three buses total. One is mine, then there is a band bus and a crew bus."

"That seems like a lot of wasted gas," she mutters.

I laugh, "It is, but there are also security guys. Liam stays on my bus with me, and there are four more that travel with

us. There are two on each bus, making the space crowded enough as it is."

"I never thought you actually traveled the country on a bus. I just thought you flew everywhere."

"I do that too," I tell her. "When there are long breaks between shows, I fly home and fly back, but this is a tighter packed tour so trips home will be minimal."

"I have no idea how to even pack for something like this."

Liam chuckles, "Trust me, lass, it's not easy, but having our own bus gives us some latitude."

"I don't have enough clothes for three months of traveling." There is sadness in her voice and her eyes are looking up at the ceiling as if she's trying to calculate something.

"What about back home?"

"Uh, no. I brought the majority of what I had there with me." She hesitates, "When I left Phoenix, I broke my lease, stored some stuff and brought everything else with me."

"You don't have anything here," Liam chimes in.

Livia shrugs. "I didn't have anything there either." She sighs. "I gave up on material possessions a long time ago." She starts to fidget with her hands and as she looks at them, she continues, "I was afraid of having to pack up and run. I didn't want to have to choose between what I wanted and what I needed. So I never let myself get too attached to anything. I always kept my music on my mp3 player, my address book in my phone and backed up to my computer, and I don't own any jewelry, and that basically left clothes."

"So then why did you break your lease?" Liam asks her. I was curious about that too.

She lets out a slow breath. "I never planned on going back

to Phoenix. If this didn't work out, I'd planned on running again. I told you this that first night."

"Well, I'm glad it worked out," I say. "I'd hate to think of never seeing you again."

She looks at me with wide eyes. "That won't happen now. I'm tired of running. Maybe going back to New York will be a good thing. Maybe I can finally put the past to rest. I've never even seen my father's grave. I haven't been to my mother's since the Christmas before I was taken. I don't know why, but I feel like I need to see them all of a sudden."

"We'll make it happen," Liam says. "You've also got a storage unit to deal with, and then there is the matter of the life insurance..."

"I haven't decided if I want it."

"Which?" I ask for clarification.

"Either," she breathes.

"Why not?" Liam asks. "The money is yours. All I did was put it in an account for you. The stuff in storage is because I think you may find some things in there you want to keep."

She shakes her head. "No, anything from that house will only remind me of what life was like before Ricci got ahold of me."

"But it's all a part of who you are," I remind her.

Her eyes meet mine, "I know, but that part of me is so far removed from who I am now that I don't see the point in dredging it up." She turns to Liam. "I appreciate you saving it, really I do, and I'll pay you back for the storage fees..."

"No, lass. I set that storage unit up so when I found you again you'd have a piece of home. I kept it going even when I wasn't sure you were still alive. But if you honestly feel that stuff is unimportant, I will have it cleaned out."

She nods. "I don't think I want it."

"You don't have to decide right now," I tell her. "We have time and once you're back in New York, you might feel differently about it. Regardless of the circumstances, your father died and he left something for you. I think you need to take the money."

"I don't even know how to handle that kind of money," she says.

Both Liam and I smile at her. "We'll help you," Liam tells her.

She nods and my heart swells at the acceptance she appears to have for all things pertaining to her father and her past. In the back of mind, I am worried we've not yet reached the peak of this issue. She's buried and denied so much for so long.

Livia is an amazingly strong woman and I commend her for being that way, but there is something under the surface and I'm afraid of what it is and what will happen when it comes out.

Regardless, I'm not going anywhere.

I'm not sure at what point it happened, but the idea of losing Livia scares the hell out of me. If she were to walk away from me, I'd never recover. Sometime over the last month, I've fallen head over heels in love with her. Now it's time to show her what real love looks like.

*"Dad," I call into the house as I return home from school.*

*"In here, baby girl."*

*I go toward the sound of his voice coming from his room. "Dad, what are you doing in the closet?" I ask him.*

He puts something up on the top shelf, a box. "What's that?" I ask.

"It's nothing, baby, just some of daddy's stuff. How was school?"

"It was good. I got my math test back," I tell him with excitement.

He raises an eyebrow at me. "Well, are you going to keep me in suspense forever?"

I laugh, "No." I take the folded papers from my pocket, looking down at the bright red A at the top and I turn it around.

"Only an A?" he teases me.

"Seriously, dad?"

He steps off the step ladder he was on and wraps me in his arms. "That's a great way to start Christmas break."

"I thought so," I say as I pull away from our hug. He reluctantly lets me go.

"I'll go get dinner started." He smiles and leaves the room. My eyes drift to the box on the top shelf.

For some strange reason, he seemed nervous that I caught him and I can't help wondering what's really in that box.

The box slips my mind as Christmas comes and goes and before I know it, the New Year is here and I return to school. The first day back was boring, as usual. Nothing exciting happened because teachers were still on vacation hangover.

Walking home from the train station, I stop at bodega around the corner from the house and pick up some snacks.

Back on the sidewalk, I notice a black van parked at the corner. I don't think much of it, other than its running and

*there doesn't appear to be anyone inside. There are no windows in the back and no business logo on the side. I shrug it off and keep walking toward home.*

*I stand on the corner, waiting for the light to change so I can cross the street. I'm alone, oddly alone. Finally the light changes, but the next thing I know I'm being dragged backwards, a hand over my mouth, and then a hood is thrown over my head.*

*I bite the hand over my mouth and the man curses at me, "Do that shit again and I'll kick all your fucking teeth out of your mouth." I don't recognize the voice, but the accent is easily identifiable. It's Italian.*

*I scream when the man throws me onto something that I can't see, and then I hear a door slide closed and tires squealing as I'm thrown backwards. I'm in the van.*

"Livia! Come on, baby, wake up."

"Wha..." I scoot away from someone I can't see in the dark room.

"Livi, breathe," a familiar voice says.

I pull in a deep breath, but it doesn't help. The memory is so real, so vivid. "Where am I?" I ask, still unable to see. The bed, a bed, the voice, Bryan. "Bryan?"

"I'm here, baby." A light flicks on and I blink rapidly trying to adjust to the sudden intrusion as the memory of the dream fades away.

"I need that box," I say, unsure what it means.

"What box?" His eyebrows knit together in confusion.

"A box my father had. It was in his closet."

Bryan's brow unfurls and he settles next to me.

"Do you think Liam kept it?" I ask him.

"I don't know. If you know what it looks like, he might be able to tell you."

I nod. "I'll ask him." I move to get up from the bed.

His hand wraps around my wrist. "In the morning. It's the middle of the night."

"Oh," I blush, looking down at my naked body. "Good point."

I climb back into bed and he wraps his arms around me. "You want to talk about your dream?"

"It was nothing," I whisper.

"It didn't sound like nothing." His voice is soft, concerned.

I swallow. "I was reliving the day they took me off the streets. But it was odd; it started a couple weeks before that. I watched my father put this box up in the closet. When I asked him about it, he said it was nothing, but I knew that wasn't true. I vowed to go after the box and look inside, but I'd forgotten about it. Until now."

"Do you have any idea what's inside?"

I shake my head. "I haven't a clue. But I feel like I need to find out."

Bryan nods then yawns. "We leave in the morning."

I sigh, "I know."

After a few minutes, Bryan's breathing evens out as he falls asleep. Me? I lay there awake, unable to turn my mind off. I can't stop thinking about that box and what may or may not be in it. I desperately want to ask Liam if he knows about the box, but Bryan was right. It's two-thirty in the morning. Liam deserves his rest; he's got a lot going on in the next couple days.

I can only imagine what's inside that box or why it made my father so nervous. It didn't dawn on me at the time, but

then again, I didn't know anything compared to what I know now.

My father worked a lot, but he tried to stick mostly to overnight shifts so he could be home when I got home from school. We often ate dinner at four and five o'clock at night because he had to run off to work for the night. Many times he wouldn't be home when I got up in the morning, so I cherished what little time we had in the afternoons and on the rare occasions that we got that time.

For some reason, things had been different in the weeks leading up to Christmas but when I asked him about it, he'd just tell me work was slow. I found that hard to believe given it was New York and the holidays. He'd been a detective for as long as I can remember and I don't ever remember having him around so much, especially close to Christmas. In hindsight, I'm glad he was there.

By the time the sun rises through the windows of Bryan's bedroom, I'm wiping away tears remembering that last Christmas with my father and I'm ready to face the storage locker Liam set up for me.

I slide out of bed carefully. Thankfully, Bryan stays asleep.

I stand there for a few minutes watching him sleep. He looks so peaceful. The last couple days have been a chaotic whirlwind of activity and this is the first time I've seen him sleep for longer than a couple hours. It's nice to see.

I go into the closet and find a t-shirt and a pair of pajama pants and then quietly leave the bedroom in search of Liam. I go to his room, but the door is slightly ajar and all the lights are off, indicating he's probably not in there. I go to his office, a little closet of a room off the hallway on the way to the studio. I knock, but there's no answer so I turn toward the kitchen and nearly collide with Liam. I nearly scream and fall over until he steadies me.

"Looking for me?" he teases.

"Don't do that to me," I pant. My breathing starts to slow to normal.

"Sorry, lass. Everything alright?" he asks.

I shake my head. "Not really. I had a dream last night. Or maybe it was a memory, I can't quite tell the difference some days."

"About?"

"My father's closet. A few days before Christmas, before he was killed, I caught him putting a box up on his shelf. I didn't think anything of it at the time, but seeing the memory, he looked paranoid, scared, when I caught him. I'm wondering if you remember the stuff that's in the storage unit."

He shrugs. "I remember some stuff. I did pull some boxes from his closet, but I don't know if there was anything in them of significance."

"Did you go through them?"

He shakes his head. "Not really. I went looking for things like guns and stuff like that, but I didn't pay much attention to his paperwork. Though..." he pauses, thinking, "Now that you mention it, there were a couple of boxes that looked like they had old case files in them."

"Please tell me you kept them?"

"Of course I did, lass. I figured anything he kept, for whatever the reason, was important somehow. Like I said, I figured one day you'd like to go through it, decide what was important and what's not."

"I'd like to see the unit."

"Are you sure?" he asks me.

"Yes, I have to know if that box is in there."

"Alright, I'll make arrangements," he concedes.

"Today?" I ask. "Bryan's schedule is clear for travelling."

"Have you talked to Bryan about this?"

I shake my head. "He woke me from the dream. I told him about the box, but I didn't say anything about wanting to go today. I just don't know if I can wait any longer," I admit. There may be something in there that is somehow important. Though I can't imagine what it would be or what it would do for anyone. Who knows, maybe it will give me some closure.

"Alright, lass. We'll clear it with Bryan."

"I'd like him to be there."

He hesitates, "I don't know..."

"Be where?" Bryan says from behind Liam.

I peer around Liam's shoulder to see him standing there half-naked in only pajama bottoms and bare feet. My mouth waters.

"I want to go to the storage unit."

"The dream?" he asks.

"Yes. I'd like to do it today."

Bryan nods. "If that's what you want, we'll go."

"Liam doesn't think you should come."

Bryan looks at Liam with questions in his eyes. "I didn't mean anything by it. I just..." Liam sighs, "I'll make arrangements."

"You just, what?" I ask.

Liam turns back to me. "I didn't know if it would be something you'd want to do on your own. I can make arrangements to have the contents moved down here and you can go through them at your leisure."

"We're leaving in a little over a week for three months. I

highly doubt that's enough time for me to go through the contents, provided you can get them to Nashville quickly. I know, for whatever the reason is, I have to find that box."

"Alright, why don't we do this? We will go to the unit, see if we can locate the box. In the meantime, Liam, why don't we work on arrangements for getting the contents shipped here for when we return from the tour. I mean, how much stuff is in this unit?"

*Bryan*

"HOLY shit," Livia squeaks as Liam lifts the door on her storage unit. We haven't even been to the hotel yet.

During the flight from Nashville to New York, Livia was bouncing in her seat with anxiety and anticipation. I thought it had to do with coming to New York, but apparently it has everything to do with this box. She insisted we come straight here and neither Liam nor I were in the mood to argue with her.

"Did you throw anything out?" she asks Liam as she steps inside the unit.

"Sure, I did. Anything that was clearly trash and most everything in the kitchen, and a good majority of your dad's stuff. I didn't think you really wanted to be sifting through his clothes when and if you ever opened this unit."

"So you kept basically everything but the kitchen sink," she snarks.

"More or less," Liam teases back.

I look around the unit. It's a large unit, probably the equivalent of two or three normal sized ones. It's ridiculously well-organized and the boxes are all labeled. "How much time did you spend on this?" Livia asks him.

"Too much time."

"I can tell," she says as she starts reading his awful handwriting on the labels.

From here I can see things marked, living room, kitchen, though there are only two. Then Livia's room takes up a good majority of the boxes lining the walls. In the center of the unit is some furniture. Dressers and nightstands, plus a couch that looks like it fell out of the seventies. Livia's hand slides along the backside of the orange, green and yellow, well-used sofa. "I hated this thing. It's so gaudy and ugly." The playfulness is gone, replaced by melancholy.

Liam gives a little chuckle. "I moved that thing three times. It's heavy as hell."

Livia continues to look around at the boxes until she stops in front of a stack labeled 'Merc'. She points to them and turns back to Liam, "His room?"

"Aye, lass."

## Unknown

"What do you want?"

"You told me to call when unit five-six-three was opened."

"Has it been opened?"

"Yes, and as far as I can tell, it's still open."

"Good."

The line goes dead.

## Livia

I pull down a box. It's the first of six that have my father's nickname labeled on them. "Got a scissors?"

"No, but I have a knife," Liam answers as he flips open a knife and hands the hilt to me.

"Thanks," I offer without delight before sliding the knife along the tape and popping the top open. Inside are miscellaneous things from my father's room- things from his night stands, some magazines, and a couple of books. My father was a sucker for true crime novels and this box has plenty of those. "Not there," I say before shoving the box to the side.

Bryan recloses the box. We don't have any tape so he alternates the flaps to close it back up. I pull down the next box and slice into it. There is nothing of significance inside. Some more books, other miscellaneous things that aren't what I'm after.

"Is there any chance you emptied the contents into something else?"

"No, I just packed stuff up as I found it," Liam tells me.

I shove the second box off to the side and go through two more boxes without seeing much, though I did find my father's badge. That was the hardest thing to look at. Dirty cop or not, he loved his job and he was damn good at it. "Until the system failed me so bad, I wanted to be a cop. I wanted to be a detective like my father," I share with no one in particular.

Neither of them replies. I didn't expect them to.

I reach for the next box and there is a noise down the hall. Liam reaches for the gun on his hip, unlocking the holster and backing up toward the door. My heart starts pounding in my chest and my hands start shaking.

I hear voices, I can't make them out, but they sound like they're happy-go-lucky types and another door closes down the way and Liam drops his guard. "Should I be worried?" I ask.

"No, lass, I just haven't been to this unit in a long time."

"Does anyone know you have it?" Bryan asks.

"Aye, my brother."

"No one else?" I ask.

"No, Livia, no one else."

I nod in understanding then go back to the box in front of me. I slide the blade of the knife through the tape and flip

the flaps. My heart stops pounding and my breathing stops altogether. Inside this box are several smaller boxes. The ones on the top I remember from my dad's closet. I flip the lid on the first one. Shoes. I roll my eyes. "For a cop, he had a fine taste in shoes," Bryan says from where he's observing at my side.

"He used to spend hours polishing his shoes. Work boots, anything that went on his feet. The man didn't own a pair of tennis shoes." I recall the memory of watching him polish his boots. It was something he did often and I actually enjoyed watching him do it. It was almost methodic, rhythmic. I understand the appeal. It's almost cathartic.

I pull the lid up on the next box, more shoes. I pull both from the bigger box and reveal another below them. "That's it," I squeak. "That's the box." I pull a nondescript brown box from inside the larger box.

"Can we take it with us, lass?"

"Yeah," I reply handing the box to Bryan who holds on to it while I reach in and open the next box only to find more shoes. I pull it out quick and flip open the last two boxes on the bottom. One has some file folders in it so I grab it. The other box has more shoes. I put the four boxes of shoes back inside and close it up. I hand Bryan the file folder box and take the other one from his hand. He doesn't hesitate to hand it over to me. "Let's go," I tell them both.

We step outside the unit and Liam pulls down the rolling door and locks it, then sets the alarm. We start walking down the hallway toward the stairs of the five story storage facility. "You seriously carried all that stuff up here?"

"Nah, there's an elevator around the corner," Liam shares, his voice lighter now that we're out of the unit. I look out the window, down in the parking lot and freeze. Sitting there in the lot is a black van, much like the van that was on the

street corner that day. It's like déjà vu all over again.

"They're here," I breathe.

"Who?" Bryan and Liam ask in unison.

"That van, it's just like…" I can't speak anymore because I can't draw air into my lungs.

"Livia, relax," Liam orders as he gets closer to me. "I will check it out, alright. But I'm pretty sure that van was here when we got here."

I nod, but I'm not sure I'm hearing him. "I knew I shouldn't have come back here."

"Livia, breathe, it's alright," Bryan consoles me.

"Come on, let's go down, I will look into it, alright?" Liam asks.

I nod, but I'm having a hard time getting my feet to move. Bryan wraps his arms around me, bringing me back to him. "You're safe, Livia, no one can touch you now. Understand me?"

I nod again, the fog clearing and reality returning. They're both right. I'm overreacting. "I'm sorry, I just…"

"No need to apologize. Okay? Let's just go."

I nod and Bryan releases me. I follow Liam down the stairs. Each stair makes me feel a little better. It's irrational of me to think that after all this time they'd be keeping an eye on something they don't even know exists, right? Right.

*Unknown*

"Do they have it?"

"I don't think so. They just have two boxes. But I'll be honest with you, it's not her."

"What do you mean it's not her?"

"It looks nothing like her. And the two that are with her? I have never seen either one of them before. Are we sure it was in there?"

"Yes, damn it. It's in there. We need to find a way into that unit."

"They reset the alarm."

"That's never stopped us before."

"If you're so fucking confident it's in there, why in the hell haven't we gone in there before?"

"Until they went back in there, I wasn't even sure it was there, or that it even exists. Now I'm confident."

"And if you're too late?"

"Oh, we're never too late."

The line goes dead.

*Livia*

"CLIMB in back with her," Liam tells Bryan as we exit the building, making a beeline for the SUV.

"What's going on?" I ask as we climb inside.

"Nothing, Livia."

"Don't give me that," I snap.

"I think it's nothing, okay? Please, just try and relax," Liam says as he starts the vehicle.

"I knew I shouldn't have come back here."

"Stop, please," Bryan orders. "I understand your fear, but you're being irrational here. After all this time, do you honestly believe someone has been watching this storage unit every day? Or that they just randomly picked today to come here?"

"No," I answer, though I don't feel the conviction behind the word.

Liam pulls out of our parking spot and gets us on our way, putting distance between us and the storage unit. "What if they've been looking for what's in this box?"

"If they were looking for it, your apartment would have been tossed when I went to clean it out after your dad's death. It wasn't. If they were looking for it, other than the alarm being on the door, what would have stopped them from entering that unit? Not to mention the fact that Declan is the only person who knows about this unit."

"You said your brother..." Bryan counters.

"Declan is my brother."

The car falls silent as Liam drives us down the road. His glances in his rear view and side mirrors doesn't go unnoticed. "You think someone's following us?" I ask.

"No, but it doesn't hurt to keep an eye out. We haven't had anyone behind us in over two miles." Just then he makes a sharp right turn, no signal, no warning. "Believe me, please?"

"I believe you. But the cops followed you for weeks back then," I remind him.

"Aye, but I knew they were there and they only ever followed when they knew I was driving. Not that they needed to. They were always aware of where we were going before we left the house," he says with confidence. "There wasn't much that transpired I was unaware of and the things that did transpire were outside my purview when it came to the investigation and I had no need to know. But when it came to the safety of you, the other girls, and me, they held nothing back."

"I always assumed when they sent in undercovers that they just kind of forgot about them," Bryan says.

"Sometimes, but with a case as big as Ricci's and with what he was capable of, no one left anything to chance," Liam says.

He makes another sharp turn, this time to the left and then we're on the highway. The farther away from the unit we get, the heavier the box gets in my lap. An ever-present reminder of something my father was trying to tell me, or keep from me. Time will tell which one. Nevertheless, this is something I need to find out about.

It isn't until Bryan's hand on top of the box stops my movement that I realize I've been pushing the lid up and down absently. "We'll be at the hotel in ten minutes, can you wait that long?" Bryan says softly into my ear.

"I'm trying."

"Livia, I know you want into it, but please, give us time to get to the hotel," Liam requests from the front seat.

"Alright," I agree with reluctance. "I'm just anxious. I'm

sorry."

"Nothing to be sorry for, baby. We understand." Bryan kisses my temple and it calms me more than I think he knows or realizes.

I knew the morning after arriving in Nashville that I was falling in love with him. Now I know I'm in love with him. I've stopped myself so many times from saying those three little words because the idea makes me feel vulnerable. If I can just remain inside this blissful little bubble a little while longer, it will mean all the difference in the world. I must believe that because this box on my lap is like Pandora's Box. I have a feeling that once it's opened, it can never be sealed again. Who knows what that will mean for me and Bryan, or my uncertain future.

After a short drive we pull outside a high-end extravagant hotel near Central Park. It's not the Plaza, that would be too obvious and too much of a tourist trap. No, this place caters to the mega-rich and famous.

Liam pulls into the valet line and we all exit the car. Bryan and I go inside while Liam handles our luggage. Bryan checks us into our room and before long we're standing inside the presidential suite.

"You sure know how to woo a girl." I shoulder check Bryan and he laughs.

"Only the best," he smirks as he gives the room a once-over. He places the box tucked under his arm on the massive dining table near the windows overlooking Central Park.

"It's breathtaking." Seeing the city sprawled out beneath us reminds me even more of what it was like to live in New York City. The constant hustle and bustle of people walking down the streets. The constant confusion of the tourists standing in front of signs or on street corners reading maps. My favorite was watching attempt to navigate the subway

system.

Sundays were always my favorite day in the city. That was usually when the tourists cleared out and the natives moved about town handling their business. The streets that housed nearly nine million people were practically empty. It was heaven on earth.

I turn away from the window that's opened my mind to reminiscing about those days and back to reality and the brown box that seems to be growing bigger by the minute in my hands.

There's a knock on the door and I jump. "Relax, baby, it's just the luggage," Bryan admonished me and I take a deep breath.

"The sooner we can get this over with, the faster I can at least attempt to relax."

"Good," Bryan smiles.

Liam enters the room with two men behind him. One is the bellman and the other couldn't be further from a bellman, but has a striking resemblance to Liam. I find myself sliding behind Bryan like an eight-year-old meeting a stranger for the first time. "You can just set the luggage there." Liam points to an empty area behind a sofa and the bellman begins to unload the baggage cart he's brought with him. "Bryan, Livia, I'd like you to meet my brother, Declan Callahan."

The other man, who is clearly Declan, extends his hand and Bryan takes it. "It's a pleasure to finally meet you," Bryan tells Declan.

"Likewise, my brother speaks very highly of you," Declan says. His voice and accent are matched to Liam's and if it wasn't for the fact that Declan is slightly taller than Liam, you'd have a hard time telling them apart.

Declan looks to me. "It's a pleasure to see you again, Livia." He extends his hand to me.

"I'm sorry, I don't remember."

Declan smiles as I take his hand. "It's quite alright. Things were a bit hectic back then. You look wonderful."

"Thank you," I blush.

Liam shows the bellman out and closes and bolts the door behind him. "I asked Declan to meet us here after we decided to stop at the unit. If whatever is in that box is personal, we will leave you to it," Liam explains.

"But if by some strange miracle there is more information regarding Ricci, I'm going to have to collect it," Declan tacks on.

I nod in understanding. "What more could there be? Don't you guys already have everything you need?" I ask skeptically.

"We do, trust me on that part, but sometimes, some things are better left out of the court's hands."

"What does that mean exactly?" Bryan asks.

Declan looks to him and then back at me. "Witnesses testifying, jury tampering, influenced judges, things like that. We've done everything we can to fight for a deal, but we haven't had any success. Ricci wants to take his chances with the courts. We, at the FBI, don't want to take that chance."

"That still leaves the question unanswered. What could possibly be left that could hand you Vito Ricci's head on a silver platter?"

"Why don't you open that box and find out?" Liam points to the brown box in front of me on the table. I step closer to the table and slide the box closer to me before pulling the lid off the top.

On the very top of the box is a folded piece of paper with

my name on it in my father's handwriting.

I look to Liam for clarification. "You didn't see this before?"

He shrugs. "I just assumed it was more shoes." I pull the paper from the box. Underneath it is a book, a black, leather-bound book.

I unfold the paper with trembling hands.

*My Dearest Livia,*

*If you're reading this, I am dead. And one of the reasons I'm dead is here in this box.*

*I've never could do right by your mother, so I am hoping, with any luck, that I can do right by you.*

*When your mother died, I questioned everything about her accident because I wasn't entirely sure it was an accident. There is another box with this one that will answer that question for you too.*

*I hope this letter finds you well. Please know I did everything in my power to protect you.*

*All my love,*

*Always,*
*Dad*

I return to the box with tear-filled eyes and pull out a black journal of sorts. Holding it in my hands I flip open the cover. There's a note stuck to the inside front cover. It reads:

*There's more to Vito Ricci than meets the eye.*

I tilt the book and something falls from between the pages.

A twenty-dollar bill?

I pick it up and look it over before sliding it across the table. The three men in the room are speechless as I notice a tab on the top of the book like a bookmark and I open the book to that page. I find another sticky note:

*Ricci's best kept secret.*

I lift the sticky note to see a ledger of some type. "I don't know what any of this means," I tell the three men as their eyes watch me intently.

"I do," Declan says.

I raise an eyebrow at him. "Care to elaborate?" I ask.

"That's the Ricci Family black book. I'd imagine there are records in that book dating all the way back to the start of the family. It's the holy grail of holy grails," Declan says.

"It says on a note in the front, 'There's more to Vito Ricci than meets the eye.' There is another note here that says, 'Ricci's best kept secret' followed by a ledger of sorts."

"Can I see?" Declan asks, extending his hand for the book.

I hand it to him and he picks up the twenty that fell out of the book.

He studies a few of the pages, his eyes roaming from the book to the twenty and back again. "Son of a bitch," Declan declares.

"What?" Liam asks him.

"You didn't know about this?" Declan turns to him.

"About what, Dec?"

Declan holds up the twenty-dollar bill to Liam. "Look closely. Very, very closely."

"Counterfeit?" Bryan asks.

Declan looks at him then back to the book and nods. "I'm not a forensic accountant and there's a lot of numbers here, but this seems to be a detailed accounting of every dollar that went out as counterfeit and every dollar returned as real cash. But what I don't get is, where's the cash?"

"The real cash?" Liam asks. I look back in the box and find one more thing inside. Another piece of paper. While the men talk, I remove the paper from the box and unfold it. There's nothing on it but an address. One I recognize.

"Yeah, he obviously managed to exchange his counterfeit for real money, but where did all the real cash end up?"

"Maybe it ended up in his accounts somewhere, somewhere that seemed inconsequential at the time," Liam offers.

"Or maybe it's here," I say to them as I hand over the piece of paper with the address on it.

Liam, like me, recognizes the address. "That's impossible."

"Not really," I say. "Think about it. What if the real reason Vito Ricci killed my father was because he knew his secret. He knew where the money was hidden and he took it from Ricci."

I start to pace, a habit when I get nervous and I start to ramble. "I knew Ricci killing my father because he wouldn't play both sides was too easy. Somewhere in the back of my mind I always knew there had to be more to it than that. Sure, Ricci would kill a man for looking at him cockeyed, but if my father was already on the inside, both as a cop and as a member of Ricci's gang, I highly doubt Ricci would kill him. Why wouldn't he just beat the shit out of him to put him back on the right path?" I take a deep breath. All eyes are on me as I continue, "What if it was because my father

had discovered Ricci's hidden secret? What if he found out about the money in some way, and traced it back to Ricci? Is it possible that my father tried to confront Ricci...?"

"Livia, slow down, but I think you may be on to something," Bryan says and I turn to him. He's opened the other box, the one with the case files in it. "Come look."

I approach and take the file from him before returning to pacing as my eyes scan over the documents in my hand.

"What's the significance behind the address?" Bryan asks the other two.

"It's her old address," Liam replies.

"We lived in an apartment building. It was small, only about ten units and a..." I stop in my tracks as two things cross my mind at the same time. The first is what I'm reading in the case file in regards to counterfeit cash being distributed by a group of teenagers and the second is the hidden alcove in the basement of my old apartment.

"A what, Livia?" Liam asks.

"Basement."

"Every building in New York has a basement."

I turn to Declan and Liam. "Not like this they don't." I walk back to the table and explain, "It's a hidden door in the wall of the actual basement that leads down another flight of stairs. It was supposed to have been sealed off because there's a train line that runs through there that wasn't there when they originally built the building. It created this little alcove space with a dirt floor."

"I have to call this in," Declan says.

"Not yet." Liam holds him off, but I can tell it's not going to pacify him for long.

"The space isn't big enough. I mean, we're talking millions

of dollars, right?" I ask.

Declan and Liam both nod. Bryan takes a seat in the chair, his disbelief evident by the paleness of his skin.

"If I'm reading this book correctly, then yes, between twenty and thirty million to be exact," Declan says.

"There's no way that kind of cash fits in that alcove and goes undiscovered for all these years. But I am willing to bet there is something there."

"But what exactly?" Liam asks.

I shrug my shoulders. "I have no clue."

*Bryan*

"THIS is not a good idea," I grumble.

"I have to know what he buried down there," Livia argues.

"Then let Liam and Declan handle it. You have no business going back there." I am trying my hardest to put my foot down with her. I don't want her going back to that apartment. I worry she's gonna get in over her head. How much more can she take on before the emotional toll breaks her? "A little over an hour ago you were cowering because of a van. What makes you think you can handle going back there?" I don't want to scare her, just protect her. I take a deep breath and try a different tactic. "And what if you're right? What if someone knew or suspected that book was in that unit and they were watching?"

My words settle like storm clouds in her eyes. "If that's the case, then they know I'm alive."

"That's in the eye of the beholder, Livia," Declan chimes in. "I can pull your file, if you want me to, but I can tell you that there is very little resemblance to the sixteen, seventeen and eighteen-year-old version of you. And from a distance? You look like any other woman."

"This is all so fucked up," Livia growls. "Go, do whatever you're going to do to find what's buried in that basement."

"You'll stay?" I ask her.

Her eyes meet mine. Anger, frustration and defeat all flash before me as she sighs. "Yes, I will stay here," she breathes. She turns to Declan and Liam and demands, "I want to know what's in that basement."

"I don't know if I can do that," Declan says.

Livia spins around and charges toward him. "You son of a bitch, my father died protecting whatever he buried in that

basement. Your goddamned idea of law enforcement left me high and fucking dry to fend for myself when you all knew damn well I was still in danger. Don't give me that bullshit, Declan. You can and you will tell me what it is my father was protecting."

"Livia," Liam warns.

She peers over Declan's shoulder. "Don't, Liam. You're in no better of a situation when it comes to this whole fucking thing. Don't start with me. I've given you everything. I've even handed you what I can only assume is Ricci's black book of all his business dealings, not to mention the fact that I handed that fucktard McMurray the trafficking ring's book."

"It was you?" Declan says in shock.

Livia looks at him and spats, "Yeah, asshole, it was me. I'm the one that handed McMurray his career building piece of evidence. I'm the one who has basically handed you the Ricci case on gold platters and getting left high and dry in the middle of fucking California is the thanks I got." She rips the book from Declan's hands. "Until I turn this over to the FBI, I will maintain possession of it. At a time I deem suitable and when I'm satisfied with the information you give me in regards to what's buried in that basement. Are we clear?"

Holy shit. If I didn't already love her, I definitely would now. Gotta admire a feisty woman who knows what she wants and does what she needs to get it.

"I am the FBI," Declan says to her.

"Not in this hotel room you're not. You are Liam's brother. He invited you here because he was in town. Not because of your FBI status. It's Sunday for crying out loud, and given the strings I know you're capable of pulling, you're not some lowlife little grunt on the totem pole. So, as far as I'm concerned, you were here as a friend and as such, this," she holds up the book, "Does not exist on an official level. So, I

will say again, are we clear, gentlemen?"

"Crystal," Declan and Liam say at the same time. Declan has a look of contempt on his face while Liam has a look of fatherly pride on his. Me? My mouth is hanging open like a codfish thrown on the dock to die.

"On that note, you guys might want to go check it out," I say when I find my voice.

Both men give me a chin lift before Liam says, "Don't open the door for anyone. Stay in the room, no matter what. If there is any remote possibility they've figured any of this out, they will be here to collect."

"I got this," I tell them. After another chin lift and a reassuring smile from Liam, they leave.

"Thank god," Livia groans before grabbing me by the shirt collar and dragging me into the master suite of the room. She slams the doors closed before pushing me up against them. She roughly pulls my face down to hers. Her lips meet mine in a kiss that fires straight to my cock. It's carnal and animalistic, almost brutal.

We merge into a teeth-clashing, lip-catching, all-consuming kiss with frenzied hands fighting for shirts and pants to be removed. I grab her wrists to slow her down. "Don't, I need this. I need you," she begs and I can't argue with that.

Somehow we both end up naked and she climbs on the bed and onto her knees. She spreads herself open and I take the not so subtle hint and climb behind her on the bed. I plunge my cock inside her dripping cunt and she cries out. "Fuck me, please," she pleads.

I've never seen this side of her. She's exposed and raw. I grab her hips and pull my cock out before slamming back inside her. "Harder!" she cries out.

I do as she asks, repeating the same motion. "Good, now faster." Bossy wench.

A shiver slides up my spine as I realize what she's begging me to do. In the back of mind, I know she needs this. If I don't give this to her...I can only imagine what will happen. I squeeze her hips a little harder, she moans. I pull back and slam in, out and in. She cries out but starts to thrust her hips in time with mine. My mind goes blank. Rage consumes me as I give her what she needs. She's begging me for a punishment I know she doesn't deserve and I'm the one who's here to hand it out.

As I brutishly thrust in and out of her, her moans turn to sobs. Tears trickle down her cheeks and I try to pull away. "Don't, don't stop, please, just...just fuck me, Bryan. Please." Through her tears she begs me and I give her everything I possibly can until I feel her pussy clench around my cock and she explodes. Screaming in a way that makes my blood run cold. When her orgasm subsides, she relaxes and falls to pieces in my arms.

She doesn't say a word; she doesn't have to. I simply wrap her in my arms and gently stroke her hair, whispering honeyed words in her ear as she cries into my chest. The tears last the better part of an hour before she finally passes out in my arms.

I gently pick her up and awkwardly pull back the covers on the bed. I lay her down and cover her up. I kiss her temple and whisper, "I love you. You're safe with me."

She snuggles into the warmth of the sheets and I move to the window and close the curtains. I turn out the light that was on when we came in before grabbing my toiletries bag and heading to the bathroom for a shower.

For the first time in more than twenty-five years, I cry. I bawl as I remember the stories she's told me about Fat Tony

and how he and his men would punish her by raping and beating her. That's exactly what she asked me to do to her just now and it breaks my heart that she was so wound up she felt she needed to be punished. My mind can't catch up to the fact that she physically and emotionally needed it. There was absolutely no way I was going to be able to talk her off that ledge. She knew what she needed and she took everything I was willing to give her.

It wasn't about me; it was all about her. About what she needed in that moment and for her, it was an orgasm forced out of her. My tears turn to retching when the idea of what I've just done solidifies in my veins. I vomit all over the tile floor of the shower.

When I finally manage to clean myself up and no longer feel like I'm the dirtiest asshole on the planet, I exit the shower and head into the bedroom. Livia's breathing is nice and even and I find comfort in that. I kiss her on the temple once more before finding my clothes and getting dressed.

I shut the door quietly behind me, giving her quiet and some time to rest. I grab my laptop bag and go to work on a few things I didn't finish on the plane.

I'm knee deep in emails when the door beeps, then clicks. My heart stops pumping in my chest and my breathing hitches until I hear Liam and his brother talking quietly as they enter.

"Where's Livia?" Liam asks and I can only stare at him, conveying without words that it's not a good topic of conversation right now.

"She's asleep," I tell him. He nods in silent understanding. "What did you find?"

"Everything," Liam says as he sits down at the table with me. Declan follows, grabbing a chair next to his brother.

"Define 'everything'."

"Livia was right. That basement isn't big enough for the money to be stored, but it was certainly big enough for these," Declan says as he pulls his phone from his pocket. He clicks a few buttons before sliding the phone over to me.

"What am I looking at?" On the screen are pictures of metal plates that appear to have the outlines of lettering. The picture isn't very clear.

"Those are printing plates," Liam explains.

"It's what they used to print their cash," Declan adds. "Scroll to the next picture." I swipe to the next picture. "From what we can tell, Ricci and his crew used smaller denomination bills, cleaned them of all their ink and reprinted them. Fives he turned to tens, tens to twenties, twenties to fifties, you get the idea. The bills would pass inspection because they had all the watermarks and would pass ink tests, but if the bills got wet, the ink would wash right off them."

"Wow, I can't..." I stammer. "My mind doesn't work like this. I can't even begin to process how this would work."

"It's okay," Liam says. "It took me a long time to come to grips with the reality that men like Ricci exist to be begin with. Once you accept that, anything is possible."

I nod. "So you said you found everything, but if all you have are the plates..."

"Scroll to the next picture," Declan directs me.

It's a picture of a letter addressed to Livia.

*My Dearest Livia,*

*If you're reading this, you've found the next piece of the puzzle. There is one more step you must take. Finding this final piece of the puzzle will be difficult, but you're a smart girl, I have faith that you can do this.*

*Love always,*

*Dad*

Below the signature is a series of numbers that make no sense to me whatsoever. "What do these numbers mean?"

"We were hoping Livia could help us with that," Declan says.

"About that..." I look up from the picture of the letter Livia's father left her and at the two men. "Do not get in her way again. Do you understand me, Declan?"

"Aye, she's a feisty one."

"She's pissed off. As she should be," I tell him with raised brows.

"Your men dropped the ball with her and you know it. She should have been, at the very least, given access to some type of crisis counseling, among other things, and your people failed to do that. How many of those girls that you rescued on your takedown are still alive?" I ask him.

"I can't answer that," Declan says.

"Sure, you can."

"No, really, I can't because I don't know."

"That's the wrong answer, Declan," I scold.

"We rescued more than three hundred girls over two days. More than a dozen of them died in the hospital from their injuries. Most of them were here illegally and those who

wanted to stay were processed as such. Those who wanted to go home were sent home. It's impossible for us to track that many women."

"How about the daughter of an NYPD Detective? Or better yet, the niece of Vito Ricci? Didn't you think it was appropriate to protect her?" Livia sneers from the doorway.

"What are you talking about?" Declan's attitude rears its head. I personally want to punch the moron, and I haven't thrown out the idea yet.

"Let it go, Livia," Liam chides.

"No, I won't let it go. I get it, believe me. You guys had your hands full after biting off more than you could chew, but what you failed to realize, or investigate, was that you had someone in your midst who wasn't just a two-bit illegal or a slutty prostitute. You had me. I was a daughter ripped off the streets. I was a girl who was forcibly raped, beaten and tortured for information I didn't have. I was a fifteen-year-old girl who was forced to watch her father die protecting the secret you two went to collect today."

"We didn't know all that..."

"You didn't bother to find out," she snaps back at Declan. "You were too goddamn busy trying to build a case against Ricci that you failed to see the innocent victims for what they were, victims. Not privy to or a party to the dealings happening within the Ricci circle, but real live girls who didn't have a choice in the matter. Not to mention the fact that they, like me, probably didn't know their rights as a victim. Hell, I was an eighteen-year old American who'd been held captive for more than two years and I didn't know."

"Let's all take a deep breath," Liam cuts into Livia's rant.

"Don't-" she starts to say but Liam stops her.

"The whole thing was fucked up from the word go. There

were too many hands in the pot and the pot tipped over. Understand that a lot of things fell through the cracks back then," Liam says.

"I'll say," Livia huffs.

Declan stands up. He's posturing and it's pissing me the fuck off. "Sit down," I snap at him.

"What do you want me to say?" Declan snaps back.

"Say you'll figure out a way to fix it," Livia says.

Declan shrugs his shoulders. "I don't know how," Declan confesses.

"Let's leave this conversation for another day," I say calmer than I was a minute ago. Livia crosses her arms over her chest. "Relax, Livia. I get where you're coming from and you're right, but you're asking Declan to fix something that's out of his scope of authority. Am I right?" I look to Declan who nods solemnly. "Then this kind of passion may be put to better use with someone who can do something about it, right, Livi?"

"I'm sorry. I'm just angry. I didn't expect to ever feel like this again."

"It's understandable, lass." Liam smiles reassuringly at her. "If this is something you truly feel passionate about, maybe it's time to crawl out of your shell and do something about it."

Liam plants a seed in Livia's mind that visibly blossoms in her features. Instead of expressing defeat, she lowers her arms and a determined posture takes over her body. "I'm sorry I never thought of that before," I mutter.

Both Liam and Livia smile at me. "Alright. Now Livia, do you want to know what they found in the basement? Or are you going to continue yelling at Declan?" I ask her.

"I'm sorry," she says again.

"It's alright, darlin'." Declan gives her a small smile to show there's no hard feelings. "I'd like to help you get to where you need to be in order to get some answers. If you'll let me."

"I'd like that," Livia says softly.

"Good, now who wants to share what you found?" I ask.

*Livia*

"DO you have any idea what that means?" Declan asks me. He's just spent the last ten minutes explaining to me what they found and showing me the letter my father wrote to me.

"He seemed pretty confident that I would be the one to find all this," I whisper. The vision of my father's face when I shouted for him in that god-awful room fills my mind. He was completely petrified. But this only makes it hurt that much more. He knew they had me and yet he still didn't give up what he knew. He was willing to die not knowing what Vito would do to me once he was dead. Then again, I knew nothing about any of this until today. Maybe my father took comfort in my ignorance.

"Livia?" Bryan's voice pulls me from my thoughts.

"I'm sorry, what?" I ask.

"You alright?"

I nod, unsure of my own voice.

"Do you know what those numbers mean?" Declan asks me.

I look again at the sequence of numbers at the bottom of the letter. They look like any series of numbers. Just random numbers.

**11222171101116161**

"Is it a combination to something? A safe, maybe?" Bryan suggests.

I shake my head. "If he had a safe, I have no clue where it would be. Liam cleaned out the house. He would have found it." I look to Liam and he shakes his head.

I keep staring at the numbers and something flitters on the edge of my memory but I can't quite place it. "It's a game," I breathe. Unsure of what I said before I said it. "It's something he and I used to do all the time. But I can't recall..." I trail off as a memory comes to me.

 

*"Daddy, daddy, look, I made you a new one."* I run into the living room from my bedroom.

*"You did?"* he says with a smile on his face.

*"I did, and I bet you can't figure this one out."*

*"You think so, pumpkin?"*

*"I know so,"* I say with confidence.

*"Alright, let me work on it and I'll let you know."* He smiles wide and I hand over a piece of paper that has a series of numbers spaced out. Sometimes it's just one or two, other times it's a whole series of numbers.

**YOURE THE BESTEST DADDY EVER.**

 

"I need a piece of paper," I say frantically.

The memory of our many games comes flooding back to me. "It's a numerical anagram," I tell them as Bryan hands me a legal pad from his messenger bag. I flip to a clean page and take a seat at the table, turning the table sideways. I start by writing out the alphabet.

**A D G J M P S V Y**

**B E H K N Q T W Z**

**C F I L O R U X**

Once I'm done with the alphabet, I go back and add numbers below the letters.

**A D G J M P S V Y**
**1 2 3 4 5 6 7 8 9**

**B E H K N Q T W Z**
**10 11 12 13 14 15 16 17 18**

**C F I L O R U X**
**19 20 21 22 23 24 25 26**

"That doesn't look like any key I've ever seen," Declan says.

I look up from my pad of paper. "I know. That was the point. At five it was numerical and alphabetical order. When I was eight, we changed it up. I used to have it all memorized and we passed notes to each other using it." I look back at the pad of paper. "I need the numbers again," I tell him.

He reads the numbers to me and I write them down.

"A, A, D, doesn't make sense. E, D either," I mumble as I process through the numbers. Slowly it starts to take shape as I move down the list.

**11 22 21 7 1 10 11 16 16 1**

**E L I S A B E T T A**

"My mother," I breathe. "Elisabetta, it spells her name. But what does that mean?" I look at Declan, then Liam and then finally my gaze lands on Bryan who has this awestruck expression on his face. To be honest, I'm surprised he's looking at me at all after what I did to him earlier, but that's a whole different discussion.

"Her grave?" Liam wonders aloud.

I shrug. "I don't even know where she's buried," I tell him.

"I do," Liam says sadly.

"That's one place you will not be able to go without me," I tell them. The conviction in my voice tells all three of them that they're not to argue with me on this.

"We can't go there without the Bureau," Declan declares. "We need equipment and technology that we don't have."

"Elbow grease and shovels?" I say cynically, raising an eyebrow in question.

"And if the money is buried with her? What then?" Declan asks. "Are you planning on taking it for yourself?"

"Considering my mother died long before this fiasco happened, I can't imagine my father digging holes near her grave burying all that money. Let alone digging up her coffin and putting it in there. He loved my mother more than life itself. He'd never do that. As much as I hate to say it, there's another clue at her grave. Whether on her headstone or buried."

"She has a point," Liam says. "Not only that, but Mercutio is buried right next to her. They would have found something when we buried him."

"What kind of equipment are you thinking about?" Bryan asks Declan.

"GPR, ground penetrating radar. It would give us the chance to see underground without breaking the surface. It will also allow us a look inside the coffin on the off chance he did bury the money with her."

"Not likely," Liam and I say in unison. "Since we all seem to be in agreement that we're looking for another clue, why not just get a metal detector and search?" I add.

"What if he didn't bury it in metal?" Declan counters.

Liam snorts, "Then odds are whatever he buried there hasn't survived the elements of the last eight years. It's metal. Merc was no idiot."

"If the metal detector doesn't work, then I get to bring in my guys," Declan throws out as a counter offer.

"Deal," I agree. "Now, where do we get a metal detector?"

"I have one at home."

"Go get it, let's go," I say while standing up. Bryan stops me with a hand on my wrist.

"I'm going to put my foot down on this. Not tonight." He stares at me, begging me without words. "Whatever is there can wait one more day."

"I agree. It's getting late," Declan says. "We can meet again tomorrow and go over there."

"How do I know you won't go first?" I say, glaring at him.

He puts his hands up in defense. "I don't know where she's buried."

"Any idiot with a computer can do some research," I counter.

"Have I done something to make you mistrust me, Livia?"

I want to roll my eyes, but I refrain because tensions are already tight. "You do remember McMurray, don't you?" I raise an eyebrow.

"On my brother's life, I will stay away. The four of us can go tomorrow. Just have Liam let me know the time," Declan vows before saying good-bye.

"I'm going to go take a shower," I tell the guys after Declan leaves.

"What do you want for dinner?" Bryan asks me.

I shrug. "Surprise me."

"Room service?"

I nod before kissing him on the cheek and grabbing my suitcase. I left him with so many questions in his eyes, but I'm not ready to talk about what happened earlier. I know his mind isn't consumed with the mystery my father has left for me. He's desperate for answers about my breakdown earlier.

I don't know what to tell him. My reaction scared the hell out of me. I don't know why I dragged him in here like I did. Declan had me wired and my reaction to him was completely uncalled for. He doesn't deserve my ire. It's not his fault I ended up in that situation, but I took it out on him anyway. Then I forced Bryan into doing something he clearly wasn't comfortable doing. I kept thinking I needed to be punished for my actions. For disrespecting Declan. I was on auto-pilot and I don't even know where it all came from. It was practically involuntary. I don't quite understand it myself, let alone being able to explain it to Bryan.

I undress and look at myself in the mirror. The bathroom light catches the glint of new skin in the scars that mar my body. Scars from being beaten. They're everywhere and I'm surprised Bryan hasn't said anything about them. Then again, they're no longer pink and angry like they were when they were fresh. I covered the nastiest ones with make-up when I was stripping. They never seemed to bother any of the johns. Then again, I played the strung-out prostitute pretty well, so they probably assumed it was part of the package.

I cover my stomach with my hands as I walk away from the mirror and turn on the water.

## *Bryan*

As soon as I hear the water in the shower turn on, I turn to Liam. "I need to talk to you."

"I'm sorry about Declan. He's a bit of a handful sometimes."

"That's not what I want to talk to you about. I think she handled herself just fine with him. Kind of offsets that theory we had before about her feeling guilty for not standing up for those girls." Liam has a smile on his face that I'm about to wipe right off. "Until you left," I add somberly.

"What are you talking about, lad?"

"The minute you two were gone, she..." I pause, swallowing back the bile that rises in my throat. "I think she's forgotten how much she did actually stand up for those girls."

"What do you mean?" he asks.

I sigh. "The minute you and Declan were out the door, she grabbed me by my shirt and dragged me into the bedroom. It started off intense, as in, full of crazy wild passion." I swallow again. "Then she..." I close my eyes; this is so much harder than I imagined. Get yourself together, Hayes. I give myself a mental pep talk while Liam waits patiently for me to continue my story. "She made me punish fuck her."

"She, what?" he says with complete shock.

I nod, "At first, it was okay, but then she started crying. She just, I don't know. It was like she was possessed by something other than herself. It was the scariest thing I've ever witnessed in my life. The moment she came, she deflated and completely broke down in tears. She cried into my chest for over an hour before she fell asleep."

"Jesus, she's in worse shape than I imagined," he breathes.

"We need to get her some help and a-sap."

"It made me sick, literally," I confess.

"It's her coping mechanism. She doesn't know any other way, but it doesn't have to be bad," he tells me.

"Explain, because as far as awful goes, it was fifty shades of it."

"Was it awful because you didn't enjoy it or because it was a sudden surprise?"

I raise an eyebrow at him. "Both, equally fucked up."

He doesn't say anything for a few minutes. He simply nods as he starts pacing back and forth. "What if, with help, that need doesn't go away?" he asks.

I shrug. "I don't know. I don't know if I can do that ever again."

"But you'd be willing to do anything to keep her happy, safe and sane, wouldn't you?" he asks.

"Absolutely, without a doubt."

"There's a chance this isn't the last time this will happen. Even with help. Some people have their own way of dealing with things. This is hers. In time, the frequency of those kinds of episodes may decline, but for now, even with help, she might not know any different."

"This is the first time it's happened. What if it never happens again?" I ask.

"She still needs help. She needs to talk to someone, someone she can trust and be completely open and honest with her that is not going to judge her. If it never happens again, then you have nothing to worry about. What happened today could have been triggered by any number of things. But if you think about it, Bryan, she's under a lot of stress, and maybe she just needed someone to take it away, take control

of it, if only for a minute." Liam stops pacing. "If it happens again, try and give her what she needs."

"I'll always give her what she needs, but it doesn't mean I have to like what I'm doing. I draw the line at hitting her, so let's hope she doesn't ask," I tell him and it's true. In hindsight, the whole situation was scarier than it was awful. Sure, I didn't come, I couldn't, but it wasn't about me. It was about her. It was about fulfilling a need within her and that was exactly what I managed to do. Next time, when I'm not completely blindsided by what she needs, it might be easier to manage.

I sigh, secretly hoping there will never be a next time.

# CHAPTER TWENTY-FIVE
LETTING GO...

*Livia*

AFTER my shower, I find some pajama pants and steal one of Bryan's t-shirts. I smile. I stole it when I was packing. It's literally one of his t-shirts, but it's ridiculously soft and what makes it better is that it's big on me yet it accentuates what curves I have. Satisfied, I leave the room.

I find Bryan sitting at the dining table with his back to me and he doesn't move when the door clicks open. His head is down and I can't tell what he's doing, but it looks like he's on his phone. I walk behind him and run my hand over his shoulders. "Hey," I say softly, "Where's Liam?"

Bryan's head comes up and his brow is furrowed like he's been deep in thought, and he seems down, forlorn even. "He went to take care of some stuff. Sit, dinner's here." He gestures toward a chair on his left, one facing the window and the Manhattan skyline.

I hate to open the can of worms, but it is inevitable. He's going to ask me about this afternoon and I am not entirely sure what I'm going to say, but his melancholy mood isn't going to work for me. "What's wrong?" I ask him.

He locks his phone and sets it on the chair to his right. He has an anti-phone rule when it comes to meals. When I asked him about it, he told me that he rarely gets away from business so he forces himself to have an unhurried, uninterrupted meal. His meals are frequently interrupted anyway. His eyes meet mine, a million questions brewing in his blue eyes.

"I'm sorry," I blurt. "I don't know what came over me."

"I do," he admits. "I'll be honest, Livi, it scared the living hell out of me. When it was over, I..." he takes a deep breath,

"I felt dirty and... it made me sick."

I fidget with my hands in my lap. I don't know how to respond to that. Bryan tucks a finger under my chin, lifting my face to look at him. "Livia, I understand why you did what you did. No, I did not enjoy it. Seeing you cry is not something I enjoy seeing, but I noticed a dramatic change in you when you woke up. You need to understand that there is absolutely nothing that you deserve to be punished for. There is nothing you can do to me or to anyone else to warrant that kind of punishment." He swallows and releases my chin. "I think the thing that got to me the most is that it took me by surprise. I wasn't expecting that." He gives me a small smile. "I like rough sex, don't get me wrong, but if you're using it as a tool to punish yourself, I don't know if I can do that for you."

My heart sinks and unwanted tears fill my eyes. My chin quivers.

He shakes his head. "Don't cry. Livia, talk to me."

"You're leaving me?"

There is a shock and hurt that crosses his face that makes the tears spill over, "God, no," he breathes. "I'm not going anywhere. This is not going to drive me away from you. Not at all."

The tears flow freely now, though more from happiness than fear of losing him. I sniffle, "Then what are you saying?"

He gives me an understanding smile. "I'm saying if what happened today is something you need, if it's something you're unable to deal without, I will make do with what I can. I just don't want to be thrown off guard like that again."

"I honestly didn't know what I was doing until it was already done." I look back at my hands. "When I was with them, I had a mouth on me, much like I do now. They always

punished me for it. It didn't matter, I'd still mouth off. I'd still piss them off and each time I got punished for it."

"Did you like being punished?" he asks me.

I shake my head and look around, looking anywhere but at Bryan. I don't know how to explain this to him without sounding completely irrational and crazy. I swallow. "When they would beat me, or worse, it was...god, this is going to sound like I'm completely fucking insane," I mutter. "I welcomed the punishments because it made me feel alive. Made me actually feel something. It reminded me that I was still alive. I was still breathing. It was..." I look at him as I find the right word, "cathartic."

"I don't understand." His voice is soft.

I stand and move behind my chair and start pacing as I try and explain this to him. "I was numb. I lived in a constant state of numbness for more than two years. I was forced to do things with my body, with men, women, sometimes multiple at the same time. Whatever they paid for, I was supposed to do it without hesitation and without question. The only way that I could do that was to disconnect my mind from my body." I shudder remembering that time in my life. "I honestly cannot tell you what any of them looked like. I only vaguely remember anything that was done to me or that I did to them. It was my way of compartmentalizing reality.

"Fat Tony, Deets, Tony's other men, when they would beat me or rape me, I felt pain, I felt fear. I felt alive. But that doesn't mean I enjoyed it because I most certainly did not, but it gave me the reality check I needed to remind myself that I was alive. That I wasn't just a shell of a human being. Does any of this make sense?" I look at him. His face is red with anger, his fists are clenched and his shoulders look stiff.

"Unfortunately," I say through gritted teeth.

"Please don't be angry with me."

He softens immediately and shakes his head in disbelief. "I'm not angry with you. I'm angry that you had to endure all that just so you could feel alive, just so you could feel anything," he breathes.

I shrug. "I am so very sorry that I made you do that today."

He cocks his head, his eyes full of emotion and unshed tears. "I'd like to be able to come up with another way for you to get that kind of release, but until we do, I will set aside my personal feelings and help you as best as I can." He takes a deep breath before standing and approaching me. His hands cup my cheeks and he says, "It won't be easy, but I understand why you think that's the only way to handle frustration, rage, anger or that you think your smart mouth needs to be punished, but I have to tell you, Livi. Watching you today, with Declan, the passion in your voice, your eyes, it was amazing to see. The only time I see that kind of passion is when I'm buried deep inside you," His voice is barely above a whisper. "I never want to punish you for displaying such true emotion. Not now and not ever. I love you, Livia."

My heart stops beating for a moment then explodes with overwhelming hope, desire and love at his declaration. "I love you," I breathe back and his lips slam against mine. Fire ignites in my veins and desire explodes inside me. I moan into his mouth and he steals his chance to slide his tongue along mine. Our breathing becomes ragged and fractured. For the first time in my life, I understand what it means to be loved- truly, madly, deeply loved. I have this man to thank for that.

He slows his kisses and pulls back, peppering my lips with a few more before he pulls back and wraps his arms around me. I snake my arms around his back, holding him to me as tight as I possibly can. I never want to let him go.

"Sit, you need to eat."

"I'm not very hungry for food," she purrs, but she winks and sits.

"Neither am I, but we haven't eaten anything since this morning." I smile at her.

She pouts. I chuckle as I uncover the food I ordered. "It smells good," she says and we dig in.

Our dinner conversation was light. We talked about the upcoming days here in New York. She and Liam have worked over the last couple of days coordinating travel times and mapping out where we need to be. Liam is from New York so it wasn't too much of a hassle, but I was surprised Livia got into it too.

All in all I expected more of a fight from her over coming back to New York, but she's handled it pretty well. I reluctantly bring up the trip we agreed to make tomorrow. "Is there time in the schedule for us to go...?" I purposefully leave off the location. She's been through enough today. I'm not sure she needs or wants the reminder. She knows without me saying the words where I'm hinting at.

"You're scheduled to be done by four tomorrow. Even if we run over, we should have time."

"Okay," I say, not wanting to force her into discussing anything about where we're going.

"I've never been there. Well, not since he died," she admits softly.

"I'm not a fan, myself."

She looks at me. "I've never even asked you about your parents."

"Divorced," I state simply.

She raises an eyebrow in question. "Is that all?"

I shrug. "My mom, she's amazing. My biggest fan and loudest supporter. Unfortunately with my schedule I don't get to see her much." I stop there.

"Where does she live?"

"Oregon, a place called Two Sisters. It's in central Oregon, so getting there is even harder. I usually drive down from Portland. When I'm in the area, I try to get down there." I place my napkin on my plate.

"I've never been to Oregon," she shares.

I smile. "Then I will take you. It's gorgeous country up there. It's a great escape."

"What about your dad?"

I sigh. "That's a complicated subject. My dad is married to my mother. He's my step-dad and a very good man. He takes good care of my mother and he practically raised me. My biological father, on the other hand, is a deadbeat idiot I haven't seen since I was eleven or twelve. Though he calls on occasion, usually when he's drunk, needs money or is in jail."

"Do you give it to him?"

"No," I say tersely.

"Any brothers or sisters?"

"Biologically? Not that I know of. I do have one brother, a younger one. You'll meet him and get to know him pretty well here in the next couple of weeks." I smile thinking about the dork. I haven't talked to him in a couple weeks. I make a mental note to give him a call when I have time this week.

"Oh? He works for you?" she asks as she sets her fork down then wipes her mouth and tosses her napkin on the plate.

"He does. He's head of the road crew. He makes sure everywhere is where they need to be when they need to be there. He directs the stage set up and honestly," I shake my head, "I have no idea how he does it, but I can't imagine a show without him behind the scenes."

"Are you guys close?"

"We've gotten closer over the years, but even being on the road, I don't see him much. He's usually on the first bus in and the last bus out. If the schedule is really tight, he flies from one place to the other. His schedule makes mine look like a cakewalk." I laugh, "But the perk to his job is he gets to schedule the date, cities and their locations. Well, he picks them now, someone else actually handles the scheduling and he only has to work for a few months at a time."

"Sounds like my kind of job." Her face lights up.

"Hey, I only gave you a job because you begged for it."

She nods, smiling. "Yes, I did. Despite the last month lounging around your house, I'm not one to sit around and do nothing. Even though we're in New York, I'm happy to be out of the house."

"That makes two of us." I stand and offer my hand to her. "So, what ever shall we do tonight?" I say playfully.

"Oh, I don't know, have something in mind?" She winks and starts walking toward the bedroom. She throws a little extra thrust in her hips as she does. Her body beginning the slow seduction that will lead to rumpled up sheets and naked bodies curled up together before the night is out.

*Livia*

"HAVE you come up with a name yet?" Liam asks as we're on our way to Declan's office. I'm not exactly looking forward to seeing him again, but I don't have much of a choice. We came into New York yesterday, despite Bryan's appointments being for this afternoon, because I need to meet with Declan.

I lost the argument when I tried to push it off for later in the week when there was more time. Liam and Bryan made very valid points and I was left with no argument. They kindly pointed out that if Bryan and I are seen together in more than a working capacity, the tabloids are going to pick it up and start asking questions. If they do that, we need to be prepared. We all agreed to keep things professional between Bryan and me in public until we had my background secured and we all had it memorized.

I agreed to that easily enough, no need to go plastering my face all over the newspapers while I'm still in New York. I don't know why, but I get this nagging feeling something is going to happen on this trip.

"I don't have many options in the way of maintaining a viable nickname of Livia, or Liv, or Livi. There is pretty much Olivia."

"Why not just use Liv?" Bryan asks. "It's a real name, at least according to the internet."

"That's hardly enough to throw anyone off. If they recognize me and see that my name is Liv... I guess I'm trying to think of something that will throw them off. Or at the very least, make them think twice," I explain.

"Names can be changed easily enough. Nicknames, pet names, things like that. So if someone happens to recognize you, I highly doubt that a name will change that much,"

Liam says.

"What if you choose an entirely different first name then put the Liv in the last name?" Bryan asks.

"Like what?"

"I don't know, Livertti?"

I cock an eyebrow at him. "That sounds like a bad cocktail," I smirk.

He laughs, "Well, you don't want to hear my idea."

"And why would I not want to hear your idea?" I ask him.

"Because you're liable to smack me."

"That depends," a light bulb fires in my brain. "Bryan Hayes, you're not suggesting I use Hayes are you?"

He wiggles his eyebrows at me. "What?" he says innocently.

"That's solvable by a trip to the courthouse, not Declan's office," I counter, calling his bluff.

"Liam, forget Declan. Find us a courthouse."

I smack him playfully in the arm. "No, Liam, no courthouse. Jeez." Bryan sobers then pouts. "You're serious, aren't you?"

He shrugs, "Maybe."

"Bryan, seriously? That's got to be the worst marriage proposal I've ever heard."

His eyebrows go up in mock shock as he stares at me. "And just how many times have you been proposed to?"

I laugh at the look on his face. "Three," I say as monotone as I can through the laughter.

"Three, seriously?"

Liam is laughing from the front seat. "Yep, all three were

from very drunk men." I snort, "One of them is very, very gay."

"Well, that helps. Not," he says, dejected. "I guess I'm going to have to up my game."

"You're sober. That's definitely a step up."

He gives me a sweet smile. "Good, and yes, you deserve a much better proposal." He lifts my hand to his lips and kisses the back of it.

"Good, now we're running out of time to decide on my name." I shake my head. "That sounds so weird."

"Didn't you pick Becca?"

I snort, "No, that was McMurray being a dick. Literally, it's not even Rebecca on the documents he sent me. It's actually Becca. I would have preferred Rebecca."

"So why not stick with Rebecca? Then you don't have to change your name with your friends. We can add in Olivia and change the last name?" Liam suggests from the front seat.

I shrug. "I didn't think this would be so hard," I tell them both.

"It doesn't have to be," Bryan says softly.

"I know, but I think the only reason it's hard is because I've gotten used to the two of you calling me Livia. I was always proud of my name."

"Then keep it," Liam says. "We'll just have Declan alter your middle name and last name. I guess in a way it's kind of moot because Bryan is going to call you Livia or some variation of that anyway. If we keep it to Livia then there isn't any confusion."

"I guess at least change it to Olivia, give it a different spin." I shrug, "I'd let Declan decide, but after my behavior

yesterday, he might pull a McMurray on me."

"What do you mean?" Liam asks.

"I was a bitch to him yesterday." I look at my hands, remembering the pain I caused Bryan because of it.

"I'd hardly call that being a bitch, Livia. You were being honest. You're frustrated and angry. I get that, Bryan gets that and Declan definitely understands that. He knows your anger is not directed at him specifically." I meet Liam's eyes in the rearview mirror and he adds, "I'm actually proud of you, you stood up for yourself. I don't imagine that's something that's happened a lot."

"No, it's most definitely not."

"Then don't stress it. The difference between Declan and McMurray is Declan is really looking for justice. McMurray was looking for a fucking pay day." Liam sighs, "This case has completely consumed my brother for the last ten plus years. When Vito and his gang were booked and officially charged, that man literally looked ten years younger. Would you believe that I'm the older of the two of us?" My jaw drops. "Precisely. That's what this case has done to him. He's worn himself thin trying to get it right, trying to make sure Vito Ricci never sees free daylight again.

"I'm sure you can put it into better perspective than maybe Bryan can, but Ricci's reach is far and wide. He has hooks in every corner of this city and beyond it. It was Declan's responsibility to see that all the loose ends were tied up in pretty little bows for the District Attorney and the Attorney General's office. If they weren't, then Ricci could walk out of jail on a technicality and believe me, no one wants that." He takes a deep breath. "My only regret is I wasn't there to help him."

"Why did you leave?" I ask.

"They didn't give me much choice. My recovery took a lot longer than I'd planned and when I was finally able to return to work, I wasn't up to speed physically. They gave me a desk job, which was fine for a while, but... I'm not much of a paper pusher, if you catch my drift."

"I understand that, but when you got better, why not go back?" I ask.

"Bryan can answer that one."

Bryan chuckles next to me. "I made him an offer he couldn't turn down. We'd been working together long enough that we worked like a well-oiled machine and I refused to let him muck it all up."

Liam laughs, "More or less. But I have the perfect job and as much as I loved working for the Bureau, I hated the institution of it. I'm not one for following rules very well,"

"You? Follow rules?" Now it's my turn to laugh. "Nope, don't see it."

"Me either," Liam says through his laughter.

# CHAPTER TWENTY-SEVEN

I STARE at my new Tennessee driver's license for the tenth time since Declan handed it to me. When Declan suggested my new last name I about fell off my chair in laughter. It was his personal way of saying 'fuck you, Ricci' and I had to agree.

"So, how'd it go?" Bryan asks as I'm finally released from Declan's office.

I snort and look at Liam. "Your brother cracks me up," I tell him.

"He always was the family clown." Liam shoulder checks his brother and they laugh.

"So?" Bryan says anxiously.

"Olivia Elise Faricci."

"Faricci? Surely you could have done better than that, Declan?" Liam says to his brother.

I laugh again.

"It made her laugh, I had to do it. Besides, if you actually think about the name, it's not only a common name, but it actually combines her original name, Fazio, with Ricci."

"Keeping with the truth more than the lies," I add.

Bryan smiles at me. "I like it." He leans in and whispers in my ear, "Livia."

I smile and wink at him. "Olivia Hayes has a nice ring to it too," I smirk.

"Yes, yes it does." He flicks his tongue along the lobe of my ear.

"Stop that," I chastise him. "We have places to be, mister."

He laughs, "Unfortunately, the only place I want to be is buried inside you."

"Fiend."

"She has everything she needs?" Liam asks Declan.

"Aye, she has her license, a certified copy of her birth certificate, a temporary social security card, and a passport is on its way to her as soon as it's printed. She has a credit history, though a limited one. She shouldn't have any problem establishing credit. Her alter-ego, Becca Carpenter, had an unfortunate accident in some Podunk town in Alabama today. However, we made some alterations to where she was from so that her friends don't freak out if they see the article. I finalize the logistics of Becca in a couple days, but she's gone."

"Did you do the other thing too?" Liam asks and I narrow my eyes at him.

"Aye, brother. It's done. The signature cards were updated and everything."

"What is he talking about?" I ask.

"Your bank account," Liam states as if it's a normal discussion.

"I don't have a bank account."

Bryan snorts, "You do now."

"Will someone explain, please?"

Liam looks directly at me and states, "Your father's life insurance."

"Oh." I'd completely forgotten all about that.

"We'll take care of that later," Liam adds.

I nod, unsure of what else to say on the subject besides not wanting the money.

We say our goodbyes to Declan and head to the SUV on the way to Bryan's radio spot and a photo shoot.

"So, where is your driver's license?" Bryan asks.

"In my purse, why?" I narrow my eyes at him.

"I want to see."

I snort, "No, you're not allowed to ask a woman to see her driver's license."

Bryan laughs, "I'm curious."

"Curiosity killed the cat, you know that, right?" I tease.

"I do, but I'm wondering where you magically have a house. I'd like to be able to visit."

I shake my head at him. "I'll show you mine if you show me yours?"

"Oh no, not going to happen."

"Good, then I'm not showing you mine." I can't help but laugh. I really don't care. He can see it, but I really want to see his now.

I laugh harder when he shifts in his seat to pull his wallet from his back pocket. He holds it in his hand for a second before he opens it up and reaches in for his driver's license and hands it to me. I smile wide. "Winning makes me giddy," I tease as I take it from him, but I'm a good girl so I hand him mine too.

I look at the Tennessee emblem that's just like mine has then my eyes find the expiration, issue and date of birth. Then my eyes wander to his name.

I bite my tongue to hold back my chuckle. It works and I find something to distract from his middle name.

### 11/2/1982

"Jesus, you're thirty-four years old? God, that's old."

"Oh yes, because you're a spring chicken yourself."

"I'm only twenty seven," I tell him.

"According to this, but you just got this, so how do I know it's real?"

I scowl at him. "For your information, it's almost accurate."

"Oh," he says looking at me expectantly.

"We flipped the day and month. So instead of April eighth, we changed it to August fourth, but the year is the same," I explain.

"So I guess that means we will have to celebrate twice."

I roll my eyes. "Technically, yes, but not August fourth. More like June eleventh and April eight."

"Why June eleventh?" Liam asks from the front seat.

"Because that was Becca's birthday. It's what my friends know."

"Well, then we can celebrate three times," Bryan says as he leans over to kiss me. I tilt my head up so our lips touch briefly. "So, about this address?"

Uh oh. "What about it?"

"Liam, did you know that someone is living in our house?"

Liam laughs, "Nope, I'll have to call the security guys and have them throw her out."

"Oh for Pete's sake, Buford." I bust out laughing and Bryan rips his driver's license from my hand.

"Enough of my driver's license," he says. I snatch mine back from him.

"Buford? Really?" I say through tears of laughter.

"It's a family name," he grumbles.

"It's very fitting." I laugh some more.

"Okay, Meadow."

I sock him in the shoulder and he grabs it. "Ow," he says in mock pain.

Liam rolls his eyes and shakes his head at our childish banter in the backseat of the SUV. I slide over to Bryan and he wraps his arm around me, holding me close. I snuggle into his shoulder for the rest of the ride.

Somewhere in the back of my mind, his non-proposal, proposal rolls takes root and disappointment washes over me. Strangely enough, I wouldn't have minded a trip to the courthouse instead of Declan's office and that scares the living shit out of me.

*Bryan*

"THE tour begins in two weeks, you have the number one single on the country charts, number one on Billboard and it's been more than a month since its release. How does that make you feel?"

I fight the urge to roll my eyes. The question is redundant and well, boring. "It feels great, Charlie. This song is special to me and to see it do so well, I just can't describe the feeling. I'm excited to take it on the road."

"Why is this song so special to you?" Charlie asks. The excitement in his face is baffling, considering we're on the radio.

"I wrote it for someone who's very important, and very special in my life. It holds deep meaning because it gave me the opportunity to express myself in a way I didn't think I'd be able to. But it also holds true for a lot of the fans too. We always say there's a reason for everything and the last few months have proved that theory true for me. I hope it has for some of the fans out there too."

"Speaking of 'Fate Has a Reason', we'll be right back with more from Bryan Hayes." Charlie cuts to music and slides one of his earphones off, and leans over to me.

"So, who is she?" he asks.

"Ah, that is something only time will tell." I wink at him. "We're keeping things under wraps for a while."

"Not even a hint." He raises an eyebrow.

I lean a little closer to him and whisper, "You wouldn't know her."

His face lights up. "Oh, I know just about everybody."

I shake my head. "No, Charlie, you know just about

everybody in the business, but I assure you there are billions of people you don't know."

He cocks his head at me. "So, she's not in the business?"

I smirk. "I wouldn't say that," I tell him and it's true. She's in the business, now.

Charlie shakes his head and his producer says, "thirty seconds," into our headphones.

"It won't stay a secret forever, my friend."

"I'm aware, and I have no intention of keeping it a secret forever, just not right now."

"What's that exclusive gonna cost me?" Charlie asks right before the producer chimes in with a ten second warning.

"Too much." I wink.

Charlie flips a switch and replaces his headphones. "Alright folks, I'm sitting here with Bryan Hayes and we're talking about his newest single, his upcoming tour, the brand-new album releasing on Friday and so much more, so stick around and we'll be right back after this commercial break."

I miss being on satellite, no freaking commercials. I want to get this interview over with.

Another half an hour goes by and I finish with Charlie then stop into their tiny studio to record a couple of opening segments for them to use for promo and we're out the door.

"Nice job," Livia says as we slide into the SUV.

"I hate those things," I tell her, "but they get a little easier."

"He was awfully pushy about who you're dating." She winks.

I smile at her. "They're all going to be that way for a while. We just need to decide when the right time is going to be to reveal ourselves." I laugh, "Charlie wants an exclusive."

Liam laughs from the front seat. "In New York?" He shakes his head. "He can't afford it."

A light bulb goes off. "What if we auction it off?" I ask both of them.

"What do you mean?" Livia questions.

"I mean, we offer the exclusive 'who's Bryan Hayes dating' reveal to magazines, television, radio, etcetera. Then the highest bidder, regardless of market, gets the exclusive rights to reveal our relationship."

"That's not a bad idea," Liam says.

"But I don't want to make money on it," Livia confesses.

"We wouldn't." I turn to her in the back seat of the SUV. "What if we donated the profits?"

"Where?" She perks up.

"The one I want you to start," I tell her.

"Me? What about me?"

"I've been thinking since yesterday about your argument with Declan and about the girls in Ricci's ring. What if you headed an organization to find them, offer protection to them and other girls who've been victims of the same kind of crimes?"

Her mouth falls open.

"That's an amazing idea," Liam says from the front seat. "Put all that passion to good use." My eyes meet Liam's in the rearview mirror, and from the narrowing of his eyes I can tell he's smiling.

"I wouldn't have the first clue how to begin something like that," she says. Her voice is a mixture of excitement and fear.

"You wouldn't have to do it alone; we'd get people involved to help you. I know that Cami's friends Derek and Dyson are well-versed in business, maybe we could enlist one of

them to help get it off the ground." I give her an encouraging smile. "I'll even donate the seed money."

Her face lights up, but she doesn't say anything. I can tell the wheels are turning in her mind about the offer and the idea I've planted in her head. I pull her close to me and wrap my arm around her shoulder. She snuggles into me and I kiss the top of her head. "You'd be great at it," I whisper.

She looks at me and smirks, "Yeah, I would, wouldn't I?"

"That's my girl." I kiss her again, this time on the lips. They're soft and warm against mine and my cock stirs in my jeans.

"Why do they do that?" I ask Bryan as he gets up from the make-up chair.

He laughs, "Because this much perfection takes magic."

I snort, "Hardly. It actually makes you look funny."

"But it shows on camera. Honestly, I would prefer this to having the images altered. At least this way the person you see in the magazines is the same person you'll see on the streets. Why do you think I work out so much?"

I shrug. "Well, I appreciate that you work out."

"Good." He kisses the top of my head.

"You keep that up and people are going to figure out we're together."

"Fuck 'em," he retorts then kisses me again, this time on the lips.

"Fiend," I laugh.

"The one and only," he teases.

"Now, go. Get this over with so we can do something

productive." I wink at him.

He chuckles as he leaves the dressing room, Liam in tow. They disappear from the doorway then Liam comes back into view. "You coming or what?" he says with a smile.

"Yup." I grab my bag and follow them down the hall to the open studio.

There are a ton of people milling about and someone, I'm guessing the photographer, is talking to Bryan.

"It's kind of fascinating to watch," Liam whispers in my ear.

"I bet," I tell him back and they're positioning Bryan in the middle of the white backdrop. "What is this for anyway?" I ask.

"It's a combination shoot. In this case, the photographer contacted Bryan about shooting several different shots. When they're edited, with Bryan's permission, he'll turn around and sell them to magazines, newspapers, things like that. Christopher, the photographer, is Bryan's primary photographer."

"I'm never going to learn all this," I mutter.

"Sure, you will, lass. It's overwhelming at first, but you'll get the hang of it."

"So what's the shoot on Wednesday for?"

"That's for a specific magazine."

"Why don't they just buy Christopher's shots?" I ask, truly trying to understand all this.

"Because some magazines, this one in particular, like to have exclusivity on the shots, whereas Christopher can sell one or all the shots he takes today. That translates to similar shots being distributed to different outlets."

"Oy."

Liam laughs, "The nice thing about today's shots is Bryan has rights to the shots too. Should he choose to use a shot for an album or a publicity still, he pays Christopher for the shot and Bryan owns it. He can then use it as he pleases. Most of Bryan's album covers are Christopher's shots."

"They've been working together a long time," I note.

"That they have. They work well together. Surprisingly, these are the only shoots that Bryan enjoys doing."

"The background is pretty boring." I tell Liam.

He gives a short laugh. "It works as a green screen for Christopher to alter the background to whatever he desires. Sometimes it's a living room or a bedroom, outside, against a car, a wall, things like that. Doing studio shots out in the elements can be pretty tricky and hit or miss. This way Christopher can sell the pose and change it up to meet the needs of the buying entity."

"Why aren't you his assistant?" I tease.

He laughs, "I am, you're just sexier."

I nod and settle in to watch the magic happen.

I watch with rapt attention as Christopher poses Bryan. He moves around him, taking one shot after another. It's so quiet in the room you can hear a pin drop, or in this case the shutter of the camera, and that's about it. This place really needs some music.

Bryan smiles and he changes positions to sit on a stool. He looks sexy as fuck.

It's another hour before Bryan and Christopher finish the shoot. They spend another fifteen minutes looking at things on a computer. I observed from over their shoulders as Christopher's assistant did some mock-ups with some of the backgrounds they wanted to use. Some of the poses, that didn't make much sense as Christopher was shooting them,

now make perfect sense when put onto the background images.

Satisfied, Bryan is released from the shoot. He comes to me and whispers, "I need to get this crap off, come with me?"

I nod and follow him. Liam's not far behind us as we head to the dressing room he changed in earlier. He opens the door and ushers me inside before entering and closing the door. The next thing I know, I'm being pressed against the back of the door. Bryan's body heat consumes me and sends tiny pulses of pleasure to my pussy.

His lips press to mine. His breathing is already ragged before he gets too deep into it. He pulls back and says, "You're so fucking sexy." He smiles. "I couldn't keep my eyes off you. Now it's time to put my hands all over you," he growls and grabs my hand, pulling me toward the bathroom.

"What are you doing?" I scoff playfully.

"You," he states in a way that tells me arguing isn't worth it.

"I'm not getting in the shower with you," I tease him back. "This takes too long to make perfect."

"Oh no, no shower for you, shower for me." He unbuttons my jeans and lowers them to my ankles with my panties tucked inside. "Turn around," he tells me. "I want you to watch."

I do as he's asked and turn around; looking at my half-naked self in the mirror while he unbuttons his pants and pushes them down to his thighs. Then he grips his cock in his hand before sliding it from my clit back toward my entrance. "Jesus," he groans, "You're soaking wet."

I smirk into the mirror, his eyes meet mine. "What can I say, that was fucking hot."

"Oh yeah?" He lifts an eyebrow that begs for further

explanation.

"Oh yeah. It's not hard imagining you posing naked."

"And what would you have me do totally naked?" he asks as he slips the head of his cock just barely inside me.

My eyes roll up and my mouth falls slack. "I'd lay you out on the floor and climb on top of you," I tell him.

"What else?" he says as he pushes inside me a little more.

"I'd squat over you, with my hands on your stomach, and my arms just wide enough for you to watch that big, fat cock entering my pussy as I bounced up and down on you," I moan as he slams inside me.

"Watch yourself, gorgeous. Watch what you look like while I slide my cock inside you."

I moan and fight to close my eyes as he pulls himself out and he slides back inside. This time harder and faster than the last.

I'm curious where this animal came from, but my pussy is clenching repeatedly around the intrusion that's slipping in and out of my body and the pleasure is so much that all rational thought leaves my mind. My eyes are crazy and unfocused in the mirror. I find his eyes, trying desperately to find something I can hang on to and his eyes narrow slightly as the pleasure he's taking from my body registers for him.

I start to move my hips in time with him. I bite my lower lip to stop myself from crying out and my orgasm rushes to the surface as he starts to pound into me harder and deeper. I adjust my legs to as wide as they'll go trapped in my jeans and he groans behind me. The angle change makes my pussy clamp down hard on his cock.

He pushes through it. My orgasm overcomes me as he reaches around me and pinches my clit between his fingers. I explode and the woman looking back at me in the mirror

has a look of pure bliss written on her face as Bryan pours himself inside me.

# CHAPTER TWENTY-NINE

*Livia*

I CLEAN myself up while Bryan showers. I realized as he was unloading inside me that all the flirting and pent up promises of pleasure got to be too much for both of us, he just took control and acted on it. It was quick and it was carnal. Everything I didn't know I needed.

As I cleaned up, I realized I felt more centered, and secure. Not to mention my anxiety level has dropped dramatically and I'm not sure if it's a result of the post-orgasmic bliss or if it's because I let myself go for a little while.

When he's done in the shower, he gets dressed in a more casual pair of jeans and his usual t-shirt with a zip-up hoodie. It's late summer in New York so the weather is warm during the day and cooler at night. None of us know what to expect when we reach my mother's grave.

We leave the studio after Bryan says a final good-bye to Christopher. Liam drives while Bryan and I sit in the back. His arm is wrapped around me as Liam navigates the New York City traffic. Due to the time of day, nearly four, traffic is quite heavy and Liam's rather flustered until we hit the bridge and cross into Brooklyn. My home.

"It hasn't changed a bit," I mutter as I look at the Brooklyn skyline and memories of living in New York City come flooding back to me.

The closer we draw to Brooklyn, the harder it is to hold back the emotions that have been threatening since we got here yesterday. "I miss it here," I confess in a soft voice.

Bryan squeezes me a little tighter, pulling me closer to his side.

"There's just something about being in a big city. Especially this one," I add.

"I've never lived here, but I understand the appeal." Bryan rests his head against mine.

"You're either a New Yorker or you're not. There is no middle ground with this city. The traffic is a mess, the subways are crowded and everything is ridiculously expensive, but it has a certain magic to it," Liam chimes in from the front.

"Were you born here, Liam?" I ask.

"No, lass. Declan and I were born in Scotland. Our parents brought us here when I was five, Declan was two. But we moved to the city and until I met Bryan, I'd barely been out of it." His voice carries a tone of reminiscence with it and I completely understand why he'd feel that way.

"Do you miss it?" Bryan asks him.

"Sometimes, but I don't miss the constant going and going. I get enough of that with you. But it's different because I get to go different places, do different things that I probably never would have done otherwise." Liam's accent is a pleasant thing to listen to, I love listening to him talk. His voice has a very soothing, fatherly quality to it. "I couldn't live here again, that much I know for sure."

"No?" I question.

"Nah, I'm too old for this shit," he laughs.

"How old are you?" I ask.

"Old enough to be friends with your father." He winks at me through the rearview mirror.

"Well, he would have been fifty-one this year," I say with a taunting tone to my voice.

"Your father was older than I am, lass."

"Regardless, you look good for your age. Whatever that is," I giggle.

We spend the rest of the ride in silence. Bryan's arm and body heat is an ever-present reminder that no matter what happens tonight, I have him by my side. I find comfort in knowing I don't have to face this alone. No matter how much I want to think this blissful feeling is only temporary, he's become an addiction for me. I don't know how I would go through the rest of my life if I didn't have him with me.

No matter the obstacles, he's proven time and time again that he's not going anywhere.

I look up at him from where I sit at his side and his eyes meet mine. I mouth, "I love you.". His lips turn up in a wide smile and he kisses my lips gently.

"I love you," he whispers against my lips before kissing me again.

Declan is waiting for us in the parking lot when we arrive at the cemetery. He hasn't been here long because he's pulling something from his trunk when we pull up next to him. There are no other cars in the parking lot which makes me feel better about being here. The nagging feeling that something's about to happen hasn't gone away and I've been on edge all day. I wonder if Liam is feeling it too. He hasn't left me alone all day, regardless of where we've been.

I guess he's really going to make good on his promise to protect me always.

"You ready for this?" Bryan asks as Liam gets out of the car.

I sit up straight and look at him before shrugging. "I think so. You'd think after all this time it wouldn't be so hard."

"Most people have had a chance to grieve their losses, you haven't."

"I grieved for my mother. Well, as much as a three-year-old could," I tell him. "By the time I was old enough to realize other kids had moms and dads, I was content to just have my

dad, so it never bothered me. It's his grave I'm more worried about seeing," I admit honestly.

"Understood. I won't pretend to understand what you're feeling because I've not lost a parent, but I'm here, no matter what."

His voice is filled with conviction, conveying to me that the words he speaks are the truth. I smile and nod that I understand his words and he opens the door and slides out of the car. Once he's out, he offers me his hand and I take it. Once outside the car, I hear Liam and Declan talking.

"What do you mean?"

"See for yourself," Declan says and he hands Liam something as Bryan and I come around the SUV.

"What's going on?" I ask.

Liam's worry-filled eyes meet mine. "We need to get this done and get out of here." His voice is shaky.

"Liam? What's going on?" I leave Bryan's side and walk over to see what he's looking at. It's a photograph.

I take it from his hands and study it. "This was yesterday."

"Aye, lass."

"The van," I breathe.

I look back at the grainy image taken from behind a window and through another window, but it's clearly Bryan, Liam and I as we left the storage unit yesterday, just before I noticed the van.

"Where did this come from?" Bryan asks.

"That's complicated, but it was an intercepted email to an email account belonging to Ricci."

"Who sent it?" I ask.

"His nephew, Victor Ricci."

"And where is Victor?" I snap.

"Until now, we had no confirmation that Victor was an active member of the family. He was barely sixteen when we took down the business and he had no ties to the family besides a name. Or at least that's what we thought," Declan explains. "After we intercepted this, we went back through some recent letters Vito had received in prison. At the time, none of them sparked much of a concern because there was little context to go on. Now we believe Victor is looking for something." Declan pulls a file folder out of the trunk of his car. "These are the letters, I printed them off. I thought maybe Livia could help us with them. See if she can put any type of context to them."

"I don't know how I'm supposed to do that," I tell Declan. "I was never 'part' of the family."

"You might be surprised at what you see when you read them," Declan says. "Right now my concern is that Victor had eyes or ears on that storage unit because it was the one place they couldn't touch."

"Is there any indication they know what was in that unit?" Liam asks.

Declan shakes his head and shrugs. "I have no idea. For all they know, you pulled some family memorabilia from that unit, but I'm taking precautions just in case."

"What kind?" Liam asks.

"I have three agents stationed at your hotel. I'm assigning myself and another agent to accompany the three of you during your stay in New York. I've been in touch with the Nashville field office and they're working on a team to keep an eye on your residence, Bryan. If Victor Ricci wants that book, he's got a lot of people to go through first."

Fear lances through my body. My body tenses and I'm

starting to freak out. "Breathe, Livia," Liam says calmly.

"Why? Why does this shit keep happening to me?" I growl. "I should have never come back here. I should have never gone to that unit or meddled in business I don't belong fucking with," I ramble.

"Livia, calm down," Bryan says as he steps in front of me and forces me to look at him. "We've got this, alright? Nothing is going to happen to you. I won't let it. Liam won't, Declan won't. Please. Take a deep breath."

I fight to pull air into my lungs. After a couple of attempts, I'm able to pull in a deep breath and hold it for a minute.

"We're not alone here," Declan says and my eyes go wide and meet his.

"What do you mean, we're not alone here?" I snap.

"Livia, relax," Liam reminds me.

Declan leans around Bryan and tells me, "I have eight different agents surrounding this place. They have solid eyes on every corner of the cemetery and even us right now." He moves around Bryan to stand next to me. Like Liam and Bryan, Declan is tall, significantly taller than my five foot eight inch frame, and he has to look down at me to make eye contact. "I may have fucked up in the past, both with your handling and how things have been handled since then, but I assure you, on my life, that I will let absolutely nothing happen to you. Please trust that."

"I'm trying," I breathe.

"That's all we ask," Declan says with a small smile. "Now, shall we get to work so we can get out of here?"

It takes a few seconds but I nod my head.

Declan grabs two shovels, hands them to Liam and then he pulls out a metal detector from the trunk. It doesn't

look like any metal detector I've ever seen before. This one is bigger and has a wider dish shaped dome on the end of it and there is a larger screen on the handle. "Considering recent information, I was able to get the FBI to provide a GPR scanner versus just a metal detector," Declan explains as the four of us walk through the gate and into the cemetery.

There are a million and one different things running through my mind as we walk with me in the middle and the three men  surrounding me. To anyone watching it looks like we're just walking as a group, but I know exactly what they've done and guilt slices through me. I've done this. I've put them in this position and if anything happens to any one of them, I don't know how I'd live with myself.

Then I remember the insurance policy in my bag on my shoulder. I'd planned, after what he did for me this morning, my attitude yesterday and then tonight, to give him what I know he needs in order to wrap up his case. Yes, he needs whatever this clue leads him to, but he also needs the book that started it all.

Liam leads us deeper into the cemetery. It's not huge by any means and there are parked cars around the perimeter. I take comfort knowing we're not alone out here despite no one being visible.

Liam turns down a row of headstones and then stops a few rows in, pointing to the ground near one of the larger of the two stones. I remember my mother's headstone had her name on the right side and a blank box on the left. I'm assuming the left has been filled in with my father's name since his passing and I wonder idly who handled his arrangements.

I can't bring myself to look at the stone. I simply listen for the machine Declan is holding to start making noise. It doesn't take long before it's beeping non-stop and I look up to them. "What's that mean?" I ask.

"Come and look," Declan says. I move in behind him and look at the screen.

"Well, that answers that question," Liam says. "She's really in there."

I shudder. "That's creepy," I tell them all. No one laughs and Declan begins moving the scanner up toward the headstone. As it draws closer, there is more noise coming from the machine until finally off to the right side of the headstone a solid box takes shape and the beeping doesn't stop until Declan turns it off.

"Livia, we need to dig," Liam says.

I nod and finally look at the headstone. Tears stream down my cheeks when I see my father's name, date of birth, and finally his date of death. I have to assume it's accurate because I don't actually know what day he died, or rather, what day they found him.

Liam and Declan go to work digging next to the headstone and I watch as Declan is especially careful with pulling up the grass. Once that's out of the way, he digs down. Liam joins him as the alternate until one of them hits something metal and they get down on their knees and start digging by hand.

Panic rises in my throat as they continue uncovering the box and I have this morbid feeling it's not what we're hoping it is. What if it is someone's ashes buried with them? I shudder again.

After another couple minutes Declan lifts a worn metal box from its resting place. No one says anything as Liam goes back to filling in the hole they just made. Declan brings me the box. "It has a combination lock on it. Any idea what the combination is?"

I shrug and look down at the tiny wheeled numbers on the

lock. There are six of them. "Someone's birthday, maybe," I suggest.

Liam finishes filling the hole and he gently places the grass back over the overturned dirt. "Let's hope no one steps here for a while," he mutters. He stands up and starts working on spreading the darker dirt around so that it doesn't look disturbed.

"Let's go," Bryan, who's been quietly observing this entire time, says.

"Agreed." Liam gives a chin lift.

He leads us back to the SUV and the safety it provides.

"Take it back to the hotel," Declan says. "I'll meet you guys there."

"Aye," Liam says before he and his brother do their manly greeting where they grab hands and bump chests. I climb into the car with the box on my lap. I look at the lock and wonder what those numbers could possibly be. I start playing with it. First, I try my date of birth.

**04 08 89**

No luck.

I try my father's.

**07 21 65**

No dice.

"This isn't going to self-destruct if I get the combination wrong too many times, is it?" I ask.

Liam chuckles, "No, lass. It's an analog lock."

"I don't understand why we can't just pry it open."

"Not knowing what's inside, that might not be the best idea," Liam says.

"Oh yes, because opening it is a brilliant idea," I snort.

"Well, your father sucked at explosives training, so I think you're safe."

I shake my head. "I don't even want to know how you know that."

I go back to the lock and Bryan leans over and asks, "What have you tried so far?"

"My birthday, dad's."

"What about your mother?"

I close my eyes, picturing the headstone and then start turning the knobs.

**12 24 69**

There is a click of the lock. "Got it," I breathe and lift the lid.

*Bryan*

I LET out the breath I was holding while she entered her mother's birthday. I noticed it on the headstone and noticed that her date of birth and date of death were almost the same, only several years later. She died on December twenty-second nineteen ninety-one.

Livia slowly lifts the lid. I flick on the overhead light to give her more light to see what's inside.

There is another note inside a ziplock bag with her name on it.

She pulls the letter from the box and underneath it are three more ziplock bags. The first has a key in it. It looks like an old fashioned one. Below that are two bags with money inside them. There is easily more than a hundred grand in there. The top one has a hand-written note in Mercutio's handwriting. "Can you spot the fake?" I say aloud.

After a minute, she hands me the letter that she was reading.

*Well done, Livia. I knew you could figure this out.*

*If you've made it this far, you won't have a problem deciphering this one.*

*I love you with all my heart.*

*One last step, I promise.*

*P.S. Do you remember my friend Liam? You're going to need his help with this one.*

**161211812522167**

"Well, Liam, it looks like my father was planning on putting you and me back together anyway," Livia says.

"What's it say?" he asks from the front seat.

I read it aloud to him.

"Hmph, that s. o. b.. Sorry, Livia," he laughs.

Livia joins him, only her laugh is strained. "There's a key, an old fashioned one, and two ziplock bags full of cash and another note that says, 'can you spot the fake?' along with another anagram."

"Can you decipher it?"

She pulls a notebook from her bag, the same one that has my schedule and other stuff tucked inside. She opens to a clean page near the back and digs for a pen. Once she has it, she writes out the alphabet again and then numbers it. It looks the same as it did last time.

Then she starts working out the numbers. First she starts with one and puts an A down. She goes to six and puts a P down on the paper. She ends up with A P A D A A before she starts again.

She has a A P H A A but then crosses out the A A and swaps it for an E and she has A P H E. She scribbles it out. Then she starts again with a T followed by an H, then an E. The E is followed by a V then a K, which she crosses out and replaced with an A.

She has

## T H E V A

"Thevadm..." she mumbles.

Then she combines the two for a U. "The vaudd...The Vee aye u..."

"The vaults?" Liam asks from the front seat.

"Hang on..." She takes what Liam has said and writes out The Vaults, then coordinates the numbers below the remaining letters. "That's it," she says.

Suddenly the car turns sharply and Liam steps on the gas. Then a phone ringing comes through the speakers. "You're not being followed," Declan's voice answers over the speakers.

"Change of plans. Do you remember that place where we used to play as kids?"

"You're going to have to be more specific than that, brother?"

"Down by the docks," Liam says.

"Aye, I remember. What about it?"

"Meet me there, now," Liam orders.

"Aye." The line goes dead.

"Care to explain?" Livia asks.

"When your father and I were kids, we used to go down by the docks and run around like idiots. There's a bunch of run-down buildings that, to this day, are still there. One day we came across this room while running through the abandoned buildings and inside were several heavy metal doors. The doors were all locked but there were keys hung next to them, oddly enough. Does the key have a cloverleaf shape on it?"

"Yes," Livia says with hesitation.

"That's it, that's where it's at."

"How do we even know it's still there?" I ask.

"Because, those buildings hadn't been touched in fifteen years before Merc and I discovered them, from there, if he

could put the money in there, then I know they're still there. Believe me, if that book is accurate, there's more than thirty million dollars in there," Liam says. There's an excitement in his voice I haven't heard in a long time.

"Is this thing big enough for that kind of cash?" Livia asks

"One of them? No, more than one? Absolutely."

"But there's only one key," Livia counters.

"I guess we'll find out when we get there," Liam says as he steps on the gas a little harder.

"They've found it."

"How do you know?" the gruff voice says into the phone.

"Because everything I've seen points them in that direction."

"Or they're leading you on a wild goose chase around the city," the voice says followed by a harsh cough.

"I promised you we'd find it."

"Then get it done."

The line goes dead.

Victor Ricci scrubs his face. His uncle has always been a harsh man, but Victor's patience is wearing thin with the old man. He's been lying in wait for the last eight years, waiting patiently for his moment to shine and this is it. This is his chance to prove once and for all, that he's a true Ricci.

He tried to warn him that Mercutio Fazio was bad fucking news, but he didn't listen to and look where it got us? It got the majority of the family thrown in jail, killed or scattered in the wind. Without the money, the Ricci family dies once and for all.

Victor's phone rings. He looks at the phone number.

"You better have something for me."

"Da. Posylaya adres." (Yes. Sending the address.)

"Good," Victor snaps and ends the call.

Only one good thing came from Vito's business dealings with Russia. Spies. Everywhere.

*Livia*

WE pull up outside an extremely run-down building in the middle of nowhere. There are very few street lights visible and the sun is setting quickly. "There are flashlights in the back," Liam says as he turns the ignition off on the car.

"Shouldn't we wait until morning?" I ask. My nerves are shot and I'm starting to freak the fuck out. I'm not afraid of the dark, but I do not like the looks of this. And I still have that bad feeling.

"The sooner we do this, the sooner it can all be over. Your father left that trail for you to find and if Victor is really after what I'm assuming is in here, then we need to find it and hand it over as fast as possible," Liam tells me.

I nod. "I'm done running," I tell them both as we climb out of the car. We're in the back of the SUV getting flashlights when headlights pull around the corner.

"Livia, get down," Liam shouts. Bryan and I duck behind the car, putting it between us and the oncoming car. Liam pulls his gun from his holster and the headlights flash deliberately. "It's Declan."

"You shouldn't be here," I screech at Bryan.

"I told you, I'm with you until it's finished. Do you understand me?"

I try to nod, but I'm trembling with fear. "I don't have a good feeling about this, Bryan. I will die if anything happens to you." Tears slide down my cheeks.

"That's why we do this together. Understand me? If we stick together, nothing can go wrong. Alright?"

I nod and Bryan cups me cheeks between his hands, pulling me up and kissing me, hard, feverishly, like it's our last kiss. My gentle tears turn to sobs, ruining our kiss. "I got

you, baby," he coos.

"I love you," I whisper through my tears.

"I love you."

"I called for backup," Declan calls as he exits his car.

Bryan and I stand and move around the SUV.

"Those two really shouldn't be here," Declan says to Liam.

"I'm not going anywhere until this is done," I tell him firmly. "I've lived in this mess for the last ten years; I need it over with. My father left that shit for me to find, and now I've found it. It's my turn to get my revenge for what Vito Ricci did to me and my father."

"Feisty, this one," Declan says with an amused grin.

"You don't have to tell me twice," Bryan teases. The moment is too tense to argue with them.

"Let's get this over with," I urge.

Liam hands Bryan and I each a flashlight and Declan pulls his from his belt.

"Liam, lead the way," Bryan orders.

Liam nods and backs up, closing the hatch on the car and we move into the building. "There was a lot of busted metal in here when we were kids. So watch your footing. But it's solid concrete so we shouldn't have issues there."

"Aye," Declan acknowledges.

Liam leads, I'm second with Bryan behind me and then Declan brings up the rear as we make our way into a dilapidated, dirty building. It's obvious this place has been exposed to the elements for more than a few years. There's rusted metal everywhere, and not a spec of drywall remains. Most of the walls are broken pieces of rotting wood.

"This place is pretty straight forward," Liam shares as he

turns a corner. The deeper into the building we get, the better shape it's in and the more dust and cobwebs we come across.

"Would now be a good time to tell you that I hate spiders?" I laugh humorlessly.

No one comments back, which is fine. The further from the entrance we get, the higher my anxiety rises until we meet a staircase. "Down there," Liam announces before starting his descent into the basement.

His feet slip a little. "Watch it," Bryan says. "Concrete or not."

"Aye," Liam says and he continues the climb down.

We all follow behind him and eventually, after three flights of stairs, we reach the bottom. There's only one place to go- straight ahead until we reach to a closed metal door.

Liam pushes on it, but it doesn't budge. "Bryan, help me."

After a few minutes of pushing against the door, it starts to budge and scrape along the floor as it opens. There is at least four-hundred pounds pressing on the door between the two of them, but it's taking forever. The longer it takes, the twitchier I get. They get it open far enough that the four of us can squeeze in.

Liam goes first, then Bryan, then me and lastly Declan.

When I get inside, Liam shines the light around and sure enough, there are three vaults per wall. Nine in total.

"Where do we start?" I ask.

"The one with the missing key," Liam says as he shines his light a little higher up the wall, toward the top of the doors.

I see a hook, but nothing is there. Liam moves to the next vault and it too is missing its key. He keeps going around the room. "All the keys are gone," Liam says.

"Well, then I guess we start here," I say standing next to

the first one on the left. I insert the key and try to turn it, but it doesn't budge. "Not that one." I slide to my right, and the second vault. It doesn't open that one either.

I repeat my actions for the third, fourth and fifth. Finally, on the sixth one the key turns. "Got it," I say and continue turning the key. The locks inside the door click and knock around as they turn until the key stops moving. I reach for the handle on the door and push it down. Nothing happens. I lift it up and it clicks loudly and the door springs open.

I pull it back, flashlight ready.

I shine my light inside and scream at the top of my lungs. I bury my head into the first chest I feel. The vision of what I just saw is burned into my brain.

"Jesus, what the fuck is that?" someone growls.

"Fuck me," Liam breathes.

"That's a corpse," Declan says.

"Yeah, but who?" Liam asks.

I groan, "I really hate my father right now."

"Declan, look!" Liam exclaims.

Something in his voice makes me look back into the vault. I do my best to ignore the corpse in the vault and see where Liam is shining his light.

"Is that what I think it is?" Bryan asks.

"Aye, lad. And a hell of a lot of it."

Underneath the corpse are piles and piles of cash. Liam shuffles something around inside the vault. "Livia, take this, start on the other vaults." He hands me a key that's nearly identical to the one I just used.

"I'm not opening anymore," I squeak.

"Aye, just find it and unlock it, one of us will open it,"

Declan says and I start back at the first one again. This time I get to the third one and it unlocks.

"It's ready," I tell the guys and Liam comes over.

He pulls up on the handle and the vault disengages. The door creaks as Liam opens it. He shines his light inside. "Clear," he announces.

"Holy fuck," I murmur when I take in the massive pile of cash inside the vault and hanging from the front of the stack is the key to the next vault. I grab it and go in search of it. This time I start on the right wall. Sure enough, the second one I try, or the eight one depending on how you count them, unlocks. Feeling confident that the first vault is the only vault with a corpse inside, I go ahead and pull it open. Again, more cash, and hanging like in the last one, another key. This one takes me back to the fourth one and I open it.

I continue to repeat this process until I come to the last vault. Number nine. Inside is another pile of cash and a letter with my name on it.

I pull the letter from on top of the cash and start reading it.


*I'm so very proud of you, darlin'. You did it.*

*I'm sorry I'm no longer around for you and I will forever curse the day that Vito Ricci took me from you. But know that I have always and will always love you. You're my shining star, my gorgeous angel. Take care of yourself and remember I will always be with you.*


I can barely make out the last few lines through my tears. Bryan comes over and wraps his arms around me. "He really is gone," I sob. Ten years of grief, ten years without closure, come crashing down on me in the middle of a dusty, dirty

room, in the basement of an abandoned building in New York City.

I know one thing for certain now. My father died protecting this secret so I would be the one to find it. He didn't do it to save his own skin. He did it to protect mine. "Shh, it's alright, love. I've got you," Bryan whispers in my ear.

"What's that?" someone says.

"Lights out," someone whispers and we're bathed in darkness. Bryan stands with me in his arms as he walks toward where Liam and Declan were standing and he gently pushes me behind him. I can't see anything but I feel the three of them converging around me.

Through a gap in their circle, I can see light moving under the door and I hear the snaps of holsters and the sliding of guns as they're unsheathed. "I called for back-up," Declan whispers so softly I can barely make it out.

"They would have announced themselves, or at the very least, called you that they were here," Liam says in the same hushed tone.

The light in the hallway grows narrower and the footsteps louder the closer they get to the door. I send up a silent prayer to my dad, hoping he'll find a way to help us out of this. Maybe it's just security. I try to calm my breathing. Bryan snakes his fingers through mine, this helps to calm me down. Aside from footsteps and breathing, it's deadly quiet in this room. A flashlight shines into the door and into one of the vaults.

"Well done, Livia."

The name and the voice send ice racing through my veins.

The guys shift, drawing their weapons and cocking back hammers. It's a sound I'd know anywhere.

My heart is racing in my chest. I can't hear anything besides the blood rushing in my ears. It feels like an eternity before the man who said my name steps into the doorway. I can't see his face beyond the flashlight, but he's standing square in the door. Ready to move or shift in either direct.

"FBI," Declan says. "Who are you?"

The man laughs, "You know damn well who I am, Special Agent." His voice in menacing and my body starts to tremble uncontrollably.

"Well, well, if it isn't Victor fucking Ricci," Declan sneers. "I should have known you were following us."

"Oh, but you did know, didn't you? You knew because I wanted you to know. How'd you like that little email to my uncle this morning?"

"You have piss-poor grammar," Declan jabs back.

"Livia, there's someone here who wants to see you," Victor sneers and there are more footsteps. These are less clear, more of a shuffle than a walk. "You might remember Uncle Gio."

My breathing stops and I squeeze Bryan's hand so hard he lets out a breath as the pain registers. "He's here to bring you back home," Victor adds.

"Fuck you," I threaten.

"Oh, I'm sure that can be arranged." I close my eyes. Despite the darkness, I need to hide myself as an old man comes into view and Declan and Liam raise their guns a little higher.

"Walk away, Victor, right now," Liam demands.

"Oh no, I came here for two things, her and my money. I'm not leaving without either of them." I hear the cocking of yet another gun and I squeeze my eyes shut even tighter. "So

hand her over and I'll let the three of you walk out of here unharmed. I'll get what I came for and you leave with your lives." Victor's voice grows harsher the longer he talks.

"Not happening," Liam declares.

"Let's see, who should we start with, Uncle Gio?"

"The skinny one."

"Noooo," I cry out and try to push my way through my three protectors. They're like the Great Wall of China and I make little progress. "Dammit, let me through," I cry.

"Let her through, boys," Victor sneers.

"Never," Declan snaps.

"The skinny one it is then."

The next thing I know, I'm being shoved to the floor and shots ring out all around us. There's a loud thud as something, or someone, hits the ground, then another one and then the gunfire stops. "Oh god," I scream.

"Livia." Bryan's voice is weak. There's another knock on the floor, this time close enough for me to feel it vibrate.

"Bryan." I scurry around and find Victor's light shining on Bryan. His black t-shirt appears wet and dark. He pulls his hand away from his side. It's covered in blood. "Bryan," I scream. "No, no, nooooo," I cry and catch him as he falls.

"No, dammit, no. Stay with me Bryan." I put my hand on the wound in his side. "Don't, don't you dare leave me." I kiss his forehead while I put pressure on his side. "I love you," I sob. "Don't leave me, please,"

*Livia*

"COUNTRY music superstar, Bryan Hayes was shot last night in an abandoned warehouse in Brooklyn. Representatives of the superstar have confirmed he was transported to Lutheran Medical Center, but we have not received an update on his condition at this time."

"Turn that shit off," I demand as I'm pacing the waiting room where I've been for more than four hours. It's all I can do to stop myself from going fucking insane.

"Livia, please, sit down," Liam says for the thousandth time. I glare at him. I've literally chewed my nails down to nothing as I wait for word from the doctor about Bryan's condition. "He'll be alright," Liam says.

I stop and glare at him. "You don't know that."

"Aye, lass, but I'm trying to be optimistic here."

I close my eyes, try to take a deep breath but my lungs are fucking broken. I return to pacing the room.

"Bryan Hayes," a male voice says and I turn to see a doctor standing in the doorway in scrubs, a surgical mask around his neck and he pulls his cap off his head as Liam and I rush over to him.

"I'm Doctor Liestner. I'm the trauma surgeon who operated on Bryan."

"How is he?" Liam, much calmer than I am, asks the question I need an answer to.

"It was touch and go for a while. The bullet went straight through, but it left quite the path of destruction in its wake. But we've been able to repair the internal damage. He lost a lot of blood so the next couple hours will tell us more. But I think he's going to be just fine."

I collapse on the floor. "Thank god, thank god, thank god," I mumble repeatedly.

Liam kneels before me. "Come on, love. Doctor says you can see him for a few minutes."

The idea of seeing him spurs me into getting off the floor. Liam escorts me to the door where the doctor is waiting to take us to Bryan. "One at a time, for now," he says and my panic returns.

"Go on, lass. I'll be here when you get back."

"Aye," I give him a small smile. He returns it and nods. I follow the doctor down the hall and he stops outside the door.

"He's got a lot of tubes in him. We had to put a drainage tube in his abdomen, but with any luck, we can take it out tomorrow. He's also going to be quite pale as he lost a lot of blood."

"Okay," I tell him and he opens the door.

"Ten minutes, then he needs to rest."

"Is he awake?"

"He's coming out of the anesthesia, so he will probably be in and out of it for a while. He's likely not to remember anything, but talk to him nonetheless."

"He's really going to be okay?"

The doctor smiles at me. "Yeah, he'll be alright. It's going to be a while before he's back in tiptop shape, but he'll get there."

"Thank you, Doctor, for everything."

He nods.

I take a few hesitant steps inside the door. There's a steady beeping noise on the other side of the curtain, otherwise it's still and quiet in the room. I pull in a deep breath and hold it

as I move the curtain aside.

I tried to prepare myself, but I didn't do a very good job of it.

"Oh, god," I quietly sob as I take in his still form. His eyes are closed; his skin is beyond pale. He has an oxygen cannula in his nose, but beyond that, he looks like he's sleeping. There's a mess of tubes in his right side, but they're on the far side from me, so I try to ignore them for now.

I approach the bed, unsure of what to do, what to say or even what to touch when I get there; I just know I need to feel him. I need to feel his warmth. I need to know he's really still here with me.

I reach his bedside; tears are streaming down my cheeks and I wipe them away before I take his hand in mine. He moans and his head moves from side to side but then he stills again. I gently sit on the side of the bed and pick his hand up and place it between my own. I kiss his knuckles. His hair is in his face so I brush it to the side and he leans his head in the direction of my hand so I cup his cheek.

"I'm here, baby," I whisper. His eyelids flutter as he fights to open his eyes. It's really bright in here so I look around the room for a switch. That's when I see a cord hanging from the light directly over him. I tug it down and the light goes out. The room, though still lit, is darker now. "That's better," I say softly.

He grunts and tries again to open his eyes, this time they slowly start to open. His gorgeous blue eyes peer up at me. "Hi, baby," I coo.

"Hi," he tries to speak, but it's more of a raspy whisper. He clears his throat. "Hi," he tries again and this time it's much closer to his normal baritone.

"You have no idea how happy I am to see those baby

blues," I tell him and I get a weak smile in return. "I'm so sorry. So very sorry," I cry.

"Shh, its okay. I'm okay," he wheezes but I can hear his conviction behind them.

"Are you in pain?" I ask.

He gently shakes his head.

"Good." I give him a small smile.

"What happened?" he asks.

"You were shot."

"I know that, silly girl, Victor...the other guy?"

"They're dead. Liam and Declan took them down before they could get more than a couple shots off."

"Anyone else hurt?"

I shake my head, "No."

"Good." His eyes flutter closed again but his hand tightens around mine.

I place my head gently against his shoulder and I cry.

I cry for my father and what he did to protect me from Vito's wrath.

I cry for the fact that my fucked-up life is no longer in vein.

I cry because I nearly got Declan and Liam killed.

Because Bryan got shot.

Because Bryan, the absolutely love of my life, is going to be okay.

I cry because for the first time since I can remember, I can take a full, unbroken breath.

I never have to run again.

Because I am alive.

Because I survived Vito Ricci's crazy, not once, but twice.

And I'm wholly and completely in love with the most amazing man I've ever met in my entire life.

"You have to get better," I say.

"Why?" he croaks and I sit up to find matching tears in his eyes.

I smile through mine and answer, "Because we have a date.".

"Where at?"

"The courthouse."

His eyes close, a smile spreads across his face and one final tear slides down his cheek.

# EPILOGUE
## ONE YEAR LATER.

GETTING shot was a reality check I wasn't prepared for.

Turns out, I'm not as invincible as I envisioned I was, and I've let too much life pass me by without taking time to stop and smell the roses. Nearly losing my life made me realize there is more to living than my music career. Though I will never stop being a singer, I've learned to pull back some. To take some time for myself and most importantly, for Livia.

When things finally settled down, I found the courage to ask Livia why she reacted to Uncle Gio the way that she did when he entered the room. She'd said she was glad he was dead because that meant I wouldn't go after him. She was right. It turns out that Uncle Gio, or Giovanni – because that's original – was the one responsible for Livia's kidnapping. He was also the man who gave his men permission to rape and beat her. His voice had haunted her for ages and hearing it again, in person, was too much for her to process.

I wanted to bring him back from the dead and kill him again.

One day, Livia plans to visit her Uncle Vito in prison, just so that she can look him in the eye and tell him, game over. For now, that's Declan's job, and from what I understand he's quite enjoying that little game.

The investigation into the money is still on-going. In all, there was thirty-seven million dollars in those vaults. Thirty-seven million dollars that now belongs to the FBI. Liam keeps hinting at some sort of finder's fee. Something about Livia being the one who found the money and the FBI didn't even know it existed, and yet she turned it over to them. But right now, it's evidence in one of the biggest money laundering schemes in American history.

Liam is, well, Liam. However, somewhere along the tour he found something he'd been missing that he didn't know was lost. I'm not sure I've ever seen him happier than he is now. Only time will tell with him.

I was released from the hospital one year ago today.

I married the love of my life three hundred and sixty-four days ago.

After a longer than expected recovery, partly because I wasn't ready to leave my newlywed bliss, the tour went on as planned, just pushed back a few months and it was the most successful tour I've ever done. I guess fans were clamoring for a chance to see the country superstar who cheated death.

The tour was so big and it was extended three times. I earned an Entertainer of the Year title for the second year in a row. It also gave me my first red carpet event to show off my wife.

"Come on, Bryan, we gotta go," Livia says from the intercom of the recording studio. I nod and look at her through the glass.

As if marrying the love of my life wasn't enough, she's never asked me to punish her like she did that day in the hotel again.

Solving that puzzle was the closure she needed to bring back the Livia she was born to be. At mine and Liam's urging, she started counseling and has made great strides in finding her happy place. Her past, not forgotten but accepted as a part of who she was always meant to be.

She slides her hand along the small swell of her stomach. I smile at her again and leave my recording studio.

I wrap my arms around her and lean down to kiss her silly.

"Fiend," she teases. "This is exactly how we ended up like this in the first place."

"Oh, you love it and you know it."

"Aye, I do."

I narrow my eyes at her. "Italian's don't say 'aye'."

She narrows her eyes back at me. "World famous country superstars don't make their wives late for doctor appointments."

I laugh, "Well then, momma, we better go."

"One more thing." She wraps her arms tightly around me, pressing herself against me as tight as she's capable.

"Anything?"

"Say it again." She gives me a playful smile.

"I love you, Livia Meadow Hayes."

There's mischief in her eyes as she says in return, "I love you, Bryan Buford Hayes."

*The End*

# ACKNOWLEDGEMENTS

RACHEL - NO matter how many times I say Thank You in side the cover of a book, it will never be enough, you've been my rock even when I didn't think I needed one. P.S. Thanks for helping me hash out Ireland's History - She really needed to know.

Emily Kidman - GIRL!!! You are a goddess for which there are no better. You keep me sane and if you didn't do that, I'm pretty sure I have a purple padded room reserved for me somewhere. So, Thank You for keeping me out of it. Though purple is pretty.

Mandy and PJ (Rachel) - Thank you for sticking by me through all my crazy! The Editing is Amazing and the Cover is jaw dropping. I LURVE YOU BOTH!!

As always - my Mom and my Son, Thank you for putting up with left overs, pizza, and take-out while I found myself submerged in the world of Ireland and Dyson. Your patience is admirable and I cannot thank you enough for the love and support you show me every single day. Love You Both!

The Wicked Wenches - THANK YOU THANK YOU THANK YOU For showing me that my panic attacks were all worth it. You were the first to read Irresistibly Undeniable and the first to remind me that I haven't lost my touch. Thank You Ladies!!!

Readers - I hope you have enjoyed Ireland and Dyson's story. This one was an emotional roller coaster from start to finish and I'm honored to have you along for the ride!

Love You All!

# ABOUT THE AUTHOR

BEST SELLING Erotic, Paranormal and Contemporary Romance author Zoey Derrick comes from Glendale, Arizona. Zoey, was a mortgage underwriter by day and is now a romance and erotica novelist full-time. She writes stories as hot as the desert sun itself. It is this passion that drips off of her work, bringing excitement to anyone who enjoys a good and sensual love story.

Not only does she aim to take her readers on an erotic dance that lasts the night, it allows her to empty her mind of stories we all wish were true.

Her stories are hopeful yet true to life, skillfully avoiding melodrama and the unrealistic, bringing her gripping Erotica only closer to the heart of those that dare dipping into it.

The intimacy of her fantasies that she shares with her readers is thrilling and encouraging, climactic yet full of suspense. She is a loving mistress, up for anything, of which any reader is doomed to return to again and again

# DID YOU KNOW...

*That several of the couples you've met in this book have their own stories...*

### CAMI & TRISTAN
With Cami and Tristan's story you will meet - Beau & Mick,
Travis & Naomi and Jolene & Tyson

Finding Love's Wings
Chasing Love's Wings

### DEREK & DACOTAH
One Week

### ADDISON, TALON, & KYLE
Claiming Addison
Craving Talon
Redeeming Kyle

### DEX & RAINE
Taming Dex
Devouring Raine

### CALVIN & ERIC (MOUSE & PEACOCK)
Defining Us

### ARYN & CADEN
Aryn's Desire
Caden's Command (Coming Soon)

# Happy Reading!

www.ingramcontent.com/pod-product-compliance
Lightning Source LLC
Chambersburg PA
CBHW071106250626
47159CB00002B/621